What People Are Saying about
Going for Broke

In *Going for Broke*, Melanie Dobson artistically paints the secret life of the compulsive gambler and then shines the bright light of help and hope. Bravo!

—Mary Hunt, author of *Debt-Proof Living*

An honest, compassionate look inside the world of a female compulsive gambler. The character was so real that she could have been one of my clients.

—Eileen Fox, MA, CACIII, gambling counselor,
Woodland Park, Colorado

Going for Broke is a fast-paced read and an addiction of its own. Melanie brilliantly captures the allure of "just one more try" and the slippery slope that leads from entertainment to destruction. Take a gamble on this book—you're sure to promise yourself, "Just one more page!"

—Alison Strobel, author of *Worlds Collide* and
Violette Between

In *Going for Broke*, Melanie Dobson pens a tale that is both touching and devastating. Through each page-turning chapter, the tension builds, pulling the reader into the very core of the heroine's struggle with the addiction of gambling. A very powerful, compelling read that had me cheering at the end.

—Nancy Jo Jenkins, author of *Coldwater*
Revival

Invite Melanie Dobson to Your Book Club

Transport your book club behind the scenes and into a new world by inviting Melanie Dobson to join in your group discussion via phone. To learn more, go to www.cookministries.com/readthis or e-mail Melanie directly at bookclubs@melaniedobson.com.

Going for Broke

MELANIE DOBSON

RIVEROAK®
Good News in Fiction

COOK COMMUNICATIONS MINISTRIES
Colorado Springs, Colorado • Paris, Ontario
KINGSWAY COMMUNICATIONS LTD
Eastbourne, England

RiverOak® is an imprint of
Cook Communications Ministries, Colorado Springs, CO 80918
Cook Communications, Paris, Ontario
Kingsway Communications, Eastbourne, England

GOING FOR BROKE
© 2007 Melanie Dobson

This story is a work of fiction. All characters and events are the product of the author's imagination. Any resemblance to any person, living
or dead, is coincidental.

The Web site addresses recommended throughout this book are
offered as a resource to you. These Web sites are not intended in any
way to be or imply an endorsement on the part of Cook
Communications Ministries, nor do we vouch for their content.

First printing, 2007
Printed in the United States of America

2 3 4 5 6 7 8 9 10

Cover Design and Photography: Koechel Peterson & Associates, Inc.
Interior Design: Karen Athen

All Scripture quotations, unless otherwise noted, are taken from the
Holy Bible, New Living Translation, copyright © 1996. Used by permission of Tyndale House Publishers, Inc., Wheaton, Illinois 60189. All
rights reserved. Scripture quotations marked NIV are taken from the
Holy Bible, New International Version®. *NIV*®. Copyright © 1973,
1978, 1984 by International Bible Society. Used by permission of
Zondervan. All rights reserved.

ISBN 978-1-58919-093-1
LCCN 2007921088

062507

Dedicated to my amazing dad

and my hero

James Walter Beroth

[Love] always protects, always trusts, always hopes,

always perseveres.

1 CORINTHIANS 13:7 NIV

ACKNOWLEDGMENTS

Writing this novel has been one of the greatest challenges of my life, and I'm grateful to all the people who've supported me and prayed for me during this process.

Thank you:

Jeff Dunn, Jon Woodhams, and the staff at Cook Communications for giving me the opportunity to share Leia's story. I can't tell you how much I've appreciated your encouragement and vision.

Jim Beroth, Christy and Gerry Nunn, Eileen Fox, Nicole Ferguson, Shannon Knight, Michele Heath, Vennessa Ng, Chad Hills, David Ransopher, Jennifer Haessly, and Chris Yates—an amazing group of friends and experts who've educated me on gambling addiction, the airline industry, and knee injuries. They chopped, colored, and expanded my ideas with their insight and expertise. Any errors are my fault.

Team Dobson (Dobby and Carolyn) for entertaining my troops while I pressed toward deadline. Your love is a reflection of Christ.

My beautiful toddlers, Karly and Kinzel, for their hugs and kisses and patience while Mommy was typing away. I thank God for the gift of two amazing daughters.

My husband, Jon, who was born to be a storyteller and can polish details like a pro. His love encouraged me to pursue my writing, and his intuitive editing helped turn this dream into a reality. My blessings overflow.

And to my Lord Jesus Christ, who offers freedom to everyone trapped in an addiction. When we are weak, he is strong!

PROLOGUE

RAIN PELTED THE SIDES OF THE AIRPLANE HANGAR AS ETHAN Carlisle loaded the last box of food into the tail of the sturdy Helio Courier. This bird had been hopping between the seven thousand Philippine Islands for more than thirty years, and it showed. Ethan had passed the rigorous training necessary to fly in the mountains of north central Luzon, but he'd never get a chance to take her up if the weather didn't relent.

He slammed the cockpit door shut and walked across the hangar to look outside. The palm trees lining the airfield sagged from the downpour. The sky glowed an eerie green.

He knew God wanted him in the Philippines, but if God didn't taper this storm, the two weeks he'd set aside to fly supplies to the region's remote villages would be a waste.

John, the supervisor for the mission operation out of Bagabag, walked up behind him and handed him a Styrofoam cup.

"How do you usually celebrate the New Year?" John asked as he looked out the hangar's door.

"With chips and salsa and a marathon of board games with a couple friends."

John nodded toward the airfield. "We may be having our own New Year's Eve party in the hangar tonight."

"I won't last until midnight."

"Go get some rest." John pointed to a small lobby at the side of the hangar. "Everyone's grounded until this afternoon, maybe tomorrow."

Ethan took a sip of the muddy coffee. "How long do you think it will last?"

"One of the missionaries called in this morning from a village north of here and said they had clear skies, but the radio's been down for an hour."

A gust of wind shook the hangar, bending the palms like they were rubber.

"Isn't this supposed to be the dry season?"

"We get storms all year." John saluted the weather with his cup. "We'll pray that it clears up in the next few hours."

Ethan squinted into the hazy sky and saw something dark move in the distance. "Is that a plane?"

John took a step forward as the black spot evolved into a Cessna 182. He groaned. "She knows better!"

Ethan watched the single-engine plane turn and dip toward the runway. "She?"

"The woman never listens ..." John mumbled as he raced outside.

Ethan stepped out under the awning as he watched the Cessna battle the wind. The plane teetered and shook as it descended and then bumped twice before it landed on the runway and taxied toward the hangar. He followed John toward the plane.

The second the propeller blades wound down, the pilot jumped out. She wore a tan T-shirt under denim overalls, and her honey brown hair was pulled back in a messy ponytail. The rain streaked dirt down her forehead and arms.

She pointed back into the front seat. "We've got to get her to the hospital."

John ran up to her, his hair and jacket soaked. "I told you to stay in Reauca until this storm blew over."

Ethan heard a woman scream inside the Cessna, and then he heard a furious chorus of clucking.

"Dr. Andrews said this woman and her baby will die if she doesn't have an emergency C-section."

The woman screamed again, and Ethan peered into the open door. A pregnant woman was clutching her abdomen, contorting in pain. And the tail of the plane was filled with crates of angry chickens.

The pilot glanced into the hangar and then turned toward John. "Did I mention she's going to *die*?"

"Call an ambulance," John yelled to one of the maintenance workers.

The pilot jumped back inside the Cessna and helped the groaning woman climb out. A mechanic rushed a wheelchair into the storm, and the four of them lifted her into it. The mechanic battled the wind as he pushed her into the hangar and covered her shoulders with a blanket. Ethan turned back to John.

"I need fuel," the pilot said.

John stepped between her and the plane. "Oh no, you don't."

"And a box of antivenom serum."

"What happened?"

"A cobra bit an eight-year-old boy this morning."

"And yet you brought a plane full of chickens instead."

"He was too sick to fly."

"I'll try to radio Dr. Andrews and tell him you'll return when the weather clears."

She planted both hands on her hips. "The boy won't make it."

"I'm worried about you making it."

"He's eight, John!"

John looked as if he was about to strangle her.

"Leia ..."

"It's only a twenty-minute flight."

He lowered his voice as he stepped toward her. "These are high stakes you're playing."

"It's worth the risk."

John turned and rushed toward the hangar. "Get me the fuel truck!"

Leia pulled a crate of chickens out of the tail, the birds squawking as rain drenched their feathers. She climbed back into the plane, and when she emerged with another crate, she glanced down at the first crate still on the ground and then back at Ethan. "We need to get them inside before they drown."

"Got it." He wrapped his fingers around the thin slats of wood, but when he picked up the crate, a chicken pecked him, and the box crashed on the asphalt.

He looked up at Leia, and she rolled her eyes. "You have to pick it up from bottom."

"Right."

He carried the four crates inside the hangar and lined the angry chickens up against the wall.

A pickup truck with an aluminum tank pulled up beside the plane, and Leia pulled out the nozzle to start fueling. John walked out into the rain with a plastic bag, opened the door of the plane, and set it inside.

He nodded toward her. "It's the serum."

She planted the nozzle back into the flatbed and rushed into the hangar, two steps in front of John. Ethan looked out at the driving sheet of rain and then at the pilot.

"I'll go with her," he volunteered to John.

She glared at him as she signed the paperwork to release the serum. "Who's this?"

"It's his first day." John flung his hands between them. "Leia, meet Ethan Carlisle. Ethan, this is our rogue pilot, Leia Vaughn."

Ethan stepped forward and held out his hand. She shook it warily, and then he followed her out to the plane. When she climbed into the pilot's seat, he opened the door to the other side. He was used to the routine—he'd been nursing second seat since he was twenty-four.

"I'll fly with you—"

"No way."

He hopped into the plane. "In case you need help …"

"I won't need any help," Leia insisted.

"… with the kid."

Apparently she didn't want to waste time arguing. She turned the plane as he buckled his seat belt.

Then she took off into the storm, the Cessna shaking and howling against the wind as they flew out of Bagabag. Ethan clenched the door handle like it was a parachute cord as they disappeared into the clouds.

"You know where all the mountaintops are, right?" he asked.

"I've got a pretty good idea."

He turned his head to stare at her. "Do you have a death wish?"

"We'll be fine if we die, but I'm not sure about the boy."

"Admirable."

"It's why we do this, isn't it?" The plane broke through a cloud and into the clear blue. "John's just blowing smoke. He's flown through worse a hundred times when someone called for help."

"Do you always fly with poultry?" he asked.

"They're payment for the woman's surgery."

His fingers wound tighter around the handle as the plane bounced in the turbulence. "I hope the surgeon likes eggs."

"He'll trade them for something else."

"Do you think the woman will be okay?"

Leia banked left, flying toward a ridge of imposing mountains. "She should make it to the hospital in time, but there's no guarantee."

Sprawled below them were miles of rigorous jungle, and a river snaked through the dense mangrove forest. They flew by a waterfall cascading into a clear pool. Nearby, lime-colored rice terraces stairstepped up a mountainside.

She pointed toward the water. "It's the Chico River."

"Gorgeous." He released his hold on the handle. "How long have you been flying over here?"

"I've volunteered between Christmas and New Year's for the past five years." Her blue eyes glazed for an instant. "How long are you going to be here?"

"Two weeks. I just got hired by Ambassador Air, so I'm starting my new job at the end of the month."

"Good company." Leia turned the plane north. "You're ... what? Twenty-eight? Twenty-nine?"

"Just turned thirty."

"Someday I'm going to fly with the majors."

He believed her. "Where do you work now?"

"At Corporate Direct. I fly charters."

"Out of Denver?"

She glanced over at him. "That's right."

"I just moved to Denver."

They were flying directly toward a mountain.

"Don't you think you better ..." he started, pointing toward the crags.

She buzzed the rocky top, missing the summit by fifty feet. "You like mountains?"

He wiped the sweat off his face. "I prefer to ski on them."

"Then you'll love Colorado."

She pointed toward a mountain in front of them. "That's where we're going."

He leaned forward in his seat but didn't see an airfield. "Where?"

"You'll see."

He squinted until he saw what looked like a thin piece of sandpaper that had been carved out of the mountainside. Their landing strip. If she didn't hit the crude runway just right, they'd plunge down into the valley. It would probably be days before someone found them.

He started to say something about the shoddy-looking strip, but her eyes had creased into slits, her gaze boring through the window. She dropped the flaps as they descended; the plane smacked the runway. They bumped over the field of rocks—wheels rattling as if they were skating across marbles—before they screeched to a halt. Ethan opened his eyes and saw the edge of the runway fifteen feet in front of them.

He whistled.

"It's a breeze." She flashed him a confident smile, but he saw her hands shake. She was blowing a little smoke herself.

She killed the engine as a crowd of natives ran toward the plane. "Let's get this medicine to the doctor."

Ethan released his grip on the door and jumped out. A man with a safari hat covering most of his blond hair ran up to Leia. Dr. Andrews.

"I knew you'd come back." When the doctor hugged her, it didn't look as if he was going to let go.

Ethan stepped up beside them and cleared his throat. "Excuse me."

Dr. Andrews released his hold as Leia turned toward him.

Ethan waved his thumb toward the plane. "Isn't this an emergency?"

Four villagers brought the boy up the hill on a stretcher as Leia retrieved the box of antivenom from the plane. Ethan lifted the child and cradled him in his arms like a baby. As the doctor administered the serum, Ethan prayed softly that God would spare the boy's life.

1

Five years later

"IT'S ONLY A GAME," LEIA MUTTERED AS SHE SHOVED ANOTHER quarter into the Golden Wonder and pulled the metal arm. Red and yellow fruit whirled across three paylines, but she didn't blink. The display slowed to a tick. Her body tensed.

This roll was a winner. She could feel it. Time to recover some of the money she'd lost this afternoon.

The spinning stopped, and a white light flashed across the screen— two grape clusters, scattered lemons, a couple of cherries, and the token gold bar. No good. Why couldn't she beat this thing? One decent win was all she wanted instead of the measly ten quarters the machine spit out when it froze on a row of silver bells.

She dropped three more quarters into the slot machine and gritted her teeth as she spun again.

This was ridiculous. There was no reason for her to get worked up. Nobody was going to die if she didn't win. Nothing was going to burn down. Besides, if she didn't increase her bet, the maximum payout was only fifty bucks. The Vicodin she took this morning must be messing with her mind.

Another spin. Another loss.

She groaned. Winning was a matter of principle now. All she needed was one row of diamonds to recoup the cash she'd lost in the last hour. If she bet a few more quarters, a row of gold would pay for her entire ski weekend.

She wouldn't budge until the Golden Wonder gave her at least a portion of the money she'd crammed into it. All she wanted was a few dollars to make up for her time and the torture of sitting inside a musty casino on a sunny Colorado day.

She wasn't supposed to be here. She and Julie Kirk were supposed to be skiing down Copper Mountain's intense moguls. They'd planned this long weekend getaway last summer, a girls-only excursion to celebrate New Year's Eve.

The first day of their trip was amazing: powder-packed runs, temperatures hovering around fifty. The only wind a light breeze from the east. When Julie begged her to stop for a late lunch, they both gobbled cheeseburgers before racing right back out. They took the last lift up the mountaintop and skied around the groomers who emerged in full force at the end of the day.

Thursday had been perfect.

Yesterday was torture.

The morning started out fine. She and Julie left the lodge early, arriving at the lift twenty minutes before it opened. They were second in line. Overnight snow flurries had left behind a brilliant white powder, and the sky was a crisp blue. They rode to the top of a black-diamond run, and Leia ripped down the bumps with Julie close behind her.

Then it happened. A purple streak startled her two seconds before the snowboarder cut her off. With no time to stop, she catapulted down the hill, skis flying in opposite directions. She landed a foot from a pine tree. With her legs knotted under her like a pretzel, she spat out a mouthful of snow and lifted her head. The snowboarder had disappeared, but her right knee seared with fire.

When she tried to sit up, she screamed with pain. Julie yelled to a ski instructor for help.

The afternoon was a blur—the humiliating stretcher ride down the mountain, waiting in the long emergency room line while she groaned with pain, and finally the diagnosis from a doctor who didn't look old enough to have a diploma. He explained that she'd fractured her tibial plateau—the top of the shinbone that joins the knee. He said the Vicodin would numb her pain until she scheduled an MRI and a visit with an orthopedist, but no driving for three months. No flying for at least five months. Happy New Year.

She stuck a fistful of quarters into the slot machine and brushed her hand over the leg that she'd propped up on a stool.

If only she could stop thinking about her injury. She closed her eyes as the machine spun, but it was impossible to focus when she lost again.

The career implications of her accident were overwhelming. She was in the midst of interviewing with Ambassador Air to fly 737s. Her dream job. She'd raced through the company's initial interview and the physical and psychological exams in December. Her simulator test was scheduled for next week. With Corporate Direct teetering on bankruptcy, she'd probably be unemployed by the end of the year if she didn't find something soon.

Pilots with decades more experience than she had were vying for jobs with major carriers like Ambassador Air. What would the company do when she told them she'd fractured her knee? Hiring another pilot would be a cinch.

She looked down at the immobilizer wrapped around her leg. She'd asked Doogie Howser what she was supposed to do with a knee injury, but the kid had only threatened her, telling her to take it easy or she'd ruin her knee. A moratorium on flying if she screwed it up.

She was supposed to be outside, enjoying the mountains and the fresh air, yet here she was on New Year's Eve, sitting in a Black Hawk casino by herself.

She looked up the aisle, a parade of whirling colored lights. *Where did Julie go?*

The crowded casino was decorated like an old saloon with painted mirrors, tinted windows, and a Western bar at the side of the room. A lemon Pledge scent clung to the furniture, barely masking the stench of body odor and fried food.

She looked above her at the loft restaurant. People clustered around the rail to watch the action below. Instead of the crystal she'd seen in Vegas, an antler chandelier hung over the casino floor, and the columns around the room were stacked with marbled river rock. If they took out the game tables and slot machines, this place could pass for an upscale fishing lodge.

She clasped three more quarters in her hands and kissed her knuckles. This was the play she needed. She could feel it.

She spun again. This time she won a dollar. Big money.

A loud whistle blared from the next aisle, followed by a scream. Someone was taking home a jackpot.

"Are you on a streak?" Julie asked as she sat down beside her and handed her a tall glass of tea and an ice pack.

Leia put the ice on her swollen knee and sipped the cold tea. "A losing one."

Julie flicked her arm with a French-manicured nail. "Aren't you grumpy today?"

"I've fed ninety bucks to this machine."

Julie lifted her drink, an orange concoction topped off with a cowboy hat. "Then you're overdue for some good luck."

Julie's black hair was pinned back in a French twist, and she wore a snug lavender turtleneck above a black fluted skirt and stilettos. With her flawless ivory skin and Barbie-like figure, Julie turned heads on both the ski slopes and the casino floor. She worked as a flight attendant for Corporate Direct, and several executives specifically requested that she be on board whenever they flew.

They never requested Leia as a pilot, but with her plain brown hair and stock uniform attire, she understood why. She didn't care if the passengers found her attractive as long as they respected her work, but they should request her. She was meticulous about punctuality, dedicated to arriving at their destination on time.

"Ethan's going to wonder where all my money went." She pointed down to her knee. "That little emergency room trip cost more than our entire vacation."

"Your insurance will cover it."

Leia sighed. "You don't want to know how big our deductible is."

"With that payment, Ethan won't even notice the money you spent today," Julie said.

"He counts every penny I spend—twice."

"Then just tell that cute husband of yours we went gambling."

"Why don't I just tell him we robbed a bank?"

"We couldn't just sit in the hotel room all day and do nothing."

"Yes, we could."

"And be bored out of our minds."

Leia rubbed her leg. When God created her husband, he gave him a heart the size of Colorado and a conscience that weighed more than a 777. She loved the strength in his grace as he softened out her many rough edges. She envied his steady moral compass and intense convictions. But his pursuit of righteousness drove him to avoid any activity that teetered on the fence between absolute right and wrong. In his orderly world of black and white, gambling was akin to drunkenness and lust.

She'd never viewed gambling as a sin. When she was younger, she even considered a few hours in a casino to be harmless fun. Ethan didn't know, but before they got married, she gambled when she had layovers in Atlantic City. She hadn't been inside a casino in four years, but the last time she visited Atlantic City, she'd left Caesars with two hundred extra dollars stuffed in her purse.

She couldn't tell Ethan about these excursions. Tiptoeing around issues like that was the secret to keeping their marriage intact.

Julie unclipped her twist, black hair pouring over her shoulders. "Just tell him we spent the day chilling in a spa."

"I can't believe I let you talk me into coming here."

"But you're having fun, aren't you?" Julie smiled as she deposited money into the machine beside Leia and spun. The game dinged as a trio of grapes clung to the second payline, and her friend let out a shriek. When she hit a button, quarters emptied out of the machine.

It figured Julie would win on her first try. She was the queen of good luck.

Leia pulled the knob again. She wasn't about to let a stupid game

beat her. After all, she'd spent the last seven years of her life at the controls of much bigger machinery, commanding G3s with her fingertips.
No slot machine was going to get the best of her.

The Golden Wonder gobbled her last three quarters.

She turned to Julie. "Could you hang on to my machine while I get
more cash?"

"No problem. Do you want me to get the money for you?"

Leia shook her head. "I can do it."

Curling her fingers over the white plastic rim, she grasped the
bucket by her side before securing both crutches and hobbling toward
the ATM at the center of the room.

Maroon-colored bar stools lined both sides of the aisle, someone
sitting in almost every one. But instead of chatting with each other, the
players were communing solely with the machines in front of them. She
hadn't thought about it before, but gambling was a lonely sport, pushing buttons and pulling knobs over and over to jockey for the big win.
A cheap thrill.

Didn't they know what real excitement was? Try jumping out of a
plane at ten thousand feet or scuba diving with stingrays off Grand
Cayman or landing on a sliver of grass—otherwise known as an
airstrip—in the remote regions of the Philippines.

She entered her PIN into the ATM. This was the last try for her, and
then she was out of here. There were a hundred other things she'd
rather be doing if she could ditch her knee injury along with the
crutches.

Forty dollars in quarters spilled out of the ATM, and Leia bent over
to shovel the change into her bucket. So far this was the only way she
could get cash in this casino. She should just stay here and withdraw
from her bank account every ten minutes so she could hear the clang of
falling change. At least she'd leave the place with some money.

As she balanced her crutches under her arms, a wave of panic hit
her. What if the casino name showed up on their statement? Ethan
would have an aneurysm.

Surely the withdrawal would just be recorded as a cash transaction.
If not, she'd have to come up with a good excuse. Not a lie, of course.

She'd use part of the money for food, so she could tell him she treated Julie to a nice lunch.

Leia turned slowly to limp back to her machine. Yesterday she'd barreled down a black-diamond run; today she could barely cross a room. What was she going to do cooped up at home for three months? It would drive her crazy.

She heard a deep laugh, and it surprised her—a lot of people cheered in this casino, but it was the first laugh she'd heard all day. She spun her head toward a card table and gasped.

All she saw was his back—thick shoulders, buzzed hair, and the familiar brown jacket draped over the back of his stool. She squinted as he leaned toward a woman next to him. There was no question. Derek Barton was sitting at the poker table, his dark hair punctuating the backdrop of platinum blonde.

She snuck backward. She couldn't let him see her. If she went down another aisle, she could sneak back to Julie and say her knee was killing her. They had to get out of here before Derek decided to work the crowd.

He laughed again. Cocky was the best way to describe Derek Barton. A *Top Gun*–type aviator and her husband's childhood friend, Derek was last person she wanted to see today. She hated when he and his attitude came to visit them. He thought the world owed him because he grew up as a military brat and now flew F-16s for the air force. Ethan overlooked Derek's audacity because her husband suffered from a condition known as loyalty. Blind loyalty. Ethan could see a million faults in the world around them, but when it came to his friends and his sister and even his wife, he didn't need blinders. His eyes were already shut.

If he ever opened his eyes, he'd be stunned to find her personal rap sheet crammed full of flaws, but he never asked, and she never volunteered. Derek was never honest about his faults either, but if he saw her in this casino, Leia suspected that the man would relish in crushing Ethan's loyalty to his wife.

He'd probably be on the phone with Ethan before she said good-bye, explaining how she'd fed their hard-earned money to a slot machine.

She'd grab Julie and escape before he turned his head.

As she turned toward the aisle, someone bumped her arm, and her quarters clanged when the bucket hit a chair.

She felt the plastic slipping from her grasp, sliding toward the floor. She tried to hang on to it, throwing down her crutches and diving for the bucket on one leg before it hit the floor.

Too late. Silver clanged around her feet as the coins bounced off the tile like icy balls of hail.

She ducked and closed her eyes. Several people leaned down to help her, but she didn't move. Maybe Derek wouldn't notice her. Maybe he'd keep on laughing with his girlfriend or score a big hand. Anything to distract him from her plight.

Derek Barton couldn't find out that she was here.

2

L EIA?"

    She heard Derek say her name, but she kept scooping up the quarters until she had recovered all the scattered coins. If she didn't make eye contact, maybe he'd go away. She could pretend the past twenty-four hours had been a horrible nightmare and return to her regular life. If only he'd keep walking to the next poker table, forget he saw her.

    "Leia Vaughn," he said again, fluttering his fingers in front of her face. "What are you doing here?"

    "Hey, Derek." She braced one hand on a chair to prop herself up, but he still towered over her. She looked up at him and then down at her crutch. When he didn't offer to pick it up for her, she bent over and snatched the crutch from the floor. "I've been Leia Carlisle for four years."

    "Where's Ethan?" The disbelief in his voice betrayed him. He knew Ethan wasn't here.

    She held the white bucket behind her back while she balanced herself on her right leg. She could play this off, couldn't she? Be polite, cordial ... and send the man on his way.

"Julie and I are on a ski trip." She propped her hip against the ATM. "We decided to stop here and eat."

"How was the food?"

She shrugged her shoulders. "I shouldn't keep you."

He nodded toward her half-hidden bucket. "You lose your lunch money?"

She squeezed the bucket to her chest. He'd found her in a casino, with a bucket full of change clasped in her arm. Even Derek could figure out she wasn't here for the cheap seafood. "Almost a hundred bucks."

"Apparently your luck has changed." He brushed both hands over his dark hair and grabbed her bucket. "I'll take it from here."

"I didn't know you gambled," she said, though all she wanted to ask was if he was any good.

"It's not something Ethan and I discuss." He winked at her. "I'm guessing the feeling's mutual."

She almost clobbered the smirk off his face with one of her crutches. How dare he assume that she was in his club? He was Ethan's friend, not hers. Her husband may have issues, but she was not above cutting ties with people who weren't loyal to her.

"I'm not trying to be sneaky," she insisted.

He pulled out his cell phone and clicked through the menu. "Great! Let's call Ethan right now and tell him what a coincidence it is that we ran into each other. And of all places …"

"You're hilarious."

"That's what I thought." He shoved the phone back into his pocket and pointed toward an empty blackjack table. "Let's win your money back."

She watched him saunter up to the cage and exchange her trove of silver for hard cash. She shouldn't be here. The second she walked out of the hospital, she should have caught a cab to the airport and flown straight to their new home.

But she wasn't at home. She was inside a casino and down a hundred bucks. It wouldn't hurt to at least try to let Derek recover the money she lost before she went back to the hotel.

She followed Derek to the blackjack table and nodded at the over-weight dealer who was outfitted in a white vintage shirt and a black bandana. Derek sat down on a stool and slid the dealer her cash.

"Give us five-dollar chips," Derek instructed.

The man exchanged the money for eight red chips.

Leia propped herself up on a chair behind Derek, and he pulled her close to him. The spicy lime scent in his cologne stifled her. She hopped off the chair and onto her good leg, scooting the seat a few inches back.

He centered two red chips in the circle in front of him and tapped the table.

"That's ten dollars," Leia whispered.

"You have to bet big to win big."

If he didn't win, the rest of her cash would be gone in three more rounds.

"You ready to get your money back?" he asked.

"I don't need you to rescue me, Derek."

"Yes, you do," he said as the dealer dealt him a card facedown on the table and a ten that faced up.

No, she didn't! He was obviously more experienced at the gambling scene than she was, but she didn't need him to do this. It was only a hundred-dollar loss ... but if he was volunteering to get it back, she wouldn't stop him. She just wasn't going to feel the least bit obligated if he managed to win.

Derek glanced at the card turned down on the table and tapped his finger on the table. The dealer hit him with one more card, an ace, and Derek announced he'd stand.

The dealer exposed Derek's hidden card—an eight of spades. He had won the first round, gaining more in seconds than she'd won in an hour.

The dealer pushed two more red chips in front of Derek. He left them stacked in the circle.

"Aren't you going to take those?" Leia asked, but he shook his head.

"No sense wasting time."

She clenched her fists. She hated giving up the reins, especially to someone like Derek who would flaunt his rescue for the rest of their lives. Depending on him for help was like climbing altitude with icy wings. No guarantees.

He won the next hand, and she relaxed her fingers. He made it look so simple. She must have a huge *L* for loser painted on her forehead.

Julie snuck into the seat beside her and squeezed her elbow.

"I just went to battle with two women trying to steal your slot machine."

"I ran into Derek at the ATM." When Leia pointed at him, Julie's brow crunched with her frown. "You remember him from my wedding, right?"

"How could I forget your charming maid of honor?" Derek leaned across Leia and kissed Julie's cheek.

Her friend winced as if a cobra's venom had burned her eyes. No flirty comeback, just utter disdain. Odd for a skillful flight attendant who usually warded off men with a playful retort.

"Concentrate on winning, please," Leia said as Julie recoiled, stepping back from the chair.

Derek's next hand was an ace and a queen. Blackjack.

"That works." Leia watched the dealer push six chips their way. Derek was up forty dollars. At least she hadn't lost it all.

"Tell me when he's gone," Julie whispered before walking away.

Leia wished Julie would stay, but she couldn't blame her. She didn't like being around Derek either, even if he was one of Ethan's so-called best friends.

She and Ethan were engaged by the time he introduced her to Derek. After their double date at the Cheesecake Factory, the man called her at home and asked her to meet him for drinks. What a pal. She didn't go out with Derek, and she never told Ethan what had happened. Ethan hung out with him every month or two, convinced that his influence would lead Derek to Christ. She hoped it would happen, but Derek was not only uninterested in their faith; he despised it. His theology—"Live to fly and then you fry." A sick motto for a hotshot.

Leia pinched Derek's arm. "Give me the six chips you just won."

"Aren't I doing a good enough job for you?"

"I'm keeping a few bucks in reserve."

He reluctantly handed her the stack of chips, and she was glad she'd asked because the dealer won the next round. Four chips gone.

For the next half hour the stack of chips ebbed high and low. Leia snatched a few chips in between plays. Extra money to beat that slot machine.

A blonde woman slipped in front of her and kissed Derek before moving to the next table. Derek didn't introduce her to Leia. He didn't need to. She knew exactly what the woman wanted, and it wasn't her acquaintance.

"You said you lost a hundred, right?" Derek asked, wiping off the lipstick stain with the back of his hand.

"That's right."

When he dumped a handful of chips into her palms, a shot of adrenaline surged through her body and washed over her leg. For an instant the pain was gone.

"All your expenses plus a little bonus."

"Thank you."

"I've got some business to attend to." He nodded toward the blonde waiting for him in the corner. "I won't say a word about this to Ethan."

"I owe you."

A disturbing smile crossed his lips. "I know."

"Well then ..." She tossed the chips into the bucket and grabbed her crutches. "Who knows when I'll see you again."

"Sometime soon." Derek hopped off the stool and yanked his leather flight jacket over his arms and was gone.

She shuffled toward the gold cage to cash out her chips and saw Julie chatting with several businessmen by the casino door.

When Julie saw her, she rushed to her side.

"You know them?" Leia asked, nodding toward the men.

"They've flown with me before. Is Derek gone?"

"Left with some blonde chick."

"He's a jerk, isn't he?" Julie asked as she grabbed Leia's bucket of chips.

"Yes, but he got my money back."

"He'll make you pay."

"How do you know that?"

Julie grunted. "Derek doesn't play nice."

"Maybe he just had a moment of compassion."

"Did he ask you how you hurt your leg?"

"No."

"Then I doubt it was compassion."

Julie poured the bucket of chips into a tray, and the woman asked how Leia wanted the cash.

"It doesn't matter." She paused. "Except I'd like twenty in quarters."

"What are you going to do with those?" Julie eyed the mound of quarters as Leia refilled her bucket.

"I'm going to play the Golden Wonder one last time." Derek may have recovered her money, but she still hadn't won. She needed to conquer that game.

Julie took the quarters from her and dumped them back into the tray. "Don't you know you're supposed to quit while you're ahead?"

Leia's hand shook as the cashier handed her a twenty. Then she followed Julie out the casino door.

It wasn't until they were almost back to Copper Mountain that she realized she'd forgotten to eat a casino lunch in case Ethan asked. Her little white lie had turned gray.

3

N OT A SINGLE BUMP ROCKED THE JET AS ETHAN CARLISLE FLEW west over the Grand Canyon. Clear skies and light winds—perfect weather conditions. He scanned the desert floor as burnt-red sands plunged into a massive purple chasm, river threads carving through the canyons. Admiring God's creation from twenty-five thousand feet was one of his favorite job perks. Today's masterpieces included redwood-colored cliffs, a misty blue lake, and a cluster of white rocky spires.

The 737-400 was packed with 144 passengers from LaGuardia, and his responsibility was to guarantee they had a safe flight. It didn't matter to him if their arrival was fifteen minutes or even an hour late. If the plane was intact, the passengers injury free, he'd done his job. On-time arrival was a bonus.

"What are you doing for New Year's Eve?" the captain asked, drinking from his glass of Sprite. The man spat the ice cubes back into his glass and adjusted his headset over graying hair.

"No plans." Ethan guzzled his water. "I wish I were in Colorado, though. Skiing with my wife."

"Isn't it about time for you two to settle down and have kids?"

"Very soon." Ethan grinned. "In exactly six months, she'll be able to quit her job."

The flight attendant knocked on the door, and Ethan handed her his water glass for a refill. He'd spread out his and Leia's future on an Excel chart, developing an intricate plan to eliminate their debt while guarding their small savings. The budget cutbacks would smart, but in six months their only debt would be their mortgage.

"Won't she miss flying?" the captain asked.

Ethan bristled. Of course she'd miss flying. She told him that every time they discussed the future. "Leia will love being a mom," Ethan told the captain.

"Sounds like she's an amazing lady."

"She is."

He knew the instant he watched Leia land the plane in Bagabag that she was amazing. She'd challenged him like no other woman he'd ever met, taking his breath away, literally, as she dodged the mountains on the way to Reauca. She was driven, dedicated to helping the Filipinos, and she was beautiful. As he watched her risk her life to carry people and supplies back and forth to the remote villages in the Philippines, he knew his days of dating were over.

After Leia rescued the pregnant woman, Ethan flew the woman and her newborn daughter back to the village the next week, in clear skies. Thank God, Leia had rebelled when their supervisor grounded her. Her tenacity to deliver the antivenom serum saved Benito's life.

Even though Leia drove him nuts sometimes, he was still crazy about his wife. And he was envious of her drive. Nothing stopped her from using her flight skills to serve the Lord. Not the treacherous runways or terrible weather or the hostile people they encountered. Not even the suave Dr. Andrews distracted her from her goals. As he ate dinner with the villagers in Reauca, he remembered thanking God that the doctor didn't live in Denver.

When he and Leia returned to Colorado, he called her the next day. Eight months later they walked down a short aisle in an Aspen mountain chapel, and he promised to love, honor, and cherish her no matter what happened during the rest of their lives.

His parents were still missionaries in Germany, but they'd flown to the States for his wedding and to visit his sister, Paige. The wedding was more like a Carlisle family reunion. His parents loved Leia, and they showered her with love and presents, since her own mother missed the ceremony.

Ethan took their wedding vows seriously. He'd promised to love and cherish his wife, protecting both her emotional and physical well-being. When she was away from him, he prayed constantly for her safety. Leia craved adrenaline like he craved caffeine.

The sun crept over the horizon, blazing shadows across the dusty landscape below them.

"Are you ready for this?" the captain asked, grabbing the microphone. He didn't wait for Ethan's answer as he called the Los Angeles Center. "This is Ambassador Air Bravo 328 Kilo requesting descent."

The radio crackled. "Ambassador Air clear to descend to ten thousand feet."

Ethan descended and reduced their airspeed, leveling the plane.

They flew by Lake Mead on the left, and Ethan glanced down at the five hundred square miles of turquoise water, culminating at the formidable Hoover Dam. Someday soon he'd rent a boat, so he and Leia could have a peaceful weekend exploring the quiet bays.

A radio operator interrupted his thoughts. "Ambassador Air, contact Las Vegas Approach, 125.02."

The captain switched frequencies and called Las Vegas. Moments later they were cleared.

"Roger, Approach Control," the captain said, the landing gear thumping toward the ground. "Ambassador Air 328, clear for the ILS 25R approach."

To his right, the lights of the Las Vegas Strip glittered like gems, accosting him every night he landed in the infamous Sin City. Whites and reds and purples competed against the dark sky; the Luxor's green laser beam blasting through center stage.

"Ambassador Air 328, contact Las Vegas tower, 119.9."

The captain changed frequency again, and the tower cleared them to land.

Ethan eyed a 757 five miles in front of them as he slowly reduced the throttle to slide down the glide slope. With no crosswinds this evening, landing in Vegas would be a snap.

"A thousand feet above ground," the captain said.

"Roger, a thousand feet above ground," Ethan repeated.

"Five hundred feet above ground."

"Roger, five hundred feet above ground."

Seconds later Ethan thrust the engines into reverse as the aircraft slapped the runway, pressing the rudder pedals with both feet until he slowed the plane and steered them toward the gate.

"Good luck to you and your wife, Ethan," the captain said as he released his seat belt and extended his hand. "Don't forget what they say about best-laid plans."

Ethan's shoulders tensed as he shook the man's hand. "I've got backup plans for my backup plan."

"I'm sure you do."

The captain shut the cockpit door.

Ethan shrugged off the man's cynicism, pulling out the checklist from the cabinet as the FAA required even though he could do the check in his sleep. Engines—shut down. Light switches—off. Parking brake—set. Fuel pumps—off. Air-conditioning—set.

He was as detailed in his personal life as he was with the flight check. He'd considered every possible scenario before constructing their family budget. No matter what happened, he had it under control.

He grabbed his flight bag and strolled through the breezeway and into the terminal. The scent of chocolate drifted down Concourse B, and he stopped at a café. He needed a drink—an iced mocha with an extra shot of espresso.

He counted his cash and then shoved it back in his pocket, pushing himself on toward transportation. They were saving money now instead of spending it on frivolous treats. Giving up his daily mocha was a small sacrifice. It would be worth it a year from now when they had a baby.

He took a sip of water from a fountain and powered on his cell phone. An envelope flashed to signal voice mail—hopefully a message from Leia. They hadn't talked since yesterday, an hour before his morning flight.

He glanced down at his watch. Six o'clock. She'd be off the slopes by now.

He hit the button for voice mail.

Instead of Leia, the message was from Derek Barton.

As Ethan walked toward the shuttle, he hit the button to replay Derek's message. Then he dialed his wife.

4

LEIA'S FINGERS FELT CLAMMY AS SHE ATTEMPTED TO HOBBLE behind Julie through the cramped restaurant. Couples lounged on Ikea sofas, toasting flutes of wine. Singles swarmed in pods, exaggerating their day's stories while downing mugs of local beer, waiting for the clock to strike midnight so they could toast in the new year.

A guy with a ponytail and an acoustic guitar belted out "Margaritaville" from a small stage in the corner of the room, and the crowd lifted their drinks as he repeated the chorus for the third time.

She was wasting away in Colorado-ville.

Julie handed her a tonic water when they sat down on two bar stools. Leia sipped the bubbly water as she looked outside the long wall of windows at a rack lined with designer skis and snowboards. Beyond that was a grand view of the snow-covered Copper Mountain. Everyone else had been enjoying the powder for the past seven hours while they'd been trapped inside a casino.

The après-ski party was Julie's idea. She wanted to pretend they'd spent the day on the slopes, but it was hard to pretend when they were the only ones not dressed in tailored ski pants and fleece.

The guitar player started "American Pie."

"Are you ready to go?" she asked Julie as she fidgeted on the stool. Maybe they could manage a walk before it got dark.

Her friend drank from her pink cocktail. "We just got here."

"I need some fresh air."

Her cell phone rang, and she looked down at the number. Ethan. She hesitated before she pressed the green button. It was time to tell her husband the bad news.

She rubbed the top of her leg as she answered the phone. "Hey."

"Do you miss me?" he asked.

"Very much."

Balancing her phone on her shoulder, she hopped with her crutches toward a window. It wasn't much quieter at the edge of the room.

"What's all that noise?"

"Julie and I are attempting to have dinner, but the place is too crowded to breathe."

He laughed. "How was the powder today?"

"I heard it was great."

"You didn't ski?"

"They banned me from the slopes."

"What?" She could hear the panic in his voice. "What happened?"

"A snowboarder tried to run me over yesterday, and I fractured my knee."

"Are you okay?"

"Going a little stir-crazy. I spent yesterday afternoon in the hospital and today recovering."

"You should have called me."

"You were in New York."

She watched the lights of the groomers smoothing a trail down the beginner's slope.

"I would have taken a sick day," he said. "Flown to Denver on the next flight."

"That's exactly why I didn't call. You had to work, and Julie's been glued to my side."

"But you're my wife," he said. "I'm the one who's supposed to take care of you."

"I'm okay, Ethan."

"The company won't consider disability, will they?"

"They'll give me time off to recover—without pay. Apparently, snow skiing is considered a high-risk sport."

"Now we know why."

She felt as if she'd been transported back to elementary school for a moment, her first-grade teacher reprimanding her for a job not so well done.

"At least you have job security," he said.

"I hope so."

"The company can't replace you over an injury."

"But if they go bankrupt, all bets are off."

"It's only a setback," he assured her. "We'll figure out a way to cut back on costs."

It always came back to money for Ethan. She knew he was silently calculating how much this injury would cost them. Their deductible plus the time she'd be off work. In less than two hours, her husband would have devised a new financial plan.

"If I get this new job, it will almost double my salary," she said.

He didn't latch on to the salary potential. "We'll tighten our budget. Rein in a few expenses."

Which meant she'd be banned from spending a cent.

"What have you been doing all day?" Ethan asked.

A man with a red vest toasted his bottle of beer in her direction, and she glared back at him. That's all she needed, a sloshed ski instructor hitting on her. "You're breaking up."

"Are you there?" he asked.

"Sorry, I can barely hear you."

"Where did you and Julie go today?" he repeated.

"We've just been resting." She ran her finger across the bar in the window. "The doctor said I won't be able to return to work for five or six months."

"Are you going to call Ambassador?"

"After New Year's. I'll beg them to postpone my interview."

"If they don't, it'll be fine."

"I really want this job, Ethan."

"Do you want me to fly to Denver tonight?" he asked.

"No. I'm hoping to catch the 6:00 a.m. flight out." Something clanged in the background, and she turned toward the stage. The Jimmy Buffett wannabe was ramping up for his next round. "Where are you?"

"On my way to the shuttle."

The singer strummed his guitar, and someone cheered from the front row. "Go home and get some rest."

"Do we have plans the last week of January?" he asked.

"Where do you want to go?"

"No place." He paused. "Derek just called, and he wants to come see our new home."

She leaned back against a pole, the cold metal chilling her skin. *How dare he!*

"When did he decide this?"

"I don't know. He said he'd been wanting to visit for a while."

"We just saw him."

"At Thanksgiving."

A couple sat down beside her, talking way too loud about the perfect conditions on the slopes. She turned the volume up on her phone.

"Is there a problem?" Ethan asked.

"I don't know if I'll be ready for company so soon."

"It's only Derek."

"Right."

ETHAN'S COMPANY SHUTTLE WAS WAITING OUTSIDE THE AIRPORT TO take the last round of flight crews to the parking lot. He rolled his bag off the sidewalk, picked it up, and carried it inside to slide on the rack. Two flight attendants and another pilot entered after him.

He nodded at the other employees as he sat down, but he was too focused on the change in his plans to talk. He turned on his Palm Pilot and opened the calculator, inputting his salary and deducting their basic living expenses. A rough estimate until he could plan it out on a spreadsheet.

He leaned back against the stiff cushion. It would be tight the next six months without Leia's paycheck. He'd been counting on her salary to help pay for their new home until he got a raise.

When the van stopped at Row E, Ethan stepped off the shuttle and walked toward his silver Honda Accord. He lifted his flight bag into the trunk, climbed into the front seat, and started his car.

With a few tweaks to tighten their budget, he'd make it work. It was only a small setback. If Leia didn't get this new job, they could start their family right away.

He wasn't happy that she was hurt, not at all, but sometimes God used trials for a greater purpose. Something really good.

Maybe this was one of those times.

As he drove out of the airport, Ethan turned southeast toward their new home in Henderson. He passed a row of casinos painted yellow and blue. Teasing. Tempting. Seducing willing people with their allure.

The stucco casino in the middle stuck out from the clutter, its white lights glittering like diamonds against the red-carpeted entrance. The sign read Casa Bonita. But there was nothing beautiful about a casino.

Ethan knew firsthand about the ugly side of gambling. It had almost destroyed his sister and her family. Paige's husband wasn't a casino gambler. Brett preferred to waste his money on high-stakes sports betting. Horse racing. Football. Hockey. The kids shooting hoops next door. It didn't seem to matter to him as long as it involved winning. His sister knew she'd married an athlete. She just didn't know how addicted he was to the win.

Ethan's heart ached for Paige. He'd spent his childhood defending her, but she told him to leave Brett alone. He didn't understand how she could sit back while her husband destroyed their family. Every time they teetered on bankruptcy, Brett promised to quit, yet his addiction to gambling always won in the end.

The last time Ethan talked to Paige, she said Brett had stopped gambling for good.

Ethan stopped at a light, and a man and woman crossed the street in front of him. The man held the hand of a toddler dressed in a lavender sundress and white sweater. Ethan glanced at his watch—8:00 p.m. What were they thinking? Their daughter should be on her way to bed.

On second thought, the family should be on its way out of this city. The Strip wasn't the place to entertain a child.

Las Vegas was an introduction to an evil no one should have to face, especially not a two-year-old girl. Once the industry captured a child, it was grueling to break free.

When he was researching the area before their move, he'd read that Vegas had the highest suicide rate in the country—suicide attempts for pathological gamblers were higher than for those with any other addiction. Maybe he should stop and tell that to the toddler's mom. Instead of a glittering pot of gold at the end of the rainbow, too many gamblers found a dingy cell—or a tomb.

Ambassador Air had given him three choices for relocation, and he and Leia had chosen Las Vegas because they could both fly out of McCarran. A convenient airport. Clean suburbs. A decent home base.

They had picked the suburb of Henderson and moved to Nevada last month. Neither of them had explored their new town yet with so many days on the road, but that was about to change. They'd slow down and enjoy family life when their first child was born. Even with all the gambling around Vegas, Henderson was supposed to be a good place to raise kids.

But every community had its dark sides. It just happened that Vegas, with all its bright lights, had a little more darkness than most cities. When Leia officially quit her job, he wanted to move to Charlotte or Dallas or Colorado Springs. Better places to raise a family.

Someone yelled from the other side of the street, and he turned to see a drunk banging on the hood of a car. What a sad life. The guy lived in a prosperous country with endless opportunities, but instead of pursuing his dreams, he and millions of people like him spent their time and money throwing their lives away.

The car behind him honked, and Ethan looked up at the green light before he sped through the intersection.

His sister needed to come to Vegas to talk to these parents who spent New Year's Eve strolling down the Strip with their kids. She could tell them that no good comes from trashing the family funds.

He shook his head as a woman holding the hands of two kids emerged on the sidewalk. Gambling. The worst possible crime against family.

5

A MIDDLE-AGED BLACK WOMAN WHEELED A CHAIR TO THE END OF the Jetway and parked it right in front of Leia. When Leia tried to hobble around the attendant, the woman pushed the chair forward, blocking her exit from the airplane.

"I've come to help you, hon." The attendant pointed down at the wheelchair as the plane's passengers poured out on both sides of them. "Give you a ride to the gate."

Leia tried to smile. "You must be picking up someone else."

She nodded toward Leia's leg. "I'm pretty sure I'm here for you."

"Who called you?"

The woman shrugged. "One of the flight attendants, I guess. Thought you could use some assistance."

"I appreciate you coming, but I don't need help."

The woman glanced over her shoulder as if she was afraid she might get in trouble if she didn't force Leia into the wheelchair. "I hate to tell you, but it looks like you do."

It didn't matter. She wasn't getting into a wheelchair. She'd made it this far; she could easily get into the Las Vegas terminal on crutches.

The woman shifted on her feet, but she still didn't move the chair. "It's my job to assist people like you."

"Like me?"

"You know." She pointed at Leia's crutch. "Impaired."

Leia straightened her arched back. "I hurt my knee in a skiing accident."

The woman raised an eyebrow.

"It's temporary," Leia insisted.

"It's really okay to ask for help."

"But I don't need it."

"Suit yourself." The woman buzzed the chair out of the Jetway like she was preparing for takeoff, leaving Leia alone to fry in the hot tunnel.

For an instant, Leia almost called for her to come back, but that was ridiculous. She didn't need a wheelchair. It wasn't like she was handicapped; she'd been skiing Copper Mountain two days ago. The injury was just an annoying distraction.

She had to ignore the pain and focus on her goal even if it was only walking forty feet into the airport.

With one hand she pushed her carry-on bag in front of her as she held both crutches in the other hand. Then she took two steps with her crutches, stopped, and shoved her luggage again.

If she could barely manage to walk up the breezeway, there was no way she could fly in a simulator for the final step in her interview with Ambassador. She prayed that they'd let her postpone.

It took ten minutes to get up the walkway, but she did it without a babysitter.

Gate C-12 was almost deserted by the time she hopped through the door, a blast of air-conditioning welcoming her to Las Vegas.

Home.

She glanced around the gate for Ethan, but she didn't see him.

The smell of pizza and hot dogs permeated the concourse. A crowd of people swarmed in front of her, pulling suitcases and pushing strollers between the gates.

Overhead, an out-of-breath TV announcer gabbed on the screen, but no one appeared to be listening. The attendant stood beside a row of chairs, her walkie-talkie glued to her mouth as she leaned against the wheelchair. She was probably reporting Leia's bad behavior in detail so she wouldn't get in trouble.

"Leia!" she heard Ethan shout, and she turned to watch her husband run toward her.

He stood about three inches above her five feet, nine inches, and his dark hair had been trimmed since she'd said good-bye to him on Wednesday. Short. Layered. Neat. He hadn't changed his hairstyle since they met five years ago. His blue-green eyes looked cobalt today above his blue plaid shirt.

It was his eyes that had captured her when they first met. And his heart. She cared deeply about the Filipinos, but she'd never cuddled with a child as he'd done with the kids in Reauca. She'd sat and watched him stroke Benito's hair while Dr. Andrews injected the boy with antivenom, wondering over and over if this guy was for real.

He was.

As they dated, he never stopped talking about wanting to be in God's will. That's what she wanted in her life too, to be in God's will, but she never seemed to get there.

She and Ethan shared a passion for their faith, for flying ... and for each other.

He almost lifted her off her feet when he hugged her.

"Nice hair," she said.

He pulled back with a horrified look on his face. "I didn't hurt you, did I?"

She laughed. "I hurt my knee, not my ribs."

"Just making sure." He kissed her. "Let's get an escort to drive us to the baggage claim."

"Not happening."

"C'mon, Leia. You hurt your leg."

"My knee."

He took the handle of the carry-on suitcase out of her hand. "Are you sure?"

"Ethan!"

"Okay, we'll walk."

They slowly made their way down the concourse, toward the baggage claim.

In the middle of the plain concourse was a row of flashing slot machines. Tinsel disguising a stark Christmas tree. She'd passed these machines a hundred times in Las Vegas and other airports but had never stopped. At the snail's pace she was traveling this morning, she had plenty of time to observe.

Every seat was filled with people who either couldn't wait to get to a casino after their plane landed or to try their luck one more time before they left town—apparently, they still had money to burn.

As she and Ethan slowly made their way past the slots, she glanced over at a man who'd just won. When the coins finished pouring out of the machine, he didn't hesitate. He snapped up one of the quarters, pushed it back into the slot, and hit the knob.

At least he was having better luck than she had had in Black Hawk.

"Isn't it sad?" Ethan nodded toward the line of people waiting for a seat.

"What?"

"These people. Wasting their lives and their money."

"Maybe they're just having fun."

"You don't believe that."

He was right. She didn't.

She couldn't tell him, but she hadn't had one second of fun playing the slots. Well, maybe toward the end when Derek won her money back, but she couldn't tell him that either. He'd have a hundred good reasons why she shouldn't have gambled, starting with his sister's husband. Brett had ruined her chances of ever visiting a casino in Vegas.

She took another slow step and then another, away from the slot machines.

The short walk to baggage took twenty minutes.

"You sure you're okay?" Ethan asked as they rode down the elevator.

She cringed. He was going to have to stop asking her that question.

"It's good exercise."

"I don't think you need to exercise right now."

Yes, she did. If she kept willing her body to move forward, maybe her leg would heal faster, and just maybe she could go back to work in three or four months instead of five.

The elevator doors opened, and they moved slowly toward the baggage claim. When two pilots passed by them, dressed in their black uniforms and gold bars, Leia sighed. What was she going to do without a job? She was going crazy already, and she hadn't been housebound yet. If she was feeling depressed in the beautiful mountains of Colorado … how was she going to survive being sequestered in their home?

There were only a few bags left to ride around the carousel. Most of the passengers from her flight had already grabbed their stuff and run.

"Are you glad to be home?" Ethan asked as he pulled her suitcase off the conveyor and set it beside her. The only thing left was her skis.

"I'm glad to see you."

"Fair enough."

"Even if I'm going to be stranded in our house."

He propped her suitcase against the wall. "It's not like you're going to prison."

She cringed. "Ouch!"

"I'm sorry, Leia. I didn't mean to …"

"I know." She hesitated. "But it feels like I'm headed to a penitentiary."

"I ordered satellite TV, so you can recover with ESPN."

"It is prison!"

A pained look crossed his face.

"I'm sorry." She grabbed his hand. "I appreciate you trying. But if I can't sit still for three minutes, how am I going to make it for three months?"

"It might be good for you to rest awhile."

The orange ski bag popped onto the conveyor belt, but his eyes were fixed on hers instead of the rotating luggage. She didn't point it out.

"Really?" The word came out as an accusation instead of a question.

"It's just that we've been talking about starting a family soon and—"

"You've been talking. Not me."

"You used to talk about it."

She lowered her voice. "You know I'm not ready for kids, Ethan."

"Sometimes God works in unusual ways, honey."

Her fingers clenched the handles on her crutches. How dare he bring God into this! How was she supposed to refute the workings of the Lord? If God wanted her to have a child, she was convinced he would tell her as well as Ethan. Ethan always played the spiritual card when he wanted something she didn't. Right now the last thing she wanted was a baby.

"Leia?" Ethan asked.

She pointed to the orange duffel as it started its third journey around the belt. "There's my bag."

6

E THAN PULLED THE CAR INTO THE DRIVEWAY OF 112 PROSPECT
Street. Their new home was a light-gray stucco with burnt-red
shutters and a terra-cotta roof. The front landscaping was typical
Nevada—a xeriscape of flat stones, white rocks, two scraggly looking
Ponderosa pines, and the obligatory yucca plant.

When he retired, he wanted to buy a cabin in the Rocky Mountains,
but in the meantime, their new place was modern and bright and had a
backyard with a covered deck and swimming pool. The four bedrooms
and three bathrooms seemed extravagant, but they'd turned one room
into an office and the other into a guest room. The fourth room would
be for Baby.

He'd handpicked this neighborhood because it was located in the
best school district in the county. When they drove down the street for
the first time, they'd seen a dad playing basketball with his son, a mom
pulling her kids in a wagon, and even a lemonade stand on the corner
with three girls running the table. He could almost smell chocolate chip
cookies baking in the kitchens. Even with the vision of a cabin in the
future, he could picture his family living in this neighborhood for a very
long time.

He and Leia had originally planned to start their family three years after they got married. But this summer would be five years, and they were no closer to having a family than they'd been on their wedding day.

Leia was stalling. At first she'd been afraid that if she got pregnant she would never be hired by one of the major airlines. Then she went and interviewed with Ambassador Air in December. She was closer to her dream than she had ever been. And he was further than ever from his dream of becoming a dad.

He wanted her to be able to fly with a major carrier—that's all she had talked about since the day he had met her. But if they were going to have a family, they needed to start soon. If she got the job with Ambassador, she'd be put back on reserve, standing by for her flight assignments. They wouldn't be able to coordinate schedules so someone was at home with their child.

She celebrated her thirty-fourth birthday this year, and he was already thirty-five. If they waited much longer to have children, people would think they were grandparents.

When he opened his car door, he watched Leia reach for her handle. Click. He locked her door before she could open it.

He grinned over at her. "I don't think so."

"C'mon, Ethan."

"You're not going anywhere alone."

He jumped out of the car and walked around the hood to the passenger side. He unlocked her door and took her arm as she climbed out. Then he retrieved the crutches from the back and handed them to her.

"Now that wasn't so hard, was it?"

She stuck out her tongue at him. "Horrible."

"Well, Mrs. Carlisle, you'd better get used to it, because I'm going to baby you as much as I can until you're better."

"That's what I'm afraid of."

"I don't think anyone is going to feel a bit sorry for you."

"I'm not looking for pity."

"And I'm not planning on giving you any. Just a few foot massages and unlimited refills on iced tea."

She shuffled toward the house. "I guess I can handle that."

"Isn't that sweet of you."

She rolled her eyes before she turned to focus on the front door.

He'd married an attractive, fun, godly woman—and one of the most stubborn people he'd ever met. He wished she'd just let him help her without complaining. He wanted to do things for her. Had wanted to, in fact, their entire marriage.

She might say she didn't want his help now, but she was going to get it. When they took their vows, he'd been serious when he said "in sickness and in health." Besides the occasional cold, this was the first time Leia had ever truly needed him to take care of her. He'd already committed to do the job, and he planned to take it seriously.

Of course he'd be traveling weekends while she recovered, but neither of them mentioned that reality. When he was home, he'd focus on her.

He took her suitcase out of the trunk and followed her slow progress toward the house.

"Yoo-hoo!"

He and Leia turned around to see a woman with light-red hair bounding out of the pink house next to theirs. She wore a lime and yellow floral skirt with a tight, sleeveless lime turtleneck top. In her arms, she balanced a plate of what looked like brownies, and he marveled that the dish made it intact as she cruised around the maze of plants and rocks in their front yard as if she'd practiced the course.

"I am *so* glad to see you." She waved the plate at him. Brownies with nuts on top.

"I'm Ethan," he said warily. "This is my wife, Leia."

The woman barely glanced at her.

"I'm Misty Knapp. Your friendly neighbor. I've been waiting and waiting to bring you a welcome gift. Baked five batches of brownies before I actually saw you in the driveway. Just finished batch number six today. Fresh from the oven."

She whisked the brownies under his nose and then pulled them back to her chest. "They're my special recipe, so don't even ask. Passed down from my great-great-grandmother on my dad's side. I bring them to all the new neighbors."

She handed him the plate like she was presenting him with a trophy. "Welcome to Prospect Street."

"Thank you," Leia said over his shoulder. The last thing she'd want to do was chitchat.

But Misty wasn't deterred. "You two are never home."

"We're both pilots," Ethan offered. "Fly out of McCarran."

"Ooh, how exciting! I love to fly, though we don't go many places these days."

When she winked at him, he felt like reminding her that not only was he married, but that his wife was standing four feet away. "After baby number three came along, we pretty much stopped touring the world, or at least the West Coast, but that doesn't mean we don't have fun anymore. We have loads of fun. There are tons of things to do around here."

She swept her hand toward their car. "Where are your kids?"

"We don't have any," Leia said.

"No kids?" Her eyes widened as she reached out to pat Ethan's arm. "Well, you should have some soon. You'll just love being parents. It's the best. They keep me laughing all day long."

He would bet that she kept them laughing too.

"So what do you like to do when you're not working?" Misty asked.

Ethan could smell the chocolate through the Cling Wrap. He wondered if it would be rude to open it up and eat one now.

"Before we moved, we were really involved with our church in Denver, but we haven't found a church here yet." He shrugged. "Haven't been home on many weekends."

"Are you Mormon?" she asked.

"Christian."

She shrugged. "It's all the same, isn't it?"

He opened his mouth to explain the differences, but Misty didn't give him the chance.

"We've got bunches of great churches around here." Misty started naming them alphabetically as if she had memorized the yellow pages.

Leia cleared her throat. "I'd better get inside."

"Of course you should." Misty fluttered her pink-painted nails.

"Here I am talking away, and you've got a broken leg. Good thing you've got such a handsome man to take care of you."

"Good thing."

Ethan wished Leia could at least feign some enthusiasm.

Misty reached out and tapped one of the crutches. "Before you go, I want to invite you to a playgroup that I have at my house on Fridays at two. You'll just love it."

"But I don't have any children."

"Oh, that's okay." Misty grinned. "The group's just an excuse for the neighborhood women to get together and gorge on sweets. The kids play while we gossip, and there's tons of good stuff to catch you up on. We may live in the desert, but news is never dry around here."

"I don't think ..." Leia began.

"She'll be there," Ethan reached out and squeezed his wife's hand. She didn't squeeze back. "Two o'clock."

"Yep." Misty winked at him. "I'd invite you too, but no boys allowed."

"I work on Fridays."

"Such an exciting career."

He cleared his throat. "So what do the guys do for fun around here?"

"Play lots and lots of golf."

"I guess I'll have to learn."

"You'd be just great at it."

"I really think I should go inside." Leia pointed a crutch toward the door. Ethan was thankful she didn't take a swing at their neighbor.

"See you Friday," Misty said as she backed across the yard.

He followed Leia up the two front steps and unlocked the door for her. The entry had vaulted ceilings with a silver chandelier hanging over the staircase that led to the second-floor loft. The living room furniture they'd picked out after they were married was a combination of taupe and dark browns. Leia had added olive green curtains, a matching blanket, and some scattered pillows that were a deep purple color.

Beyond the living room were an open kitchen and steps leading down to a family room with their entertainment center and sliding glass doors that opened to a cement patio and the swimming pool.

He unwrapped the plate, snagged a brownie, and engulfed it in two bites. Kudos to Misty's great-great-grandmother.

"Why did you tell her I'd go to her group?" Leia asked as she eased into their new brushed-leather chair and flipped out the footrest.

"So you can meet other women in our neighborhood."

"That woman's more interested in relating to you than to me."

"Don't be silly."

"I'm not."

"You have to make new friends, Leia."

"I will make friends, but not with the neighborhood flirt."

"She wasn't so bad."

"You say that only because she was wearing a tight shirt."

He sat down beside her. "You know me better than that."

She sighed. "I'm not worried about you."

He held out the plate to her. "She may talk a mile a minute, but she makes a mean brownie."

Leia took one off the plate and nibbled a bite off the end. "Not bad."

"I bet the two of us will finish these before we go to bed." He smiled at her. "So does your knee stop you from doing anything else?"

She locked his gaze. "Just what are you suggesting?"

"That you help me check out the guest bedroom."

"But we already checked it out."

"I don't think the results came back correctly."

"It may take me fifteen minutes to get upstairs."

He grinned. "I can wait."

7

THE ERRATIC CLUNKING FROM THE MRI SCANNER TURNED THE SOFT ROCK music in Leia's headphones into a disturbing alternative beat. The hospital gown irritated her bare skin, creating a persistent itch under her left shoulder blade. If only she could scratch her back like a dog with an annoying flea.

But she wasn't supposed to move. She was barely allowed to breathe.

The metal tunnel enclosed around her like a coffin, and her skin felt hot in spite of the cool air pumped into the vault. She pretended she was in the vintage open-air biplane that she flew the summer after her college graduation.

She'd flown guests at the Ohio State Fair, the chilly breeze invigorating her as they cruised the clear blue skies. Some of her riders wanted the rush of a roller-coaster ride on their short flight. She'd dive into a lazy eight and shoot up in a heart-stopping chandelle. Other riders wanted calm. She'd cruise above the fairgrounds at sunset so they could watch the downtown lights of Columbus flicker against the dusk.

It didn't matter to her whether she conducted a thrill ride or a tranquil flight as long as she was in the cockpit. She controlled the destiny of her passengers, maneuvering the plane with the touch of a control stick, rotating the nose in and out of the wind.

But today she wasn't in charge. The radiographer outside the scanner was controlling her fate while she played corpse.

"Okay, Leia." The radiographer's voice blasted through the music in her headset. "We need you to hold your breath again and count to ten."

She closed her eyes as a loud clang rang in her ears, the coil circling her knee. She felt as if she were trapped inside a steel drum, someone hammering the sides.

"You can breathe now," the radiographer said. "We'll be about five more minutes."

The cold air eased back through her nose and down through her lungs. Chilled metal. Like the icy arm of the slot machine in her fingers.

She was back in Black Hawk for an instant. White lights flashing. Buzzers ringing. The Golden Wonder tempting her with its fruit.

She'd been so close to tasting the big win that it was palpable. Just seconds from lining up the gold bars on the screen when Derek had interrupted her show.

What would it have felt like to score?

She'd ridden a wave for a few days after her win in Atlantic City. But her winnings had been piddling compared to the ten-thousand-dollar jackpot on Black Hawk's machine.

"We're done," the radiographer finally said, and the conveyor bed rolled into the glare of fluorescent lights. She took a deep breath. The air tasted like ammonia.

The man offered his hand, and she reluctantly let him help her up.

"Do you need something to drink?" he asked.

"No, thanks." She stood up beside him. "How long until you have the results?"

"The orthopedist put a rush on the MRI." He checked his watch. "The radiologist should read the results in the next hour."

She changed into gym shorts and a white T-shirt, and Ethan escorted her out of the hospital and into his Accord.

"How are you doing?" he asked as they drove toward a café for lunch.

"I'm hoping this has all been a colossal mistake. That the ER doctor was wrong."

"But your knee—"

"Maybe it's just a sprain, and I'll only be off work for a few weeks."

"And if he was right?"

She cringed. "Then I'll be catching up on reality TV for a long time."

"Let's get out of the house this weekend." He grabbed her hand and squeezed. "Maybe we can try out a new church."

"I'd like that."

"And go have a picnic at Lake Mead."

"You're too good to me, Ethan."

When he stopped at the light, he leaned over and kissed her.

Ethan might be taking a couple weekends off to help her, but he'd be flying again the next weekend. And the next. What was she going to do without him to chauffeur her around town? She'd never stayed inside for four days her entire life. Even as a girl she was always escaping the house to ride her bike or play kickball or fly the blue-and-white-striped remote-control plane that her dad bought for her tenth birthday. Her mother complained almost every day about Leia's tattered clothes, torn and grass stained from hours playing in their wooded backyard, but her dad said Leia was born to be outside.

Sometime around her eleventh birthday, her mother folded a closet full of pink dresses, lavender-laced hose, patent-leather shoes, and white bows into two cardboard boxes and carried them up into the attic. Leia never wore pink again.

Her mother might not have been able to keep her inside, but Leia's knee injury had shut her in and locked the front door.

♠ ♥ ♣ ♦

THE SILVER TOP OF DR. ROSENTHAL'S EXAMINATION TABLE GLEAMED IN the overhead light; the dark blue curtains covering the room's only window were pulled tight. Leia laid her head back against the flat pillow on the table as Ethan inched back the curtains to look outside.

A quick knock, and Dr. Rosenthal walked into the room. Leia watched the wrinkles crease around the doctor's eyes as he read her chart. He looked nothing like the emergency room doctor who'd cared for her in Colorado. This doctor's gray eyebrows matched his hair, and the wrinkles around his mouth meant decades' worth of experience. At least she hoped he had experience. He was supposed to be the top orthopedist in Las Vegas.

The ER doctor back in Colorado had looked barely old enough to read a medical journal. Definitely not old enough to interpret an X-ray. If only Dr. Rosenthal would tell her that all was well. That Doogie Howser made a bad call. On her next visit to his office, she could drive herself.

The doctor nodded toward Ethan and then turned to her. "How are you feeling?"

"Pretty good on this medication."

"Vicodin?"

She nodded as he made a note on her chart.

"Any side effects?"

"No, sir."

"Depression?"

She only hesitated for an instant. "No."

"You've been icing it?" he asked.

"Constantly. And I'm keeping it elevated too."

He looked at Ethan first before glancing back at her. "Between the medication and the isolation, I want you to let me know if you experience any signs of moodiness or unexplained sadness."

Ethan looked as if he was about to say something, but she didn't give him time to speak.

"How long until I can drive again?"

He flipped on the computer screen in front of her, and she squinted at the 3-D picture of the tendons, bones, muscles, and ligaments around her knee. With the click of the button, the picture revolved, and Dr. Rosenthal shook his head solemnly.

"It's displaced. Twelve weeks if we can correct the fracture with arthroscopic surgery."

"Surgery?"

He pointed at the screen. "You have a tibial plateau fracture."

She didn't even realize she'd been holding her breath until she sighed, her hope dashed that maybe it was only a tear.

"We need to wait a week for the swelling to decrease, and then I'd recommend you move right into surgery to realign the bones since it's a displaced fracture."

"What if it wasn't displaced?" Ethan asked.

"The bones would still be aligned, so you wouldn't need surgery."

Leia leaned toward the doctor. "How long will it take me to recover from surgery?"

"It depends on your knee, but it usually takes six to twelve months for complete recovery with physiotherapy. Possibly longer."

"When can I fly again?"

"We'll have to see how the recovery goes, but probably about six months."

"And snow skiing?"

"I don't recommend it."

She stared at him stunned. "Ever?"

"Not if you like having a knee."

Ethan turned to the doctor. "What are the risks with surgery?"

He handed Ethan a stack of stapled paperwork and then looked at Leia. "Here is some information, but the main risks include swelling and stiffness of the joint, bleeding, blood clots, infections, or continuing knee problems.

"The recovery can be both painful and frustrating because you will be immobile for the first few weeks and unable to do much activity during the first three months."

"What about physical therapy?" Ethan asked.

"She'll be going three times a week."

Ethan glanced through the first page. "Can we review our options before we make a decision?"

Dr. Rosenthal closed his file. "Of course."

Leia looked down at her knee. There was no way she was going to prolong it. Get it operated on and then move on.

"I want to schedule it today," Leia said.

Ethan flipped to the second page. "We can call in the morning."

Leia stood up on her left leg. "I'm not going to wait."

8

ETHAN DIDN'T UTTER A WORD ON THEIR DRIVE HOME. LEIA glanced over at him, but he didn't cough or sigh or even look back at her. How could he possibly be angry at her for scheduling her surgery? She didn't need any other options. Fix her knee and get back into the cockpit. The road to recovery was clear.

He pulled into the driveway and waited for her to open the door. When she got out, he put the car into reverse.

"I'm going to the store," he muttered.

"Ethan ..."

He didn't look at her. "I want you to get better, Leia, but I thought we could at least visit another doctor. Get a second opinion."

"I'm sorry, honey." She leaned back into the door. "The Vicodin is talking for me these days."

He stared at the garage door. "I'm just trying to help you."

"I want to be done with this surgery."

"It's *your* knee," he said before he backed out of the driveway.

Leia shrugged off his attitude as she wobbled through the garage. She appreciated Ethan's caution when it came to their finances or their house, but he was right—it was her knee, and she didn't need to wait for another doctor's opinion. She would have had surgery today if Dr. Rosenthal had given her the option.

The message light was blinking when Leia retreated back into the living room, and she hit the button.

"Hey!" Julie said. "I'm on my way to Vail for a long weekend, and I'm missing you. As soon as your leg is better, we'll head to the Caribbean or somewhere else that bans snowboarding."

Leia groaned and deleted the message.

She moved toward the stairs and limped up the steps, one hand on the banister, the other dragging her crutches. She finally made it to the top, but she hadn't felt this exhausted since she summited Pikes Peak.

Inside the master bedroom, she sat down in the office chair beside the bed and turned on the computer that Ethan had moved from the office to the bedroom desk so she wouldn't have to travel far to check e-mail.

The bookshelves above the desk were painted white, and she'd decorated the room with pale blue curtains and a bedspread printed with tiny white leaves. A Palladian window with a window seat lined the wall at the foot of the bed; the view below was of their swimming pool and the neighbor's backyard. A small window beside their bed looked out onto the road in front of their house.

She turned on the computer in front of her and roamed through her Rolodex until she came to the number of Victoria August, her chief pilot at Corporate Direct. She dialed the number and left the message that she'd injured her knee and needed surgery before she could return to work. Hopefully she would have a job to return to when she recovered. She followed the call by faxing Victoria a written statement about her injury and Dr. Rosenthal's letter.

Then she picked up the business card of Jeff Morton, the Ambassador Air recruiter she'd met with in Denver last month. She had to tell him that she was bailing out on her scheduled simulator ride. All she wanted was for him to understand.

She dialed the number slowly and tried to smile into the phone when the recruiter answered.

"Hi, Jeff. This is Leia Carlisle."

"Leia! I was just thinking about you."

A good sign.

"I'm afraid I'm going to have to reschedule my sim ride on Thursday."

"That shouldn't be a problem. Would Friday work?"

"Actually, it may be a few months before I can come."

He paused. "Have you changed your mind?"

"No ... I injured my knee."

"Yikes. How did you do that?"

"Snow skiing."

"The worst possible sport for a pilot."

"I've never had a problem with my knees before."

"Let me check the schedule," Jeff said. "I'll call you right back with a new date."

"Thank you."

She said a quiet prayer of thanks when she hung up the phone, and then she checked her watch. It was only four o'clock.

What was on TV at four? Soap operas? Daytime talk? Probably nothing she wanted to watch.

She opened her Internet browser and surfed a few news Web sites, checked the weather one more time, and then researched tibial plateau fractures. As she read the horror story of one woman's botched operation, she logged off the site. Probably better to have no information before she headed into surgery. Everyone felt obligated to share when something went wrong.

She tapped her thumb against the edge of her desk. Julie was probably bumping down a mogul right now, screaming into the wind, while Leia was alone in her bedroom, reading about knee surgery. Leia searched for pictures of the Vail slopes, clicking on a shot of a skier blazing through fresh powder. What if she could never ski again, never feel the breeze against her face as she sped down a mountain?

She needed another track. A distraction. She typed in the search words *Black Hawk*, and a picture of the casino she'd visited appeared on the screen. If only she'd won something from that silly slot machine, she could chalk the day up to entertainment and move on. And she would have beaten it if only Derek hadn't swooped in to rescue her. All she'd needed was a little more time.

At the side of the screen was a listing of online casinos. She clicked on a Web site called Slot Heaven, and red and yellow lights flashed on the black screen. She skimmed the intro—if she wanted to play the slots, she could play for free or use a credit card to win cash.

She'd play for free. No strings attached. Easy entertainment while she waited for Ethan to come home.

She was scanning through the list of slots on the site when she saw it. The Golden Wonder. The machine that ate all of her money and wouldn't spit a cent of it back. The game that wouldn't surrender.

She toyed with the edge of her mouse, watching the arrow swim back and forth across the screen, but she didn't open the link.

9

Leia pulled her hair back into a sloppy ponytail, brushed her teeth, and tried to scrub the orange Cheetos stains off her hands. It was after lunch on Friday, but she still hadn't dressed for the day. Or for yesterday. Why bother with clean clothes when all she'd done the past three days was hang off the side of a couch? Every time she moved, she could feel the muscles in her body morphing into lumps of fat.

She'd tried to keep her mind occupied in spite of her inability to move. She'd read two of the mysteries Ethan had checked out at the library, watched five movies, read their entire stash of aviation magazines, and spent the rest of the time surfing ESPN, the Weather Channel, and the Travel Channel.

Ethan had stuck with her through two of the movies, but then he'd gone jogging. Not that she blamed him. He could only handle the couch potato schtick for an hour or two.

She limped onto the scale and then back off to try again, but the results were the same. She'd gained three pounds since she busted her knee. Three pounds in a week! She was used to burning off whatever she ate when she played basketball at the gym. Watching TV burned about a calorie an hour, though she must have sweated off a few extra calories when she'd moved from the couch to the refrigerator to find something else to eat.

Three pounds a week. Twenty weeks.

She wouldn't be able to fit in her uniform when she returned to work.

The telephone rang, and she heard Ethan answer it.

He opened the bathroom door and handed it to her. "For you."

"Hello," she answered.

"Happy Friday! It's Misty Knapp, your friendly neighbor."

Leia grimaced. Like she would forget the woman.

"Hi, Misty."

"Just wanted to remind you that playgroup is in a half hour."

"I'm not sure—"

"You just have to come today," Misty interrupted. "I've told everyone that you're going to be here, and they're dying to meet you. We don't know any other girls who can fly. You must have a million juicy stories."

"I think I'll—"

Misty gasped into the phone. "What am I thinking? I'm so sorry. You can't get over here on your own, can you? Can Ethan help you?"

"He was just getting ready to run an errand."

"No problem. I'll be at your door in twenty minutes."

"I don't need—"

"It's no problem at all," Misty said. "I'll see you in a few."

The phone clicked, and Leia tucked the receiver into her pocket. Either the woman was entirely clueless or she was really good. Leia guessed it was the second one. Misty Knapp was a master of manipulation.

Leia reached for her crutch by the sink and climbed over the pile of dirty laundry cascading down both sides of the hamper and across the floor.

It wouldn't kill her to go to Misty's chocolate fest, she supposed. The walls in their new home were closing in on her anyway after a week of being trapped inside. She'd only stay an hour, and Ethan would be happy. But not one minute more.

Moving into the bedroom, Leia opened the closet door and stared

Leia wrapped her orange-tinted fingers around a chocolate éclair, and she bit into the creamy treat as she tried to listen as the women traded scantily dressed versions of what they termed "news." Forget attending a playgroup. She'd been conned into playing studio audience for the neighborhood soap opera. She actually longed for the quietness of her house, for her couch. In a half hour, Samantha Brown would be exploring a vintage hotel on the Travel Channel.

One of the toddlers smacked the baby who'd been sleeping in a car seat on the floor, and a wail escaped the girl's lips like a siren. Angeline told her daughter she'd be fine and kept talking as if her cries weren't echoing around them in surround sound.

God help her. If this was what it would be like to be a mother, she was never having children.

"So what do you think, Leia?" she heard Misty ask.

"I'm sorry." She snapped back into the conversation. "About what?"

The women giggled as Misty playfully rolled her eyes. "About coming to my party next weekend. We sell the best candles in the world, and you can even host a party if you want. The weekend after that is gourmet cookware. You won't have to shop for Christmas this year."

Christmas? Who was thinking about Christmas in January?

"I'll check my schedule," Leia said. She'd create something. Anything. A taxi ride and a dentist appointment if necessary. If she stayed home, she was certain her neighbor would peep into the windows and call her bluff.

"Pregnant woman potty break," Angeline said as she hopped down. "I made it thirty minutes this time."

Misty toasted her with her hot tea. "A record."

The second Angeline left the room, Heather leaned into the group. "Does anyone else think her haircut is awful?"

"It's horrendous," Misty agreed while the other women nodded their heads.

"Should we tell her?" Danna asked.

"No way," Heather said. "Never tell a pregnant woman the truth."

Leia leaned back against her chair and hoped Angeline had made it to the safety of the bathroom before her new hairstyle was chopped into pieces. She checked her watch. She'd been here fifty-eight minutes.

She stood up. "I've got to go home."

"We're not done for another two hours." Misty patted the empty bar stool.

"I'm going to attempt to make dinner for Ethan and me."

Misty winked. "You don't strike me as the homemaking type."

Leia's knuckles turned white from the grasp on her crutch. Angeline appeared back in the kitchen.

Leia turned her head from Misty to Angeline. "Could I get the number for Sadie's Salon?"

"Sure."

"Everyone was just saying how much they loved your hair."

Angeline didn't see Misty's glare as she scribbled the number on the back of a receipt and handed it to her.

"See you next week," Angeline called as Misty followed her into the living room.

Leia didn't answer, but she heard the conversation resume quickly about their favorite places to get a haircut. They were probably chomping at the bit to pulverize her. What would they say when she walked out the door? *That Leia Carlisle is one dull chick. She didn't feed us an ounce of gossip. And did you see her hair? It's even worse than Angeline's. She's in desperate need of a good cut. And I'm certain she's gained at least three pounds since she injured her knee.*

Misty plastered another smile on her face as she opened the door. "Hopefully we'll see you next Friday."

Leia smiled back. "I'll let you know."

She was never going back to Misty Knapp's house. It didn't matter if she never made another friend in Henderson. At least, she'd still have her sanity.

Ethan was waiting for her in the living room when she opened the front door.

"So?" he asked.

"Even the Vicodin couldn't stop my head from pounding."

"It couldn't have been that bad."

She stretched out her leg on the couch. "The kids were out of control, and every time one of the women left the room, the others tore her apart like they were fresh meat."

"You're exaggerating."

"I was trapped inside a saga of *Desperate Housewives*, and I couldn't change the channel."

He sighed. "So you're not going back?"

"Never."

10

CHURCH ON SUNDAY MORNING WAS A BUST. LEIA KNEW IT WASN'T a fit the moment they walked into the stained-glass sanctuary and she sniffed a warring mix of cologne and hairspray. It was a shallow observation—the people were probably the nicest people in town, but with all the dark suits and shimmering dresses, she felt like she was attending an Oscar party instead of a worship service.

She was hoping for an instant connection when they walked through the front door. Their church in Denver had been a haven of believers who were trying to be authentic and journey together through the joys and potholes that life offered. She didn't have anything against suits or hairspray, but as she listened to the sermon, she wondered if the glitz was only a flashy Band-Aid for a room filled with hurting souls. What if God washed away all their makeup along with their sins? What beauty and sorrow would be revealed?

She longed for their community back home. Even if her marriage sometimes seemed like a show of smoke and mirrors, she had a couple friends who seemed to love her in spite of her scars. No makeup necessary.

The woman who had known her best was their elderly neighbor in

Denver. Ella Turner had succumbed to heart disease two years ago, but before she died, she rode with Leia and Ethan to church almost every weekend. When Ethan was out of town, Leia would order pizza and knock on Ella's door and then spend an hour or two listening to her expound about her love for Jesus, her anger at the local government, and her shock over the price of gasoline.

Leia had been on a trip to Minneapolis when Ella journeyed to heaven. She'd been like a mom Leia always wished she'd had, and Leia grieved quietly for weeks. After Ella died, she and Ethan decided that if they couldn't fly supplies to churches in the States, they could at least drive people to church who didn't have a car. Thus began the Carlisle chauffeur service—delivering elderly people to church and then treating them to lunch before they went home.

But they didn't have anyone to take home today. She doubted anyone in their neighborhood needed a ride to church.

Ethan redeemed the afternoon by driving to the cliffs above Lake Mead. He turned off Lakeshore Road, and she could see the water below reflecting in the sun and the white mast of a sailboat riding the breeze.

"So what did you think about the service?" he asked.

She shrugged her shoulders. "It was okay."

"What was wrong with it?"

"I'd rather listen to Doppler radar than another one of those sermons."

"He spoke the truth."

"I was the only woman in the sanctuary who wasn't wearing a dress."

He swerved around a pile of stones. "Since when did you care ..."

"And no one even said hello."

"The couple behind us did."

"When they were forced to greet their neighbor."

They passed an empty pullout, and Ethan took a quick U-turn on the deserted road and drove back into the small lot that overlooked the bay. "We're not going to find another New Community, Leia."

"I know. I just think we need to keep looking."

"The unending church hop."

"It's the first church we've tried!"

Her expectations were probably too high. She and Ethan would never find the same church they'd had in Denver, but she was hoping for a place where the pastor was passionate about teaching the Bible, the music was upbeat, and someone organized small groups so she could meet other women who didn't spend their Fridays steeped in gossip. And someplace she could wear jeans.

When Ethan parked the car, a gust of wind shot up the ridge, stirring the clusters of wild grass and creosote bush in the wild space in front of them.

Leia zipped up her windbreaker and hopped out of the car on her left leg. Both crutches under her arms, she limped over the curb and through a huge gape in the guardrail. A monster truck must have plowed through the metal barrier.

Ethan carried a green cooler and a blanket beside her as they moved across the rocky field, her crutches wobbling over the dusty scree.

She peered over the precipice beside Ethan as she peeled back the hair that wrapped around her face. For an instant she was back in Reauca, bumping along the treacherous strip. Neither of them had gone back to the Philippines after they got married. Somehow they'd become satisfied with the status quo.

Ethan pointed down as two boats sped out of the bay. "It must be at least two hundred feet to the water."

"Too bad we don't have a hang glider."

He stepped back. "A good blast of wind would push us over this cliff."

"Or we could just jump."

Ethan whipped out the blanket, the breeze capturing the corners like a kite. "There's an awful thought."

He pulled the blanket back from the cliff, securing the corners with stones as he spread it across the rocky red ground. Then he took out turkey sandwiches and apples from the cooler and set them on the blanket while she cracked open two cans of Diet Coke.

He tore open a bag of chips, and she scooped out a handful. "Are you homesick?" she asked.

"A little."

"Me too."

She'd never had a problem meeting people, but making new friends was another issue. She was starting from scratch, and she couldn't even drive. Even if they did find a church, Ethan wouldn't be around to take her on the weekends. How was she supposed to make friends when she couldn't leave the house?

She needed a real friend. Not someone like Misty who squeezed every drop of information out of her so-called friends before moving on.

He took a sip of his drink. "Are you nervous about tomorrow?"

She shrugged. "I want to get this surgery done."

"You're allowed to be nervous."

"But I'm not."

He leaned toward her and whispered, "Does anything ever scare you, Leia?"

Being out of control.

Ethan's cell phone rang, and he pulled it out of his pocket, glancing at the screen. "It's Derek."

Leia cringed. Derek Barton scared her too.

Ethan answered the phone.

"When are you coming to visit us?"

He paused. "Sure. The twenty-second should work fine."

She grabbed Ethan's arm, shaking her head.

"Hold on a sec."

He pushed the mute button on the phone and covered the speaker with his palm.

"What's wrong?" he asked her.

She searched for an excuse. "What if I have physical therapy on the twenty-second?"

"C'mon, Leia, he'll understand."

"But …"

Ethan was already back on the phone. "The twenty-second works great."

Just perfect.

"Did Derek do something wrong?" Ethan asked after he ended the phone call.

She shrugged. She hated a man like him having any power over her, and now he knew her secret.

"He's cocky."

"He needs Jesus," Ethan retorted.

"But he's not interested in Christianity."

Ethan pulled his jacket over his arms. "You don't know his heart, Leia. God sent Jesus to save people like Derek, not condemn them."

Leia propped her right leg up on a pillow. "I have no doubt that God may be trying to save him, but even God can't force Derek to accept the truth."

"If God can save murderers like the apostle Paul, he can certainly save Derek."

"I'm not doubting God's ability, Ethan. God can do anything. It's Derek that worries me."

"That's why we have to demonstrate God's love to him."

"You don't understand."

He leaned close to her. "What don't I understand?"

His telephone rang again, and he looked down at the screen.

"It's Paige."

She nodded as she pushed herself up and limped back toward the car, listening as Ethan counseled his only sister. Paige was the other person in his life who could do no wrong. Leia had never heard him criticize his sister or her lack of strength to stand up when her husband was hurting her and their kids. Ethan almost thrived on her lack of self-respect as he stepped into his big-brother boots and attempted yet another rescue.

Paige didn't need rescuing. She needed to learn how to be strong.

Leia stared out at the window as Ethan told Paige she needed to come stay with them in Henderson for a few weeks. He didn't even bother to ask if it was okay with her.

Paige turned the offer down like she always did, and Ethan spent the rest of their drive home talking about his niece and two nephews—Paige had three kids under the age of five.

Ethan called Paige at least once a week, and when they didn't talk, he worried about her. The Carlisle kids had rarely seen their parents when they were young, so they stuck together in boarding school. Leia had heard all the stories about Ethan warring for his sister even when she didn't need his help. Paige was now a capable adult, but Ethan still treated her as if she were about twelve years old. Ethan didn't need a baby; he already had a kid.

When he dropped her off in the driveway, he put his hand over the phone. "I'll be back in a half hour, tops."

She slammed the car door shut with her elbow. He was being optimistic. By the time he finished the call with Paige in the grocery store parking lot and then compared the price, size, and weight for every product on their list, it would take him at least forty-five minutes to get home.

She pushed herself back upstairs to the closest thing she had to a friend right now. Her computer.

She opened her e-mail program and hit the receive button. One new message today. This one from Eva Dellman. Her mother's best—and these days her only—friend.

The subject was simple: *Your Mother.* She could only imagine what had happened now.

She slid her mouse over the message to open it but then hesitated and moved the mouse away. Eva only e-mailed when something was wrong with her mom. She didn't know if she could handle the latest about her mom's obsession.

Curiosity won the battle. She took a deep breath and slid the mouse back over to click it.

> I wish I had good news for you, Leia, but I'm afraid
> that I don't.

Of course, she didn't have good news. Eva never e-mailed her unless something bad had happened.

> Your mother was arrested at Christmas. She made

> me promise not to tell you about this incident until
> she was sentenced, but the judge gave her another
> year today, a felony charge.
>
> She won't have access to e-mail in prison, but I
> know she would appreciate it if you'd write. She
> talks about you every time I see her.

This latest incident! Only Eva would call her mother's fascination with crime an incident. When she wasn't incarcerated, Sondra Vaughn couldn't keep her fingers off jewelry, books, makeup, and even lingerie that wasn't hers. Growing up, Leia had assumed her parents were wealthy since they never had a shortage of stuff in their house. Everything from her mother's expensive wardrobe to their home's decor was in a constant state of evolution. Every time the stuff started to ooze out of their closets, her dad made them take a trip to Goodwill.

During Leia's freshman year in college she got a call from an attorney telling her that her mother had been picked up at Lazarus for stealing a pair of pink gloves. She was stunned, convinced that it couldn't be true until the lawyer said the whole thing had been caught on tape.

Leia was hurt at first and then irate. Sondra Vaughn was a devout Presbyterian and a respected bank officer in their Columbus suburb. It wasn't as if she needed anything—especially a pair of pink gloves. Her dad's life insurance policy provided well for them both.

But the pink glove "incident" was only the beginning. By the fourth time Sondra was arrested, even her expensive attorney couldn't make the crime go away. Leia went to the court hearing, and the judge looked apologetic when he said Sondra seemed like a model citizen, but shoplifting was a serious crime. It had to stop. Instead of fining her again, he sent her to jail.

Her mother's friends were shocked when they heard about the three-month sentence. Eva was the only one who stuck by her side then and for the next fifteen years as Sondra traveled in and out of prison as if it were her annual trip to Club Med.

Leia's mother had written to her several times about the empower-
ment and thrill she got from shoplifting. She said she didn't want to do
it; she just couldn't seem to help herself.

Leia hated weakness. Even before she found out about the shoplifting, she'd vowed never to be like her mom. A pair of pink gloves
hardened her contempt and severed their relationship.

She deleted Eva's e-mail, pulled it back out of the trash bin, and
then threw it away again. No reason to read it twice.

She switched programs, surfing the Internet for a few minutes,
checking the weather and news. She tapped her fingers on the keyboard. For some reason it felt wrong to go onto a gambling site on
Sunday, but that was silly. She wasn't doing anything wrong.

She typed in the address for Slot Heaven. The oranges and blues on
the screen shimmered like the light through the stained-glass window
at church this morning. But here she felt welcome. Safe.

When she hit the start button, the screen started to whirl. Then she
heard the garage door open. She glanced at her watch as she shut down
the computer.

Ethan had actually made it home in less than a half hour.

11

LEIA'S HEAD SWAM AS SHE FOCUSED ON THE BEDROOM WINDOW IN front of her. She tried to pull herself up on her elbows, but she collapsed back against the pillows. Her knee screamed in pain; her throat almost heaved. She'd taken OxyContin before she left the hospital—almost an hour ago. The pain relief should kick in any second, but she'd have to do something else about the nausea. She hadn't thrown up since she was in junior high, and she didn't want to break that record today.

She closed her eyes, her mind spinning. The surgery had lasted for more than an hour. She remembered smelling chlorine and blinking into a bright light when she entered the operating room this morning, unnerved because she hadn't succumbed to the anesthesia. She was about to complain to the surgeon when she woke up in the recovery room with an IV in her arm and Ethan by her side. He'd handed her a saltine cracker, and she'd pushed it back. Eating was the last thing she wanted to do.

The staff released her into Ethan's care that afternoon, saying her pain had stabilized, but it didn't feel stable.

"The hard part's over," she heard Ethan say, but she didn't open her eyes.

"You've got to be kidding me."

His hand stroked her hair. "Does it hurt?"

"Like it's been stripped and burned."

"The pain should go away in the next two or three days."

"I'm praying for one."

"Me too," he said. "You need to eat something."

"Not until my stomach decides it wants to eat."

"Take this." He opened her hand and set the Phenergan tablet in her palm. She swallowed it. She'd tried to be strong—rejecting the nausea medicine since she never got sick. Silly her.

"Will it knock me out?" she asked.

"I don't think so, but you'll be able to open your eyes."

"And I want to do that because ..."

He kissed her forehead, and she peeked out at him through one eye. He was smiling down at her, and she knew he was in his element. Pampering her. Coddling her. He thrived on being a caretaker. If he hadn't pursued aviation, her husband probably would have become a registered nurse.

She tried to open her eyes again and saw a vase with peach roses sitting on the window seat. When the roses started rocking, she squeezed her eyes shut.

She put her hand on her forehead. "Did you get me flowers?"

"Julie sent them to you with an invitation to ski Telluride next week."

"Isn't she funny."

He put a cold washcloth on her forehead. "Maybe you'll be able to ski again someday."

"You heard what the doctor said."

"You never know ..."

"Right now all I want to be able to do is walk down the Jetway and into the cockpit without a crutch."

He propped up her knee on a pillow. "Do you need anything else?"

She hesitated. Why was it so hard for her to ask?

"Ice," she finally said. "I'd really like a couple pieces of plain old ice."

"No problem."

She also wanted a Sprite but decided the ice would do.

The doorbell rang as Ethan stepped outside the bedroom door.

"Who's that?" she asked.

He turned back toward her. "No idea."

"If it's Misty Knapp, don't let her con you into coming upstairs."

"I'll guard the front."

He shut the bedroom door, and she heard voices downstairs. Seconds later she heard Misty's voice streaming across the loft.

Ethan opened the door, shrugging as Misty breezed into the room. The woman couldn't stand being on the sidelines.

"You must be starving!" she exclaimed.

"Not really."

"Then let's change that."

She propped a TV tray painted with daisies on the bed and then slid an insulated bag off her shoulder. Apparently she'd forgiven and forgotten Leia's remark at her chocolate party. Or maybe it was easy to overlook a barb when she was hunting information.

Misty arranged fried chicken and mashed potatoes on a plastic plate and set a couple packs of salt and pepper beside it.

"I would have brought butter, but I figured the extra fat was the last thing you needed right now." She pinched Leia's cheek, and Leia slapped her hand away.

Had anyone ever been clobbered with fried chicken?

"I can't eat until tomorrow."

"Well, then …" She picked up the tray and handed it to Ethan. "I bet you're famished."

Ethan snapped a piece of chicken off the tray and took a bite. "It's delicious."

"My mother's specialty."

Ethan glanced over when Leia groaned. "Leia needs her rest."

"Of course she does. And I've got a nest of hungry birds waiting for me at home." She turned to Leia. "I guess this means you won't be coming to my candle party."

Leia glared at her.

"No worries." Misty waved as she backed toward the door. "You can catch the next one."

Leia took a deep breath when Ethan followed her out of the room. Mercifully, she was alone.

The nausea rolled through her stomach again, and then it started to subside. She inched herself up on the stack of pillows and grabbed the remote control on the nightstand. With a flick she turned on the TV and flipped past the news, a gardening show, and a story about the *Brady Bunch* actors. Stopping at the Weather Channel, she stared at the Doppler radar map of the United States. A swarm of red patches dotted the Pacific Northwest—severe weather for flights in and out of Sea-Tac. Light precipitation over Southern California and Dallas. Snow in New York and Boston.

She clicked over to the Travel Channel. It was featuring a special on New Zealand's South Island. She watched the show for ten minutes before shutting it down. It didn't help her state of mind to see healthy people heli-skiing, ice climbing, and biking around fjords and across pristine mountain paths. She wanted to toss their expensive packs and mountain bikes into the sea.

Ethan opened the door and stuck his head inside the room. She suddenly felt as if she were at the zoo. Or in the zoo—the keeper was checking on the caged animal to make sure she was drugged and fed. If she was good, maybe he'd let her go out and play.

"Do you want to watch a movie?" he asked, holding up a DVD.

"What is it?"

"National Treasure."

"We've seen that three times."

"I'm trying to be helpful, Leia." He turned to leave.

Her eyes glanced at the computer beside the bed. If only Ethan would run an errand or two, she could escape without actually leaving the room.

But she couldn't go online as long as he was in the house. At least a movie might distract her.

"Okay," she agreed, "let's just watch the movie."

He turned it on and sat down on the bed. As she watched the characters risk everything to uncover the treasure, her mind wandered. She was ready to take some risk. Or at least face a challenge that didn't involve getting out of bed. The computer taunted her. It was right there. A foot away. Yet it might as well have been a hundred miles away with Ethan on the other side.

She fidgeted through the movie, counting the minutes until it was done. As the credits rolled, Ethan's eyes closed.

"Honey," she whispered.

He didn't move. "Yeah?"

"I'm hungry."

His eyes crept open. "Do you want some of that chicken?"

"I'm craving a cheeseburger."

"In-N-Out?"

Her stomach rumbled. "Definitely."

He sat up and tugged on his jeans. "Good thing I love you."

She kissed his cheek. "You're the best."

He grabbed his wallet off the nightstand and moved toward the door.

After he left, she swallowed another OxyContin to ease the burning in her knee and carefully slipped her wrapped leg out from the sheets. On her good leg, she took one hop toward the desk chair and propped her right leg up on a pillow.

She was hungry, but she was more interested in checking out Slot Heaven than eating. She set her alarm clock for thirty minutes before she logged on to the computer. The Web site chimed as she read through the instructions, and then she passed on the screen invitation to input a credit card number. She picked the Golden Wonder, and a glowing box on the side of the screen filled her account with five hundred bucks in play money.

She leaned back in her chair, her fingers brushing the keyboard. The room was so quiet. Surreal. It was nothing like the chaos in a casino. Here she was at peace. She spun the slot machine and savored the rush of anticipation as she waited.

The game ate her two-dollar bet, but she didn't stop to think about the loss. It wasn't like she was using real money. She could bet a hundred dollars if she wanted and still not lose a thing.

She upped the ante to five dollars and spun again. The machine ate that too.

She took a deep breath. Losing was just part of the game. It made winning so much more fun.

On her next spin she won back three dollars, and then she lost six. She spun again. And again.

The clock beeped beside her, and she slapped the button to shut it off. The thirty minutes had passed in a warm, soothing blur. It didn't even matter that she'd lost two hundred dollars in her dash to win. She was just glad she hadn't used her credit card.

AFTER HER FOLLOW-UP VISIT WITH DR. ROSENTHAL ON FRIDAY, Ethan drove them to a small coffee shop near the hospital. Scattered across the cozy room were antique tables; faded rose cushions attached to high-back chairs; and open steamer trunks packed with books, magazines, and wooden board games.

Leia followed Ethan to a corner table in front of the ornate fireplace. Sepia-tone pictures of royalty lined the dark mantel, and a basket on one side was filled with firewood.

Leia reached down and touched the firewood. Dry but real. She couldn't imagine it was ever actually cold enough to use a fireplace in Vegas, but the wood was a nice touch.

Ethan pushed her seat in behind her. "Iced tea?"

"Peach."

"You got it," he said as he turned around.

Ethan had spent the week turning their house into part hospital, part hotel. He bought a dozen ice packs for her knee and stacked them in the freezer. He stocked the refrigerator with groceries. He did the laundry. He borrowed a stack of books from the local library, rented a couple of new DVDs.

And now he was leaving her alone … for four days.

She glanced over at him standing beside the café's shiny front counter. He wore dark Levi's with a burnt-orange shirt that buttoned up the front, the collar of his white T-shirt lining the top. The young barista twirled the tip of her blonde ponytail as she smiled at him, but Ethan didn't seem to notice as he took the drinks from the counter.

No matter where they went, women flirted with her husband. It didn't seem to matter that she was sitting near him or even right beside him. And when they found out he was an airline pilot, the women swooned.

Even after four and a half years of marriage, she still wondered why Ethan had chosen a tomboy as his wife. At the beginning of their relationship, she'd admired him and enjoyed his company. Her heart even fluttered a few times when he touched her shoulder or squeezed her hand, but she'd never slobbered over him. She still thought Ethan deserved to be with someone like the drooling barista or Misty Knapp or the two ex-girlfriends who still called him, even though he'd asked them to stop.

"Your tea, my love," he said as he slid her drink across the table. The barista glowered at her, and she grinned in return. She wanted to mouth, "He's mine," but figured that was obvious.

Ethan set a small cup in front of him, and Leia eyed it. Usually he had a large mug filled with frothy milk, chocolate, and espresso.

"Where's your mocha?" she asked.

"I decided on coffee today with a shot of chocolate."

She raised an eyebrow. "You never order plain coffee."

He took a sip of it. "It's not bad when you add lots of milk."

"What's going on, Ethan?"

"I'm just trying to cut back right now. Save a little money."

"We can afford your daily mocha."

At least she figured they could. Ethan was the one who handled their finances, but her income was supposed to go directly to their savings and retirement accounts as well as funding an occasional vacation and weekend getaway. They'd decided when they got married to live on one income in case one of them lost their job in the unreliable field of aviation. Her accident was just a temporary setback. She'd be getting a paycheck again soon.

"Coffee's fine," he said as he took another sip. "Have you heard back from Ambassador yet?"

She shook her head. Jeff Morton hadn't even bothered with a courtesy call to say he was still working on rescheduling the rest of her interview. Hopefully he'd just gotten behind—she wouldn't be able to fly anyway until the summer.

"What are you going to do while I'm gone?" Ethan asked.

"Run a marathon."

He ignored her comment. "Do you need me to get you anything else?"

"The tea's fine."

"I meant before I leave this afternoon."

She reached over and squeezed his hand. "You've already turned the house into a resort."

"I'm just—"

"Where are you staying tonight?" she asked.

"New York."

She stirred another packet of Splenda into her tea. "There's a low-pressure system moving through Ohio."

"I'll be in New York before it comes through."

"Snowstorms across the Midwest."

"I know, Leia." He smiled. "I watched the weather with you."

She sighed. "I wish I were the one flying out today."

"If you were going with me, we could eat at Le Rivage."

"Hardly the place to eat on our new budget."

"I'm only kidding," he said. "I was just thinking about our second anniversary."

She would love to eat at Le Rivage tonight. Lobster bisque and bay scallops baked with Gruyère sounded much better than the delivery pizza she'd be settling for.

"Do you remember?" he asked.

"What?"

"Nothing." He checked his watch. "I have to be at the airport in an hour."

She stood up and tucked her crutches under her arms. "We better go."

Twenty minutes later Ethan parked the car in the driveway and helped her to the front porch. Unlocking the door, he shoved it open for her but didn't go inside.

"I'm going to miss you," he said as he pulled her close to him. She kissed him, resting her head on his shoulder. "Now I'll be able to see you every time I come home."

"It's only temporary, Ethan."

"Then I'll enjoy it for now."

He kissed her again, and then he walked toward the car. She stood at the door and saluted him with a crutch as he drove off.

After she shut the door, she leaned back against the frame. The room was eerily quiet. She'd have to blast the Weather Channel for white noise.

12

AFTER THREE DAYS OF WATCHING MOVIES AND BAD TV ALONE, Leia opted to take action. She'd been avoiding the computer since Ethan left for his ride. A phantom called guilt had haunted her since she'd sent Ethan out for a cheeseburger even though she wasn't doing anything wrong. She hadn't even used real money to play.

Yet Ethan wouldn't see it was a game. To him, gambling was personal.

She'd tried to avoid the computer for him, but today it called her with fervor, the Golden Wonder mocking her defeat.

She was ready for a battle. And she was going to win.

It was Sunday again, but there was no one to take her to church. No one in the state of Nevada seemed to care that she was alone. She yearned to escape to a place that the TV screen couldn't take her. A companion who wouldn't judge her for craving a high.

She stared at the computer screen in front of her.

There was nothing wrong with her desire to succeed. God knew her heart even if Ethan wouldn't understand her need for a mental retreat. Her husband was far away—flying over Louisiana or Mississippi this afternoon. He was enjoying his day in the sky. What was the big deal with her having a little fun even if she was grounded? It was her time, her space. And she was supposed to rest. All she had to do was lift a couple fingers to play.

She slid her mouse over the Golden Wonder icon and clicked it. Brightly colored fruit and silver bells rolled across the screen, dangling like the steady swing of a hypnotist's watch. She couldn't keep her eyes off the chain.

She blinked when the spin stopped. Two cherries and a gold bar.

She had won!

A surge of power raced through her arms, tingling her shoulders. She didn't hesitate. She tapped the mouse to spin again.

Another win!

The hands on the wall clock spun as quickly as the silver credit meter on the screen. In a couple of hours, she was up $1,150!

So this is what it felt like to beat the machine. To be on top again.

The exhilaration pumped another rush of adrenaline through her chest. The energy she'd needed to get out of bed was only a few steps away, on her desktop. She could almost feel her strength returning. The satisfaction she'd craved for much longer than a week was finally hers.

If she played with actual cash, she might actually make some money this time around.

With a quick roll back of her shoulders, she reminded herself that the free area was designed to get her hooked so she would bet cash. She probably wouldn't make this much when, *if*, she entered a credit card number.

But there was no harm in pretending. She could keep winning without costing Ethan a dime.

The telephone rang in the background, and she put her hands to her side, checking her pockets for the cordless. She'd left it downstairs.

No sense even trying to run for it. Besides, it was probably Julie calling to brag about another glorious day of skiing Vail. She could almost hear her friend's exact words—fresh powder, crisp blue sky, and the feel of the breeze against her face as she plowed down the mountainside. It wasn't fair.

Leia tapped the mouse with her thumb and watched the slots whirl around again.

A blast of adrenaline raced through her body as the tick slowed and then displayed her win.

She smiled. Some people ran away when they were faced with conflict, but God had created her with the need to confront every new challenge and conquer. Here was a way to do it without having to leave her house. A simple device to escape her frustration without hurting a soul.

She hit the button. This might not be as much fun as skiing, but it sure beat another evening of TV. One hundred fifty channels, yet nothing was worth watching. As long as the phone quit interrupting, the game would distract her mind from the pain that hammered her knee.

She smiled. *Knee? What knee?*

Why did people even need to go into a sterile casino? They could play at home and not pay a cent.

Another hour or so vanished, and her stomach growled. She glanced up at the clock beside the desk. Seven! Where had the time gone? She pulled down the menu to shut it down but opted to put it asleep instead. Just in case she wanted to play later.

Grabbing the crutches beside the desk, Leia slowly walked out of the bedroom and down the hardwood staircase. Her kitchen looked dull compared to her neighbor's cascade of color. She'd painted one wall tan, and the rest were the original eggshell, decorated with barn-wood frames that displayed the Colorado wilderness shots they'd taken over the years.

On the wall beside the breakfast table were shots of vibrant yellow aspens in their full fall bloom and a wildflower meadow near Ouray. A picture of a broken-down cabin by a rocky stream was above the sink, and a photo she'd taken of the snow-covered Collegiate Peaks hung at the end of their light-oak cabinets. She missed the rugged beauty of the Rockies.

Opening the refrigerator door, Leia examined her limited choices for dinner. Leftover pizza delivered two nights ago, a few slices of turkey sandwich meat, a half carton of blueberry yogurt, and four eggs.

Ethan would have to visit the grocery first thing tomorrow and stock up before she starved.

She took the eggs out of the carton and cracked them over a pan before turning the stove on high. What gourmet utensil would Misty Knapp select to scramble her eggs? She bet the woman could talk for a full hour about Leia's lack of domestic skills.

When she stirred the eggs, yolk splattered across the stove.

Make that two hours.

The phone rang again, and she hopped to the edge of the counter and picked it up.

"Where have you been?" Ethan snapped when she answered.

She checked her watch again. Seven thirty. "Nowhere."

"I tried to call you three times."

She fidgeted with the phone cord. "I'm not ignoring you, Ethan."

"I was just worried about you. You're supposed to be at home."

"I'm fine."

The eggs popped, and she limped back toward the stove. A raw burning smell drifted from the pan as she turned over the eggs; a crusty brown covered the bottom. Misty would probably faint.

"Our flight's delayed, so I don't know when I'll be getting back."

"Where are you?"

"Houston, but we're waiting for a plane from Chicago. They're being pounded by a snowstorm."

She looked outside the kitchen window at the sunset reflecting off the dusty mountain range in the distance.

"I know you're going crazy at home."

She sprinkled salt and pepper on the crispy eggs. "I'm fine."

"How's your knee?" he asked.

"Tolerable as long as I take my meds."

And even better when I'm online.

She spooned the eggs onto a plate and looked down at her half-burnt meal. She didn't suppose blackened eggs would make her neighbor's gourmet list.

How long would it take her to climb the stairs with the plate of eggs? If she could balance it right, she could eat her dinner by her computer and play a few more slots before she went to bed at eleven—or twelve.

Ethan broke the long silence. "We'll go do something fun this weekend."

"Bungee jumping?"

"I was thinking low impact."

She sat down on the last step of the staircase. There was no way she could get upstairs with the brace, the phone, and her plate of eggs.

"Don't wait up for me," he said. "It'll be long after midnight before I get there."

"No problem," she said before hanging up. She left the phone on the top of the banister as she climbed back upstairs with dinner. She didn't feel like talking to anyone else tonight.

13

ETHAN RUBBED HIS EYES AS HE STROLLED WITH HIS FLIGHT BAG out of the airport and onto the shuttle. In three more days he'd be back at the airport. With his four-days-on, three-days-off schedule, there was barely enough time for him to enjoy a break. It took him an entire day to recover from his trips and another half day to prepare to leave again. Not much time in between, but if Leia was up to it, he would take her back to Lake Mead on Wednesday or Thursday.

He glanced at his watch: 2:04 a.m. If the driver headed toward the parking lot in the next few minutes, Ethan would be home and in bed with his wife before three.

The shuttle doors opened, and an Asian woman with dark hair pulled back into a sleek ponytail walked up the steps. He'd flown with her a few months ago. Mary? Maggie? He remembered that she brought her own green tea to drink during their flights together, but he couldn't remember her name.

"Hi, Ethan," she said as she sat down across from him. "Let me guess, weather delay?"

"You got it."

Three more people entered the shuttle and sat down beside

them. The driver opened the doors for one last person and started the engine.

"I thought you were based out of Denver," she said as she took a sip from her covered Styrofoam cup.

"We moved here four weeks ago."

"I've been here for five years, so it's practically home." She slid off her shoes and stretched her toes. "How do you like Sin City?"

"We actually live outside it."

She shrugged. "It's all the same, isn't it? A casino on every corner."

"We tried to move as far away as possible from the Strip."

"Have you been to the new Regal Palace yet? It has an underwater tunnel leading to the casino floor."

Why did people assume you had to be a casino junkie to live in Nevada?

"I haven't been to any of the casinos."

"You're kidding me." She wrapped her manicured fingers around her left arm and leaned toward him. "You don't gamble?"

"I've never gambled."

Even in the faint overhead light, the question in her eyes communicated clearly. She didn't believe him.

"Is that so strange?" he asked.

"The only people who don't gamble are recovering addicts."

"And Christians."

"Hardly." The sarcasm in her laugh made him cringe. "They're pulling slots right next to the rest of us."

As the shuttle pulled away from the curb, he debated pursuing that topic, but it wasn't the right time or place.

"I don't get it," he said instead.

"What?"

"How someone could throw all their money away on gambling."

She cleared her throat. "Most people just gamble a little for fun."

He leaned forward. "Then there are others who lose everything."

"If it's an addiction."

"Yeah …"

"You don't believe that?" she asked.

He'd read an article about gambling addiction after Paige told him that Brett had a problem. The reporter said it was a psychological disorder, and if a casino was located within ten miles of an addict, it spelled disaster. Good ole Vegas.

But he still couldn't fathom why anyone would hurl their life savings away on a horse race or, even worse, borrow money just to dump into an industry that was already reeling in about $70 billion a year. Not good odds for the gambler.

He glanced out the window—Row B. His car was parked in G. "I don't understand why people don't pack up their wallets after they lose a few dollars and walk away."

The pilot to his left looked over at him as if he were crazy.

"Gambling is more addictive than drugs or alcohol," Mary-Maggie said. "Gamblers never crash, so they ride their high until the money runs out."

He rubbed his hands together. "They're throwing everything away."

"For a rush."

"A man could ruin his family like that."

She turned away from him. "It's not just a male problem, you know."

"Primarily."

"Not anymore."

"Don't you two have anything else you can talk about?" the other pilot asked.

Mary-Maggie leaned toward the man. "It's hot tonight, isn't it?"

"Beats the icy cold up north," the pilot responded.

The safe arms of the weather … Apparently, he'd just learned how to kill a conversation in Nevada.

Mary-Maggie nodded to Ethan when he slipped his bag off the shuttle's shelf and walked down the steps into the dimly lit parking lot. He hadn't meant to be rude. He was genuinely curious about how anyone could risk everything to pull a slot machine handle or play cards.

He got into his car, plugged in his iPod, and strummed his steering wheel as James Taylor sang "Fire and Rain." Turning out of the airport parking lot, he struggled to stay awake as he drove home.

When he pulled into their driveway, he looked up at the bedroom window and saw a light.

Maybe Leia had decided to wait up for him after all. She used to do that a lot during their first year of marriage, teasing him when he walked through the bedroom door. He opened the garage door and drove inside.

He used to wait up for her too after a late flight, but they'd grown older and more enamored of their sleep.

He grabbed his blazer and flight bag from the front seat and hopped out of the car into the warm garage.

He wanted to see her tonight. Pull her close to him. Kiss her gently before they fell asleep. When he'd talked to her on the phone earlier, she'd sounded tired and confused, lethargy smothering the energy that typically poured out of her and exhausted him. He wanted to give her a hug and tell her how much he loved her.

He pulled his suitcase out of the trunk and stopped to unbutton his shirt. Mary-Maggie was right about the temperature. It was hotter here than it had been in Houston.

It was a short walk through the house, to the stairs.

He called out toward the bedroom before he bounded up the steps. "I'm home."

♠ ♥ ♣ ♦

LEIA JUMPED IN HER CHAIR, SHOCKED BACK INTO REALITY. HER GAZE shot up to the clock, and she gasped. Where had the night gone?

She blinked twice. She was in her bedroom, the desk lamp on.

She clicked off the light and glanced back at silver numbers glittering in the right-hand corner of the screen.

She'd won more than nine grand in play money. If only she had a few more minutes, she'd top it off to ten.

Ethan's shoes pounded up the stairs. It was too late now to mess with the computer. She had to get into bed.

With a click, she quit Internet Explorer and jerked the mouse to the top of the screen to put the machine to sleep. Close enough to off.

Ethan's suitcase tapped the floor with a soft clunk, and she heard the wheels scraping across the hardwood.

Leaping forward on her good leg, she sprang toward the bed, steadying her breathing as she froze on top of the covers.

She clenched her hands beside her chest as Ethan opened the bedroom door. Her fingers were still trembling from the rush, the feeling that she was alive again. She wasn't ripping down a powdered mountain, but she'd escaped to another place. For twelve hours.

She'd planned to shut down the computer and climb into bed the second she heard his car pull into the driveway, but her mind had been so far away that she hadn't even heard Ethan open or close the garage door.

Her husband tiptoed across the floor.

Why hadn't she been more prepared? She should have set an alarm, shut down the computer, and gone to bed at midnight, hours before he got home. All he had to do was open her online history, and her games were over.

She'd have to be more careful next time. Even if she hadn't spent a penny online, Ethan couldn't find out what she was doing. If he walked in while she was playing slots, he'd … well, irate wouldn't begin to describe his reaction. He'd be livid.

She could try to make him understand how playing cured her boredom, stifled her urge for something challenging. It was a diversion that watching TV or reading a mystery couldn't match for satisfaction.

But he wouldn't understand.

Once she was mobile again, she wouldn't need to gamble online. She could go to a lake or the mountains or drive all the way to the Grand Canyon if she wanted. This was only something to help her pass the time.

He walked across the floor, and she opened one eye, peeking out into the darkness as he leaned over the computer. Click.

She held her breath when he revived the screen.

14

ETHAN ROLLED HIS SUITCASE ACROSS THE LOFT AND OPENED THE bedroom door. He glanced around for the light, but the room was dark, Leia breathing softly on the other side of the bed. Strange, he could swear he had seen a light. A street lamp must have reflected off the glass.

He looked down at his wife in the moonlight. She wore a T-shirt and jean shorts, and her soft hair tumbled over her face. She must have been too tired to pull on her pajamas.

When he leaned over to kiss her cheek, something crunched under his feet. He reached down to pick up the ice pack that had fallen off the bed.

He'd really wanted to tell her he loved her. That everything was going to be okay. If she'd let him, he would hold her in his arms and remind her that he was here to care for her. Of course leaving her home alone was hardly taking good care of her, but he had no other choice if he was going to provide for her as well. Quitting his job wouldn't be good for either of them.

He threw his navy uniform jacket and pants across a chair and walked toward the bathroom to brush his teeth.

As he passed by the computer on the desk, he saw the source of the light—blue and orange flashes from their screensaver traveling across the screen. Odd. Leia always turned it off before she went to bed.

He leaned over the desk and shut it down.

WHEN THE COMPUTER DINGED, LEIA RELEASED HER BREATH. HE'D only turned it off. No harm done.

Tomorrow she'd erase her online history, so he wouldn't stumble across it. Everything would be fine once she brushed over her tracks.

Candy-red apples and shiny gold bars and purple grape clusters rolled through her mind. Tick. Tick. Tick. Like the flash of a camera, they'd illuminate and then disappear.

She smiled in the darkness.

It was the best night she'd had in a long time. She didn't care if the money was fake. She was winning, conquering, soaring. Now she understood why people spent hours at a casino. It wasn't for the food or the people or the stale air. It was for the thrill of the win. The ability to thrive no matter what was happening at home.

Ethan turned off the bathroom light. She listened to him walk back out of the bedroom.

She propped herself up on her elbows. Where was he going? She repositioned her knee and lay back down, waiting in the darkness for him to return.

When he did, he tugged her shorts over the immobilizer, lifted her leg, and stuffed a pillow under it. Then he set a fresh pack of ice on top of her knee and covered her body with a fleece blanket. She didn't move.

He crawled into bed beside her and put his arm around her. She snuggled close to him, quietly thanking God for the kind man he'd given her.

"It's me," he whispered in her ear.

"Hey," she murmured as if he'd just woken her up.

"You fell asleep with your clothes on."

"Too tired to take them off."

"I put a new ice pack on your knee."

"I can feel it."

"Do you need any medicine?"

"No."

"Go back to sleep." He kissed her hair. "I love you."

"I love you, too."

He rolled over, and she heard his breathing deepen. He'd be snoring soon.

Their neighbor's porch light shone through the long window at the base of their bed. She rolled over, and her eyes caught the light against their wall. She wouldn't be able to get much sleep tonight. She probably wouldn't have slept at all if Ethan hadn't come home. If only she'd bet real money on the slots, she would have been up nine thousand dollars. Money in the bank. A couple of big wins and she could easily make up for the loss of her salary.

If only she could get back online and at least summit the ten-thousand mark. Lying here was a waste of time.

It took another hour before she calmed the spinning in her mind.

"GOOD MORNING," LEIA WHISPERED TO ETHAN WHEN SHE WOKE UP AT eight. She'd been dreaming about hiking up Pikes Peak, scrambling over a scree field to summit the mountain.

Ethan mumbled something back she couldn't understand and turned over. He usually slept ten or eleven hours after a long trip.

She sat up and started to fling her legs over the side of the bed when pain shot through her leg like cracking ice. She heaved her leg onto the floor and limped toward the bathroom door. How many more mornings would it hit her that she was trapped? That her mind was willing, but her body was weak? After her night climb up the peak, she'd forgotten that she couldn't run or even walk. Her leg, her brain, her entire body was ready to flee the house—every part of her except her knee.

Using the desk as her support, she hopped toward the bathroom on the other side of the room. As she splashed water on her face, the last critical seconds on Copper Mountain came back to her in slow motion. The rush of the powder. The blur in the corner of her eye. Flailing. Stumbling. Shooting forward when she tried to stop. And then screaming that her leg was on fire.

If only she'd waited, taken the next seat on the lift. She would have been thirty seconds or so behind the punk who spun her life out of control. Amazing how a mundane thing like waiting in line at a ski lift could alter the direction of her life.

She dried her face on the towel and threw it on top of the pile beside the hamper. Ethan could take the piles downstairs today, and she'd spend her day washing and drying. Great fun. Laundry.

If only Jeff Morton would call with a new interview date. She'd at least have something to push toward when her knee healed.

She was ready to join the Ambassador crew even though she enjoyed the adventure of flying charters. Right now she never knew where she was flying until she arrived at the airport for work. Last month she'd spent the night in Aspen, Portland, Park Valley, Biloxi, and Jackson Hole. Even though she'd be on reserve for a year or two at Ambassador, all of her layovers would be at the major hubs.

Giving up the variety and a little freedom was a small sacrifice. The salary would be much higher with the commercial airlines even though she wasn't doing it for the money. Her dad had always wanted to fly with the majors. If he were still alive, he'd be so proud that his daughter was finally joining the ranks.

She was ready to get back in the cockpit. She missed the sweet smell of jet fuel on the tarmac, the rush of pushing back from the gate to launch a flight. There was no room for monotony when she flew— either in the air or when she arrived on the ground.

She and Ethan used to spend at least one weekend a month flying a Cessna out of Denver's Centennial Airport, heading west toward Leadville or Montrose or Durango. In the winter they'd ski during the day and spend the night at a quaint bed-and-breakfast, breathing in the mountain air on a wide porch until past midnight, her with a mug of hot tea in her hands and Ethan with a fancy espresso drink. In the summer they'd throw on their backpacks and hike all day, camping out by a mountain lake and eating freeze-dried roast beef and potatoes for dinner.

The process of selling and buying a new home had stolen all their free time during the fall. They hadn't gone anyplace fun together in months. Maybe she could talk Ethan into hopping on a plane with her and heading to Santa Barbara. She'd even let him wheel her around if he'd go.

Her fingers shook as she tried to brush her teeth. Excessive adrenaline. Energy with no place to go. If she couldn't get online, she needed to get away from here before she went crazy.

One step at a time. She'd start with breakfast. A bowl of Special K.

She attempted to creep across the bedroom floor, but her crutch smacked the side of the metal chair and clanged against the desk.

Ethan sprang out of bed like someone had yelled *fire*. "What happened?"

She lifted her crutch. "I'm sorry."

"No problem." He sank back into the mattress as she stepped toward the door.

"What do you want to do today?" he asked, his voice barely audible.

"Something different." She sat down on the bed beside him. "I think we should go to California. Stay in a bed-and-breakfast in Santa Barbara or Morro Bay."

He groaned. "I don't want to be anywhere near an airport."

"We could drive," she insisted.

His head shook against the pillow. "We're saving money right now, Leia. Not spending it."

Money. Her constant reminder that she was out of work until her knee healed. One less paycheck and a bigger house payment for the Carlisle family. She was hardly holding up her end around here.

Maybe she could make a little extra cash while she was recovering, and they could stay at the Four Seasons near Santa Barbara when her knee recovered or spend a weekend sailing in the Pacific. She could almost feel the rush of wind against her face.

Ethan turned over and pulled his pillow over his head. She eyed the door, but she wasn't hungry anymore. She had to be proactive if she was going to get out of this house anytime soon.

She hopped back toward the computer and sat down.

She could set a limit. Fifty dollars. A hundred maybe. She'd decide later. If she started losing money, she would just stop playing. But if she played as well as last night, the sky was the limit.

With the chime of the computer, she turned it on.

Ethan looked over the top of the pillow. "What are you doing?"

"I'll be quiet," she said. "Just wanted to look up a few things."

If she had a credit card in her name, Ethan would never know where her extra money came from ... or maybe she would tell him eventually that she was winning some cash on the side. Either way, it was much better than hustling gourmet cookware or candles.

He stuffed his face back under the pillow as she surfed for credit card companies. She'd thrown away a million applications that had come as junk mail. Surely someone would want her business.

She scanned through sites of Visa, MasterCard, and American Express and selected a cash-back card with no annual fee. It took less than five minutes to fill out the online application and submit it. Now she just had to wait for approval.

She clicked over to her e-mail and checked for messages. Still nothing from Ambassador. How long should she wait to call Jeff again?

She fingered his business card, slid it back onto the desk, and turned down the volume on her computer.

Instead of erasing her online history, she pulled up the Web site she'd been slamming away on yesterday. She looked at the slot in front of her and then back at Ethan sleeping in bed. She'd play only for a few minutes. When he started to wake up, she'd shut it down.

She tilted her head to the right to stretch her neck, and then she pressed the start button.

Ethan coughed, and she jumped, closing the Web site before he opened his eyes.

What was she thinking? She clicked through the preferences on her computer screen and quickly erased the Web site history. He'd never know the difference.

Her stomach rumbled.

Before she started her trek down to the kitchen for breakfast, she flipped back to her e-mail one last time. She had a personal note from the credit card company.

She'd been approved.

15

ETHAN KISSED HER ON HER CHEEK AS HE WALKED OUT OF THE house with his flight bag in one hand and his cell phone on his ear. He waved back at Leia before opening the car door and getting inside. She glanced down the street as he backed out of the driveway. Two garage doors opened. A mom loaded her kids into a minivan. An SUV cruised past their house. And then a motorcycle sped by.

She wasn't leaving the house, but like all their neighbors, she had someplace to go.

Leia shut the front door and locked it. There was no time to waste. Ethan would only be gone until Tuesday.

She pulled herself up the stairs and into the bedroom.

This time she wasn't worried about being bored during his four-day trip. With Ethan gone, she could play slots all afternoon.

She grabbed a pillow from the bed and stuffed it on the office chair, propping her leg back up on the bed. Then she turned on the computer, logged into the gambling Web site, and chose the Golden Wonder.

The one-armed bandit was going to pay.

She unfolded a piece of paper she'd been carrying in her shorts pocket and entered the number of her new credit card onto the site. She had a fifteen-thousand-dollar limit, but she'd use only a hundred or two to get started. The card was only the key to open the vault. Once she had money in the casino bank, she'd never have to use it again.

She deposited a hundred dollars into her account and launched her game.

With her leg propped up on the bed beside her, she spun the reels on the slot machine. In a dizzying race for the win, silver bells, red fruit, and golden bars flew across the screen before ticking to a halt.

She closed her eyes and murmured a prayer that she'd win this game. That's all she wanted. To beat it once. Earn back the cash it had devoured in Colorado.

Two cherries linked together at the top of the screen, and she choked back a yell. It was good enough for her. Not a jackpot, but a decent win. The site credited her twenty dollars. Cash in the bank.

The telephone rang, and Leia snatched it. Maybe Jeff Morton had finally decided to call back.

Instead of Jeff, she heard a woman's voice on the line.

"You have a collect call from inmate Sondra Vaughn."

Leia choked on an ice cube and spat it back into her glass. She hadn't talked to her mother in two years.

The monotone voice continued. "This call may be monitored and recorded at any time. The charge will not exceed three dollars and forty cents for the first minute and forty cents for each additional minute. If you will pay, press three now."

She hesitated. What would the voice say if she explained exactly why she couldn't speak to her mother? She'd never been able to talk with her in the safety of their home, before her mom's first "incident." How was she supposed to chat when her mother was locked away in prison?

"Are you there?" the operator asked.

"I ca …" She hesitated, envisioning her mother alone in a cold dim room. One call for the week, and her mother was calling her.

"Are you refusing this call?" the operator asked. Her finger was probably on the button.

"No." Leia took a deep breath. "I'll take it."

With one click the intermediary left the line.

Leia fidgeted with the mouse.

"I guess you know where I am," Sondra said.

"Eva e-mailed me."

"I wanted to tell you I'm sorry. I hate hurting you."

She pressed the button on the computer and watched the fruit spin. That's what her mother said every time she was caught. The first time she had said it, Leia had actually believed her.

"You're only hurting yourself, Mom."

"I'm seeing a psychologist this time," Sondra said. "He says I have an impulse control disorder."

"Okay."

"He also says he can help me beat it."

"I really hope he can."

The payline flashed, crediting her three dollars, but she barely noticed the win. She spun again.

"It can be hereditary, Leia."

"I've never stolen a thing in my life."

"Not shoplifting. The impulse control disorder."

Now her mother was making excuses for her weakness.

"That's ridiculous."

"I just want you to be careful."

"This is your problem, Mom. Not mine."

A metal chair scraped across the floor in the background.

"I have to go," Sondra said.

Leia hesitated. "Good-bye."

The formality of the word sounded icy, but she didn't have the courage to say she loved her mother. At least not in a way that sounded real. How could she love someone when all respect for that person had disappeared?

Leia stared at the computer. For an instant she wanted to shut it down, rip out the cord, never gamble again. But she was earning money in spite of the odds. And she wasn't like her mother. She hadn't stolen a thing.

Her mother had always been needy—needy for approval from people she didn't even know. She dressed the best, pushed her daughter to be the best, owned the biggest house on the block, and stole the most elaborate decor.

Her mother's immersion into the city's social core won her scores of acquaintances, but few friends. The acquaintances vanished the day Sondra Vaughn's facade crumbled. She wasn't even close to being the perfect wife and mother she portrayed. Everyone except Eva disappeared in the following years when they realized Sondra wasn't going to change.

She had never understood her mother's infatuation with Columbus's elite. And Sondra had never understood that her daughter would rather play hoops than attend one of her teas. When Leia was forced to go to a tea party, she'd inevitably end up with Earl Grey splashed across her lacy blouse and sugar cookie crumbs in her hair. It wasn't pretty.

On the weekends that she wasn't required to attend one of her mother's events, she spent hours in the workshop with her dad. She'd sit on a bench, watch him plane a new piece of wood, cut curves with his band saw, clamp together the carved pieces, and seal the finished product with tung oil. Then she'd ride with him in his black F-150 truck across the state to deliver the custom furniture. He never lacked business. Even as a child Leia realized the money he made was pretty good. It just wasn't enough for her mother.

On their drives she and her dad talked about basketball, snow skiing, her plans to attend Ohio State, and their favorite topic—aviation. He had dreamed of being a pilot, but his vision was 20/300. Perfect eyesight with his glasses, but the FAA would never let him get his license. If he'd been born a few decades later, laser eye surgery would have corrected his vision so he could see the world from the cockpit. Almost every time she flew, Leia thought about his dream.

Three days before her fifteenth birthday, a semi broadsided her dad while he was delivering a walnut dining table and chairs to someone down in Dayton. The truck rolled. He died instantly.

The only reason she wasn't with him was because her basketball team was preparing to play their biggest rival, Worthington High, on

Saturday. Her coach had scheduled an extra practice after school, and she had called Dad at home to tell him to go to Dayton without her.

They won the big game against Worthington. She kissed the basketball for him before she shot the winning goal.

Mother and daughter mourned their loss alone in their separate bedrooms. They didn't say much even when they came out. David Vaughn had been the family referee for years, the only one who understood both of them enough to make the family work.

Leia spent the next two years focusing on school and sports, and she fled to college without a tear. She doubted her mother cried either. They were both free to pursue their own interests without explaining to the other where they were going.

No wonder she and her mother barely knew what to say to each other today. They hadn't really talked since her dad died.

She bet eight dollars on the slot and spun again. This time she lost.

No problem. It was early. She could play all night.

Actually, she could play for the next four days if she wanted. Ethan was jetting across the East Coast. Julie was probably back skiing in Aspen or Vail. Misty was home taming her hyper brood. Most of her Colorado friends had probably forgotten her by now. And her mother was in prison.

No one was there to stop her.

She spun again.

The rays pouring through the bedroom window turned amber and then charcoal.

She flipped on the light beside her desk so she could see the keyboard. No light necessary for the computer screen.

The reels flew by with every flick of the mouse. The bright colors spilled into a murky puddle of gray so that when she didn't win she barely knew what she'd spun.

If she lost, she bet again. If she won, she took a deep breath, basking for an instant as the silver number displayed her new winnings. Then she spun again.

Just a few more months and she wouldn't need to win online.

Her high would be her days in the cockpit, guiding her plane as she jetted through the air. Taking off. Landing. Pushing her craft to be on time.

But in the meantime, it almost felt like she was flying.

The number in the right corner of her screen ebbed and flowed through the night.

The paylines crossed in front of her, mesmerizing her with each spin. Her thoughts were lost inside the bells. Her brain on hold. Risk waved her forward and drew her like a magnet. Stress melted with every win; the quest drove her ahead with every loss. She could ride this high forever. A wave that never crashed.

As the hours went by, her winnings seeped away until she only had fifteen dollars left in her account. She bet it all and spun one last time.

Three gold bars lined her screen.

Jackpot.

She'd done it! She had beaten the game!

Bells rang, and she turned up the volume on her computer. It was almost as if she were back on the casino floor, except this time she was the one with the win.

Red and white and purple firecrackers exploded across the screen as her computer celebrated. She wanted to call someone, but not even Julie would celebrate with her. Gambling was a social event for her friend, not a secret pleasure.

She might be alone, but she was happier than Charlie when he found the golden ticket to Willy Wonka's chocolate factory. She'd summited her mountain. Landed her plane. Accomplished her goal.

The silver numbers on the side of her screen flipped and displayed a new number: $1,200.

Not quite her ten thousand from the other night, but still not bad.

She read through her cash-out options—transfer the winnings to her bank account through an online transfer service, keep it in her casino account to use later, or request a personal check in the mail. Nix the bank account option. She could never get that past Ethan.

The casino could send her total winnings in a check when she reached three thousand. She'd use the money to pay for small expenses like groceries and gas, cushioning their budget with a little extra, so Ethan would never know the difference.

She had beaten the Golden Wonder!

Julie would take her bucket of quarters and run for the door, but Leia couldn't stop playing now. Not while she was ahead.

She played for another hour until she nodded off at the keyboard. The computer beeped, and she jumped in her seat.

The clock on her computer screen read 6:28 a.m. She kissed the computer screen and crawled into bed, smiling to herself as she fell asleep. She'd play again when she got up.

16

WHEN ETHAN ARRIVED HOME ON TUESDAY, LEIA WAS SACKED out in bed. With her pajamas on. He woke her up at 3:30 p.m., worried that she might be sick. She finally crawled out of bed and took a quick shower before coming downstairs. She plopped down on the couch and hadn't moved since.

Leia had hurt her knee. She'd postponed an interview for a job she really wanted. And she was stranded in a new house, in a town where she didn't know a soul.

It was rough. The pits. But Ethan couldn't understand why she didn't pull herself out of the mire and at least try to make good use of the time.

He wiped the crumbs from a ham-and-cheese sandwich off the kitchen counter and filled a tall glass with the iced tea he'd just brewed. He stirred Splenda into the tea and set the sandwich and glass on a tin TV tray. Balancing the tray on one hand, he stepped down to their family room.

He stood beside the couch. "You hungry?"

She didn't answer, flipping the remote from the Travel Channel back to the weather. He glanced at the TV screen. Severe thunderstorms were planted across the Ohio River Valley. Snow showers in northern California. Zero precipitation in Las Vegas.

He leaned toward her. "Leia?"

She jumped. "What?"

"I just asked if you were hungry."

"No, you didn't."

He set the tray on the floor and cleared a stack of magazines off the coffee table. Then he set the tray in front of her. "Are you sick?"

"No."

"I'm glad to hear that."

"Did you eat dinner yet?" she asked.

"I'll wait until Derek gets here."

She turned the channel to Fox News. "Wasn't he supposed to be here at five?"

"His flight was late, but he's on his way."

"Why aren't you picking him up at the airport?"

"He refused the ride." Ethan grabbed the sandwich from her hand and took a bite. "The guy's as stubborn as my wife."

"Not really funny."

The last time they'd seen Derek was at their house in Denver. He'd spent their festive Thanksgiving Day eating turkey, potatoes, and pumpkin pie; watching football; and flirting with one of Leia's single friends.

Ethan knew Leia had never been fond of Derek, but she usually tolerated him. This time she didn't even want him in their home.

Had Derek said something to her over Thanksgiving? Ethan couldn't remember anything out of the ordinary. Derek was always the loudest one in the room, but he didn't think he'd ever been cruel to Leia.

"I realize you don't like Derek." Ethan sat down beside her. "But I appreciate you letting him stay with us for a few days."

"Do I have a choice?"

He straightened his back. "Of course you have a choice."

"Really?"

"I wish you'd tell me what's going on—"

A car honked outside, and Leia waved him toward the door. "He's here."

Ethan walked toward the living room. He'd known Derek since they were second graders at the International Boarding School in West Berlin. Derek had tried to beat up another kid, but Ethan had stepped in and thrown a punch that Derek never forgot. They spent the next seven years at IBS—some days as rivals, others as best friends. The rebel and the missionary's kid.

Ethan remembered every detail of his school, though he barely remembered his family's apartment in West Berlin. His dad and mom were Bible smugglers, and for fifteen years they slipped back and forth across the Communist border, carrying banned literature in their car.

Derek's dad was a major general in the air force, his mother a busy socialite attending military functions across Europe. Derek claimed they chose boarding school because they wanted to give their son a better education than the base schools could offer, but all the students knew the truth. They all experienced it. Derek's parents wanted to get rid of their son.

Derek and Ethan grew up together at the school, and both decided to pursue their dream of flying—Ethan with a commercial airline and Derek in the military. Ethan talked about his faith every time he and Derek got together, and Derek still tried to tempt him to the dark side. Twenty-five years had passed, but neither had succeeded in converting the other.

Ethan opened the front door and watched Derek climb out of the taxi, kissing the hand of an exotic-looking woman who stayed in the backseat. She handed him a business card and fluttered her fingers at him as the car drove off.

Ethan bounded down the steps and smacked his friend on the back.

"Who's that?" Ethan nodded toward the taxi as it turned right at the stop sign.

"Didn't catch the driver's name."

Ethan picked up a duffel bag. "The girl."

"Danna something. Apparently, she lives on the next street."

"I thought for a minute there that you were surprising us with a wife."

"Sharing a taxi." Derek laughed. "You know I don't do marriage."

"And here I had high hopes that you'd changed your mind and found a Mrs. Barton."

Derek clutched his chest as if his heart had been ripped out. "Leia was the only good one left, and you snatched her."

"I can't apologize."

"You should." Derek nodded toward their stucco house. "Nice digs."

"A step up from the old dorms."

"I'll say." Derek strutted toward the front door. "So where's your woman?"

Hopefully she was already hiding out in her room.

"Cooped up inside. She fractured her knee on New Year's Eve."

"How did she do that?"

"Snow skiing." Ethan pointed toward the door.

Derek opened his mouth, but closed it before he said a word.

"What?" Ethan asked.

"If you can't say anything good ..." Derek clipped.

Ethan stopped. "You're going to have to play nice this week. Leia's on edge."

Derek shrugged. "I was just going to ask what she was doing with all her free time."

LEIA TOOK ANOTHER BITE OF THE HAM SANDWICH AND SET IT BACK down on the plate. Even though Ethan had smothered it with mayonnaise, it tasted like sandpaper. She turned off the TV and picked up the latest *AOPA Pilot* magazine from the stack on the coffee table. At least she could look like she didn't care that Derek was here for three miserable days.

She turned to an article on electronic flight instrumentation systems and skimmed through the bullet points about satellite-delivered weather data. She'd already read the article, but she needed to look nonchalant, content ... busy. She couldn't let Derek see her sweat.

Before Ethan came home last night, she'd won another eight hundred dollars online. Her winnings over the long weekend totaled $3,850. She'd requested a money order last night, and according to the Web site, it would be in her mailbox in five days.

Black Hawk was ancient history, the minor leagues.

If only she could leave it and Derek behind.

The front door opened, and the men's voices echoed down into the den. Derek's presence alone was enough to damper anyone's joy.

She took a deep breath. If Derek exposed her guilt, Ethan would be horrified. She'd tell Ethan that Julie had surprised her by taking her to the casino. She'd never have gone on her own.

Yet if she said that, she would sound like a victim. Ethan knew no one could convince her to do something she didn't want to do.

She'd tell him about the check coming in the mail, and maybe that boost to their income would soften him. A little.

"Leia Vaughn!" Derek shouted as he strutted into the room.

She put down the magazine. "Carlisle."

"It's been way too long since I've seen you."

"Forever." She waited for him to blast Ethan with his news.

Derek slid into the leather chair beside the couch and hiked his boots up on the coffee table. "Sorry to hear about your knee."

"I'm recovering."

"I was just asking Ethan what you've been up to since you're stranded home alone."

He gave her a probing look. Did he guess that she'd been gambling online? He couldn't possibly read her that well. No one had a clue.

"Ethan's kept me entertained with a steady supply of books and satellite TV."

"Sounds rotten."

"I manage."

Ethan cleared his throat. "Do you want some iced tea? Just brewed it."

"Nah, I'm fine." Derek stretched his arms. "Unless you've got a beer?"

"You'll have to go out for alcohol on your own."

"The strangest thing happened a few weeks ago." Derek stared at

her as if she might flee on her one good leg. "I was playing blackjack at
a casino in Colorado and saw someone who looked just like you."

She clenched one of the couch's khaki green pillows. "What are the
odds?"

"Crazy, huh? She was even on crutches."

"Bizarre."

She took a bite of her sandwich, and it tasted even drier than it had
minutes before. Obviously he enjoyed torturing her, or he'd just spit out
his revelation.

Derek's eyes didn't veer from her face. "Maybe we should all go
play cards this weekend since you guys live in the gambling capital of
the world."

She wiped her sweaty palms on her jeans as Ethan shook his head.
"You know we don't gamble."

"Times change." Derek winked at her. "People change."

"You can stop terrorizing the invalid," Ethan said. "If her knee felt
better, she'd kick you."

The two bucks in front of her were crashing antlers to claim their
territory. Fortunately her buck won for the moment. Derek stopped
prodding her.

"Do you want to go out for dinner?" Ethan asked.

Derek stood up. "I could eat a whole pizza."

Ethan turned to her. "Leia?"

She set her sandwich back on the plate. "Go have some guy time."

She'd gladly entertain herself while they were gone.

17

A KNOCK ON THE BEDROOM DOOR JERKED LEIA BACK INTO REALITY.
She slid the mouse to the side of her screen, the slot machine fading to black. She'd made $350 in the past two hours, but she couldn't claim it without logging out of her account. If Ethan needed to get online, he'd have to wait.

She'd spin one more time and be done.

Someone knocked again.

"Yeah?"

"It's Derek." His voice was muffled, but she didn't attempt to open the door. She could hear him just fine.

"What do you want?"

"I have a question for you."

She stared at the desktop picture of a Hawker 1000 soaring over the Grand Canyon. Ethan had rescued her the last three days by taking Derek on a driving tour of Las Vegas, a boat ride at Lake Mead, and out for a round of golf on their neighborhood course. Derek had entertained himself in the evenings though he never discussed his late-night escapades over breakfast.

She had hid out in their bedroom while the guys were home and while they were gone.

She only had one more hour to go before they both left for the air-port. She and Derek had made it seventy-two hours without mentioning her casino trip.

Her finger tapped the mouse. "I thought you and Ethan were play-ing golf."

"We're finished. Can I come in?"

"No."

He cracked open the closed door, his head peeking inside. She should have locked it.

"Where's Ethan?" she asked as she pushed her left heel against the floor. The chair rolled back.

"What have you been doing up here?"

"Working."

He stepped inside her bedroom. He wore jeans and a tight brown T-shirt. "You look too guilty to be working."

"It's really none of your business."

He raised one of his eyebrows, stepping toward the bed. A tremor shot up her spine, and she shivered.

"Ethan?" she called toward the open door.

Derek sat down at the edge of the bed and leaned toward her. "He went out to hunt down lunch for you."

"Why didn't you go with him?"

"I told him I needed a nap."

"So nap."

"The thing is, I lied. I'm not really tired."

She wondered if Ethan's baseball bat was still under the bed.

"Then go watch TV or something."

"I wanted to keep you company. You've managed to be invisible since I arrived."

"That's funny, because I just want you to leave me alone."

He grinned at her, and she wondered how many women had melted at that smile. He'd tried to charm her before, and it failed miserably. "I don't want you to be bored, Leia. We've seen what boredom can do to you."

"Why don't you just tell Ethan you saw me in a casino?"

"I don't have incentive to tell him yet." He stood up, his stare honed like a rifle on her face. "I'm waiting to make good use of this information."

She glanced away. "Do you really think I care?"

"Yes, I do."

If the mouse weren't attached to the keyboard, she'd throw it at him. "You're a real winner, Derek. A genuinely nice guy."

"Maybe if you got to know me a little better you'd think so."

He walked toward the chair. She'd clobber him with her good leg if he tried anything. At least she'd injure it doing something worthwhile.

"Now that you have some free time, I'll have to stop back when Ethan's not home."

"Not interested."

"I might be able to talk you into it."

This time she wouldn't look away first. "You can't blackmail me into sleeping with you."

The edge of his lip crept up. "Who said anything about sleeping?"

He touched her shoulder, and she slapped his hand away from her.

"Ethan will ban you from this house if I tell him what you're suggesting."

He leaned so close to her that she could feel his breath on her neck. It burned.

"He won't know who to believe."

"You overestimate your abilities."

Her words didn't stop him. "I'll tell him you propositioned me, and when I add a little truth to the mix, he won't know who to believe."

"He'll believe his wife."

"You think?"

"I know it."

He shrugged and whispered, "I promise you'll have fun."

She picked up the phone. "I'm calling Ethan."

He curled her hand in his and squeezed. "I'll forget I ever saw you in a casino."

"It's not worth it, Derek."

He took one step back and let go. Her hand ached, but she didn't rub it. She glared at him, the phone against her ear.

"When it is, you let me know."

She heard the garage door open, and she shuddered as Derek marched toward the door and slammed it. She couldn't move from the edge of her chair, but when she looked down at the edge of the bed, she saw the tip of the aluminum bat. Next time Derek took a step into this room, she'd use it.

"Hey, Ethan!" she heard him call down the stairs.

She stared back at another jet cruising across her computer screen. She certainly had weaknesses, but Derek Barton was not one of them. The man always wanted what he couldn't have, and he certainly couldn't have her. The very thought made her want to heave. It would destroy her and kill Ethan.

This was the last time Derek was staying with them when she was here. She'd make up some story to Ethan, tell him she had to go out of town.

She clicked on her mouse, and the silver meter flashed on the screen. Her winnings were still intact. At least she hadn't lost that while Derek was presenting his sick plan. She hit the button and won again.

Her body relaxed. Her mind eased, her anger subsiding as she moved into the zone. The rush of her next win warmed her chest and arms. She was in control.

Her high ended the instant she heard footsteps on the stairs. She put the computer back to sleep and leaned over to pull the bat out from under the bed. The aluminum felt cold in her fingers, the weight empowering.

Ethan opened the door.

"You planning to play ball?" he asked, eyeing the bat in her hands. She tossed it onto the bed.

"I'm warding off unwelcome guests."

He walked toward the dresser and pulled out the handle of the suitcase he'd packed last night. He nodded toward the computer. "Derek said you were working."

"Just surfing a few sites I wanted to see."

"I'm getting ready to take off."

She nodded toward the door. "Tell Derek I said good-bye."

Moving quickly around the bed, he rolled the bat out of his way and sat down. "He's going to hang out here for a few more hours and sit by the pool. His flight doesn't leave until tonight."

"Ethan …"

"I told him you weren't in the mood to swim."

"I think he should go with you."

She wondered if her words sounded as desperate as she felt. The monster wanted blood.

But Ethan didn't get it. He kissed her shoulder and stood up. If only his lips could cool the burn from Derek's touch.

"I'll call you when I get in tonight."

When he stepped toward the door, she relaxed the tense muscles in her fists. She could take care of herself. She was in control.

"Where are you flying today?"

"New York and then Boston."

"Clear skies on the East Coast tonight," she said.

"Thanks."

He tugged on his suitcase and rolled it out into the hallway. He didn't even bother to shut the door.

A surge of anger bubbled in her stomach. Her husband knew what kind of man Derek was, yet he ignored his friend's faults, pretending Derek was a better person than he really was. But Ethan knew his buddy slept around, always had. And while he was never blatant about his little escapades, he bragged in his own sly way.

He wasn't being sly anymore.

Ethan was leaving him in their house while she was home alone. Was her husband really that naive? Maybe he thought that Derek would be loyal to him because they'd been friends for so long. Loyalty from Derek? Hardly. The guy looked at everything as a competition, and he wanted to trump Ethan in every area, including stealing his wife and then tossing the spoils overboard. It was disgusting, and her husband put on his blinders and played along.

She fidgeted in her chair as she looked out the back window. Maybe the truth was that Ethan really trusted her. Thought she wouldn't do anything immoral.

She spun the slots.

He really shouldn't trust anyone.

Derek might have conned his way into staying at her house, but there was no way he was coming back into her room. She limped toward the bedroom door and locked it. And then, for good measure, she shoved the nightstand in front of it.

She moved back toward the computer when someone twisted the knob. Then knocked.

"Go away!" she shouted.

There was silence for a moment before she heard Ethan's voice. She hobbled back to the door, moved the nightstand, and unlocked the knob.

Ethan eyed the nightstand as he walked inside and plucked his watch off the top.

She moved back to the computer and put the monitor to sleep before he saw it. He watched her closely as he wound the watch around his wrist. Then he walked toward her and kissed her lips.

Before he stepped back out the door, he turned toward her. "Derek's riding to the airport with me."

18

L EIA DREW BACK THE CURTAINS ON SATURDAY MORNING AND glanced out the window for the fourth time. The red flag on the mailbox was flipped down; the mail carrier had come and gone. She'd been waiting all week for the casino check. Every time she opened their box, she rummaged through the stack of junk mail, looking for the one envelope that would prove Slot Heaven wasn't a farce. That her persistence was going to make up for the income she'd lost.

Each time she'd been disappointed, but maybe today was the day.

She stepped out the front door and moved slowly down the stone pathway toward the street. Stratus clouds plastered the sky like gray molding, but there was no threat of rain. Perfect weather to be outside if you could ride a bike or jog or play a pickup game of basketball.

She opened the mailbox and pulled out the stack of letters inside.

The envelope on the top was from the credit card company. She opened it up and scanned down the charges. December 31. Black Hawk. $40.

She stuffed the bill in her back pocket. She'd write out the check, tell Ethan that she'd paid it. He had enough on his mind these days to worry about their bills.

She flipped to the next letter. A blue-tinted envelope with a Slot Heaven logo as the return.

She ripped it open and pulled out the check. The type was bold, made out to her for $3,850.

Score!

"Leia!" she heard Misty call, and she turned slowly toward her neighbor's house.

Misty was standing on the porch, a bouquet of flowers waving like a red pennant in her hand. She set the flowers on a bench, bounded down her front steps, and ran across the yard.

She hugged Leia's shoulders. "Where have you been?"

Leia took a step back, tucking the casino envelope into the center of the stack. "Resting."

"You had company this week." Misty pointed at her like she was withholding pertinent information.

She waved Misty's finger out of her face. "A friend from Colorado."

"Danna shared a taxi with him from the airport."

"I bet that was a treat."

"She hasn't stopped talking about him since."

"I thought you said she was married."

"Doesn't matter to her."

It doesn't matter to Derek either.

"We missed you at playgroup last week. Angeline's baby is about to pop out, and she swears he must be huge." Misty winked. "She's gained forty-five pounds."

Misty closed the mailbox for her. "Hey, I need to run a few errands today. You want to tag along?"

"I need to go to the bank."

"No problem."

Leia paused for a moment. Who knew when she'd be able to get out again to cash her check? Even if she was stuck in a car with Misty for a few hours, it was worth the headache.

"I'd appreciate a ride," she said.

Misty glanced down at her watch, baby-blue flowers pasted around a yellow band. "You want to leave in a half hour?"

"Sure."

Leia turned back toward the house. She'd never imagined she'd succumb to running errands with Misty, yet her problem was solved.

She poured a glass of tea and opened the dishwasher. She'd stuff the money into an envelope and use it to buy groceries and supplies over the next few months, so Ethan wouldn't have to bear their entire financial burden. Maybe she could convince him to let her take over all their bills, so she could pay them in cash. Then she wouldn't have to deal with questions about the extra thirty-eight hundred. She'd sneak it into their regular budget in small increments.

Leia finished putting the dishes away and reached for the mail. Flipping through the stack, her heart stopped when she saw the last envelope.

She stared at Ambassador Air's forest green logo. Jeff Morton said he would call her back. Sending a letter instead was not a good sign.

She ripped it open.

Jeff didn't mince words. After considering her qualifications, the company had decided not to hire her for the first-officer position. They hoped she would find other employment soon.

Not qualified? *Right.*

She collapsed back against the refrigerator door. Why didn't he just say it was all about her knee?

She ripped up the letter into slivers and threw it into the trash. Then she sunk down on the kitchen floor. Tears welled in her eyes, and she blinked them back. She hadn't cried since Ella died, and being turned down for a job wasn't even close to the pain she felt at losing her friend.

But she couldn't hold back the tears.

Apparently it didn't matter that she'd logged forty-three hundred hours of flight time or that she had an impeccable record or even that her husband had worked for the company for five years. She kicked the trash can, and it rolled across the floor.

So she didn't get the job. So what? There would be other openings. Other interviews. She wasn't going to let a rejection stop her from applying again. She'd get on with the majors someday.

In the meantime, at least she had a job.

She stuffed the casino check into her pocket, rubbed the tears out of her eyes, and pulled herself off the floor. Misty was peeking through the front window in the living room, and when she saw Leia, she tapped on the glass and waved.

Misty flashed a smile the moment Leia opened the door. "You ready to paint the town?"

♠ ♥ ♣ ♦

MISTY BRIEFED LEIA ON EVERY BUSINESS THEY PASSED ON HER RACE to the bank, shoveling out dirt on each owner and the scoop on an employee or two.

She waved toward the floral shop across the street. "Amanda Grayhill runs the place. Her ex-husband set up her business and then spent his free time carousing around town while Amanda brought home the bacon. She ditched the man but kept the shop."

Misty turned toward the bank's drive-through, and Leia pointed to the stone building. "Can we go inside?"

Misty nodded at the long window. "Those tellers can do everything you need these days, so you don't have to get out of the car."

"I need to speak with someone in person."

Misty turned her head, eyebrows raised. Leia figured she was dying to know what made her such an exception, but she wasn't going to volunteer the reason.

"I guess we have time." Misty pulled into a parking space. "Where was I?"

Leia didn't want to hear another word about Amanda or anyone else's problems with their ex.

"How do you know everybody in town?" she asked.

Misty smiled at her. "Born at Sunrise Hospital and grew up near Henderson. I was Clark County Fair Princess, Nevada's Junior Miss, and my high school's homecoming queen."

No surprise there. The past of her so-called friends was always tarnished while her perfectly polished history gleamed. Apparently her life was perfect, while everyone else's was falling apart.

Leia got out of the car, and Misty tailed her into the bank. For a minute Leia thought Misty was going to march up to the counter with her and destroy the very reason Leia needed to be at the bank alone, but Misty stopped to talk to the receptionist.

Leia smiled at the bank teller, a college-age guy with stringy blond hair and a silver stud in his left ear. She slid the check and her account information across the counter.

He typed her account number into the computer. "Do you want to deposit this into your checking account or savings account?"

She looked over her shoulder. Misty was still talking to the receptionist.

"Neither."

He glanced down at the check and back up at her.

"You want the whole thing in cash?"

"Yes ... please."

She dared him with her eyes to question her earnings. He knew who the check was from. The only person who did. And he knew she'd won this money by gambling.

But this was Nevada. There was a casino on practically every block including one across the street from the bank. Surely she wasn't the only one who cashed winnings instead of depositing them.

"I need to get a supervisor for approval," he said.

She could feel Misty watching her from the corner of the room, surprised that she wasn't peering over her shoulder to check out the mysterious transaction. Then again, if she turned around, Misty might be right there. Leia kept her eyes on the teller as he walked back into the teller cage, a woman dressed in a black suit right behind him.

"Good afternoon, Mrs. Carlisle."

"Good afternoon."

The woman turned the check over, ran her finger under Leia's signature, and then flipped it back.

"We don't usually cash checks this size."

Leia smiled. "I was hoping you could make an exception."

The supervisor scrolled slowly through her account on the computer. She looked at Leia and then back at the computer screen before she told the teller to cash her check.

"It's been a pleasure serving you," the supervisor said to Leia before she walked away.

The teller counted the cash and slid it into an envelope. Leia grabbed it before it touched the counter and stuffed it into her purse. As she turned, she saw the supervisor shaking Misty's hand.

The money tucked safely inside her purse, Leia grasped it as if it might fly away. She'd never carried this much cash before. It didn't seem legal.

"You do know everyone," Leia said as they walked out the front door.

"That was Allison Wilde," Misty grinned. "The runner-up for homecoming queen."

19

MISTY FLEW OUT OF THE BANK AND ONTO WATER STREET. LEIA clutched the handle as her escort whipped the car right and swerved to miss a pedestrian. Palm trees lined the sidewalks on both sides of the street, and the women drove past an elite resort with a manicured golf course and a line of stucco shops with terra-cotta roofs.

"I have to get all my errands done by four," Misty said as she hit the gas, cruising through a yellow-red light. "My husband invited some big client over for dinner."

"Ethan's coming home tomorrow."

"I don't know how you two do it, staying away from each other for so long."

"We coordinate our schedules, so we're home together as much as possible."

"Your schedules will have to change when you have a couple of munchkins with sore throats and runny noses."

"We're not having kids anytime soon."

"I love my rug rats, but three is enough. I've done my part to populate the world.

"Speaking of kids ..." Misty pointed at a store to the right, a brown building with a hunter green awning and a wide porch lined with a log hitching post. *Frazer's Outdoor Adventures.*

"I have to stop here and get Brandon a sleeping bag. His Boy Scout troop is camping at Pyramid Lake this month."

She pulled into the driveway and opened her car door. "You wanna go in?"

"Definitely." Leia slid out of her seat and shivered when she stepped outside. The temperature had dropped by at least ten degrees since they'd left the house. If she hadn't been stunned by Jeff's letter, she would have remembered to grab a jacket.

"Sam and Jenny Frazer run this place," Misty said as Leia hopped across the pavement behind her. "They're a strange couple, but it's the best outdoor shop in the county. Jenny dresses like she's trapped in the last century, but people overlook it. They all just marvel that she's stuck by Sam."

They climbed up on the porch, wooden planks creaking under the weight of Leia's crutches.

"Sam used to be a big business guy downtown, drowning in dough. He lost it all gambling, and their family was homeless for, like, a year." She took a breath. "Well, not homeless exactly. I guess they lived with friends."

Misty's hand was on the doorknob. "They started this business during his recovery, and as far as I know, he's stayed clean."

The purse on Leia's shoulder suddenly felt heavy, the envelope of cash weighing it down as Misty opened the door.

"Hey, Jenny!" Misty called to the woman standing behind the counter. "You look great today."

Jenny Frazer wore an olive green flannel shirt with a lilac T-shirt underneath. Chalky brown hair curled around her face in loose rings. Cradling the telephone in one hand, she waved at them as she answered a caller's question about camping stoves.

Leia walked beside Misty to the counter, and Misty tapped her fingers on a stack of flyers as she waited for Jenny to hang up.

Leia looked around the store. The place had a high ceiling in the middle with steps on both sides that led to a second floor filled with jackets and ski pants. A rugged climbing wall in the center of the room was covered with red, blue, and yellow handholds; and on each side were rows of bicycles, kayaks, backpacks, and camping gear. For an instant, she felt as though she was back in Colorado.

"Nice to see you, Misty," Jenny said as she hung up the phone. Her eyes sparkled when she smiled, her skin a clear ivory. The only makeup Leia guessed she wore was mascara. Quite daring for someone in her fifties, but she pulled it off perfectly. She didn't know what Misty was talking about with the clothing comment. The woman looked great. But then maybe Leia was stuck in the past decade or two.

Misty introduced her quickly before she talked business. "I need a sleeping bag for my son."

Jenny pointed to the back of the store. "We have a whole row of navy and red bags for boys."

Leia started to follow Misty toward the section, but the woman was gone. Leia rested her back against a wooden post as she turned back toward the store owner.

"So you're a friend of Misty's?" Jenny asked.

"Neighbor. We just moved here from Denver."

Jenny flipped through a pile of papers and picked one out of the middle. She circled something on the page and set it beside the register.

"Our family skis the Rockies at least once a year." Jenny pointed toward her brace. "How did you hurt your knee?"

"Skiing Copper."

"Bad weather?"

Leia shook her head. "The weather behaved perfectly, but the snowboarders didn't."

"Ouch! Did you crash?"

"Almost. He whizzed past me, but I bit it."

Jenny swiped the snowboarding magazine spread out on the counter and hid it behind her back. "I guess I shouldn't tell you I board."

"Not a good idea."

Jenny laughed. "I used to ski."

"So you've made an alliance with the dark side."

"I tried something new and loved it. No turning back for me."

Leia looked over her shoulder and saw Misty roaming through the racks of sleeping bags.

Jenny eyed her wedding ring. "Have you and your husband found a church yet?"

"How do you know I go to church?"

Jenny winked at her. "God shows me who my sisters are."

"We're still looking." Leia sighed. "We had a great church family in Colorado."

"You should come visit our church." Jenny cleared off a corner beside the register and began stacking a batch of flyers. "We've got a lot of young families and a great group of skiers who hit the slopes every year."

"You ski together?"

"Absolutely. If your knee is better, we're going to Arapahoe Basin in May."

"My doctor doesn't see much skiing in my future."

"Yikes!"

"Exactly."

Jenny picked up a pen and piece of scrap paper and handed it to her. "Write down your number. We can pick you up for church tomorrow if you want to go."

"You don't have to ..."

"I want to."

Leia scribbled her number on the paper. "I'm usually the one taking people to church."

"God gives us the opportunity to learn about his love in the most unusual ways."

Jenny took the paper as Misty rounded the corner with a violet bag in tow. Leia cringed. She could only imagine the hounding the poor boy would have to endure when he rolled out his ultrabright bag.

Misty elbowed Leia as she scooted around her.

"Will this keep Brandon warm?" She heaved the sleeping bag onto the counter, scattering the flyers onto the floor. "I don't know what the guides are thinking, taking the kids on a campout this time of year, but I can't talk Brandon out of it. And, believe me, I've tried. It's just crazy to spend the night in the freezing cold."

She didn't give Jenny the opportunity to answer her first question, so Jenny slid the tag over the scanner.

"A hundred and twenty-nine," she said.

Misty shook her head. "And crazy expensive. Do you know what I could spend a hundred and twenty-nine dollars on?"

Leia looked over at her, wondering who was supposed to answer.

"A million things," Misty concluded as she pulled out her credit card. "Starting with a new dress for tonight."

BY THE END OF THE FOURTH ERRAND, LEIA STOPPED PROCESSING Misty's turbo-spiel. While the woman gabbed about the teal charmeuse dress she was coveting from Bloomingdale's and her special caramel cake that she'd made to impress her husband's boss, Leia wondered what had happened to Sam Frazer. How could a smart, successful businessman lose everything through gambling? Why hadn't he just stopped before he spent all their cash? She understood the thrill of winning, but every gambler needed to have a limit during a downturn.

She'd decided to set a personal losing limit of $500. Her playing would stop if she ever crossed that line. Fortunately, she didn't need to worry about it right now. She was still riding the high of her big win.

Misty pulled into a gas station, and Leia turned off the radio, waiting in blessed silence as her neighbor filled her tank. She glanced into the windows of the station and saw a row of progressive slot machines and video poker terminals. It seemed they were everywhere around this town—gas stations, rest stops, grocery stores, coffee shops. She saw the back of someone in a denim jacket pull the arm of a machine. She understood the thrill of beating a game. She knew the magnetic pull of playing in the solitude of her home, escaping the loneliness for a win. And she could even comprehend the draw of the lights and music and cheap drinks on the Strip.

But playing in a grimy gas station when grand casinos were sprinkled around the city like sand? It made no sense to her.

20

L EIA ATE A BAGEL WITH CREAM CHEESE AS SHE WAITED ON THE front porch swing for Jenny and Sam Frazer to pick her up for church. After Misty had dropped her off yesterday, she'd opened the cash envelope, spread her winnings across the burgundy comforter on her bed, and ran her fingers over and over through the dusty green mound. The online casino was no scheme. The game was for real.

She played for five hours straight last night, but she lost a hundred bucks. Not a crushing defeat considering the money she had won last weekend, but she'd fight to get it back this afternoon. She brushed the crumbs off her khaki pants as she pushed the swing back and forth with her good leg.

After taking four dresses off their hangers, trying them on, and then tossing them on the bed, she'd picked a white blouse and a light green sweater to go with the pants. The sweater masked the ten pounds she'd gained since her accident, but nothing could mask the giant immobilizer on her leg. At least she was going to church with Jenny, and Jenny didn't seem like the type of woman to wear a dress any day of the week.

A metallic blue Toyota 4Runner pulled into the driveway, and Leia picked up her purse, starting her slow journey toward their truck. Jenny jumped out of the passenger door and rushed toward her. She was dressed in corduroys.

Jenny hugged her, and her husband, Sam, introduced himself as he opened up the back door. His dark hair was tinted gray, but he oozed raw youth with his confident smile, Wrangler jeans, and cowboy boots.

She climbed into the backseat beside two teenage boys. They shook her hands—Luke and Paul. Good biblical names. Luke was the older one, his hair draped over his eyes and ears like a shaggy brown curtain, and he was dressed in camouflage pants and a red T-shirt. Paul's blond hair was short and spiked, and he wore green-tinted sunglasses, a black shirt with a silver logo, and jeans.

Forget motherhood. She suddenly felt old enough to be a grandmother.

Sam pushed the truck into reverse and bumped the back tire over the curb.

Luke grabbed the handle over his head. "Drive lately, Dad?"

The front wheel bounced over the edge.

"Ignore them," Sam said, but it was hard to ignore the red and green.

"So how did you spend the rest of your Saturday?" Jenny asked as Sam turned down the street.

Leia smiled. "Bored out of my mind."

"You don't strike me as the kind of person who rests well."

"You nailed it."

Leia steadied herself as Sam raced around a corner.

"Tell you what." Jenny turned her head around. "Our church is hosting a spring carnival in April to help a church in Indonesia. We need someone who can handle a few details from home."

"A few?" Sam laughed, and Jenny punched him in the arm.

"What kind of details?" Leia asked.

"Organizing rides or food or volunteers. Whatever you'd enjoy."

"Do you need anyone to fly in supplies?" Leia quipped.

"I think we'll have to use you some other way."

Leia glanced out the window. A month ago she would have laughed at the idea of organizing rides for a carnival. Not that she didn't want to help the church. She just preferred overseeing a mission trip or coaching a basketball team. Something where she could use her interests and expertise. She'd never even liked carnivals as a kid.

But she needed something to do. Her computer may keep her busy while Ethan was traveling, but she needed a project while he was at home. Ethan's annual checkride for his pilot's license was in April anyway, and he'd spend the month in his office, poring over flight manuals instead of taking her someplace fun. Working with Jenny would occupy her time.

Leia pulled the edge of her sweater out from under Luke's leg. "Just let me know what you want."

"Wonderful." Jenny clapped her hands. "Our first meeting is on Friday."

Sam looked at her in the rearview mirror. "Do you have any idea what you're getting into?"

"Apparently not."

"It's probably a good thing."

Jenny flicked her husband's arm. "Don't listen to this man."

Leia marveled at their easy banter. After what Sam had done to their family, she was amazed that Jenny could not only forgive him, but also still love him. And their teenage boys were actually going to church on a Sunday morning. There must be some sort of parental award for that.

She quietly thanked God for introducing her to Jenny. An honest, down-to-earth, positive person who seemed to love God and care about other people. The kind of woman she needed to have as a friend.

Sam pulled into the parking lot, and Leia looked out the window. Calvary Church was a moderate-sized, rounded brick structure with a steel cross braced above double glass doors. There was a playground on one side and a cream-colored rectangular building on the other that looked like a reception hall. A simple respite in a glitzy town.

Jenny turned around in her seat again. "When is your husband getting home?"

"Probably around five. His flight's delayed in Chicago."

"Why don't you come over for lunch after church? I'm baking chicken."

Sam reached over and squeezed his wife's hand. "You don't have to make anything today, sweetheart. Let's stop at Boston Market and pick up some sandwiches to go."

"It's no bother," Jenny said.

"I insist."

Jenny turned back to Leia. "Do you mind sandwiches?"

"I vote for sandwiches," Luke said.

Leia met Sam's pleading eye in the mirror. "Boston Market sounds great."

♠ ♥ ♣ ♦

LUKE AND PAUL DISAPPEARED TO THE LEFT OF THE LOBBY WHEN they walked through the church's glass door, and Leia followed Sam and Jenny toward the sanctuary.

Jenny introduced her to one of the women on the carnival committee. The woman wore a black sleeveless dress with a burnt-orange scarf knotted around her neck and tortoiseshell glasses. Her blonde hair was pulled back in a French twist.

The woman shook her hand gracefully, welcoming her to their church. She reminded Leia of the elegance that Princess Diana exuded during her royal years. Poise without the pain. While she seemed nice enough, Leia couldn't relate to perfection.

"What was that lady's name again?" Leia asked Jenny when they sat down.

"Caroline Coffer."

"Like Coffer Steaks?"

"Exactly"

Leia had never eaten there, but the high-end restaurants were scattered across Clark County. Caroline wasn't only sophisticated; she was probably quite wealthy.

"She looks as if she'd just stepped off a page of *Glamour*."

Jenny didn't answer, shifting in her seat as she opened her bulletin and started reading.

Leia glanced around at the white walls. The church building was as

simple inside as it appeared from outside. Blue chairs were lined up in
about fifty narrow rows. In the front was a wooden lectern with a vase
of calla lilies on each side, behind it a baptismal with a cross on the
wall. On each side of the sanctuary, the morning sunlight warmed the
room through two stained-glass windows.

In spite of the simple decor, the place was packed before the worship started.

Leia sang along with the contemporary music, the words projected
on two screens. She clapped softly, praising God for his faithfulness,
basking in his light.

The young pastor stepped up on the low platform and opened his
Bible. Leia could almost feel the breeze from the hundreds of Bible
pages turning with him to Philippians 3:9.

"No matter what we do to serve God or how hard we try to avoid
sin, none of us will ever be good enough to be saved," he began. "That's
the very reason God sent his son to die for our sins."

He glanced down at his Bible to read. "'I no longer count on my own
goodness or my ability to obey God's law, but I trust Christ to save me.'

"The beauty of salvation is that God offers it to us as a gift," he
explained. "And once we accept the gift of salvation, God doesn't let us
go. He loves us and pursues us even when we drift away from him. He
doesn't stop loving us even when we choose to sin."

She squirmed in the plastic seat. Some sins were spelled out in the
Bible. Others weren't. Was gambling a sin?

"How do we know if we're living in sin?"

Leia held her breath, waiting for his answer.

"God convicts us at a gut level when our actions threaten our relationship with him. If we ignore his voice, he steps back and waits for us
to return. He won't force us to love and serve him, but he is a God of
grace, and he promises to forgive us when we ask him."

Leia stared down at her Bible. Maybe God hadn't left her. Maybe
he'd only stepped back.

"In the book of Acts, Paul writes, 'For in him we live and move and
exist.' Our soul longs for God when he isn't near. When we wake up in
the morning, he gives us the strength we need to face our day."

Lately all she'd thought about in the morning was beating the Golden Wonder. The pull of the competition gave her the strength to face her day.

She looked up at the stained-glass window beside her—two lambs sleeping next to a lion. Vibrant yellow rays shot out from the lion's body. Rays of hope. She needed hope, the reminder that God still cared for her in spite of his silence over the past few weeks. Of course, if she was honest, God had been silent over the last four years. When she married, she'd gained a husband and lost the intimacy with her heavenly Father. It was almost as though Ethan had become her god instead.

She shivered. The sun slid out from behind a cloud, and the pieces of cut glass shimmered again. The yellows and blues sparkled like casino lights celebrating a jackpot.

A ray of sunlight lit the fabric on the empty chair next to her, and she brushed her hand over the smooth material.

What would it be like to play slots at a casino on the Strip? Enjoy the lights and cheap food and the steady chime of the slots?

Jenny held out the edge of a hymnbook toward her, and Leia clutched the faded green cover in one hand as the piano started playing "Have Thine Own Way, Lord."

"Have thine own way, Lord," she sang. "Have thine own way. Wounded and weary, help me, I pray. Power, all power, surely is thine. Touch me and heal me, Savior divine."

If only God would use his power to heal her knee. Take away her pain. Give her life back to her. But she realized she was asking for her way, not God's way. What did God want her to do?

AFTER EATING CHICKEN FROM BOSTON MARKET, THE ENTIRE FRAZER FAMILY rushed out their back door, down the porch, and to the side of the house where Sam had installed a basketball hoop on a concrete court.

Jenny pulled a lawn chair out of the garage and set it up on the grass. She pointed at Leia. "We reserve the best chairs for our guests."

Leia eyed the nylon strips on the chair and then looked back up at her friend. "What are you playing?"

"Probably H-O-R-S-E."

Leia pointed her crutch toward the basket. "Can I join you?"

"When your knee heals."

For an instant she was back in Ohio, lacing her Nikes in their driveway, stretching her hamstrings, slapping her dad's hand before he tossed her the ball. "I can play on one leg."

Jenny started to protest, but Leia pointed at the immobilizer on her leg. "It's not like I can do any more damage."

"I bet the doctor would disagree."

"She's fine, Mom," Paul said. "Maybe I can actually have some competition today."

"Be nice to me." Leia laughed. "I'm still injured."

Paul dribbled the ball and made a basket. He ran, scooped it up before it hit the grass, and tossed it to Leia. "We don't play nice."

With one crutch Leia hopped up to where Paul had been standing, eyed the basket, and shot. Score.

She winked at him. "Good."

The whole family joined the game. Sam racked up the first *H*, followed by Luke and then Jenny. Leia and Paul remained letter-less as the rest of the family added an *O* and an *R*.

"We have to decide if we're going on the church's mission trip," Luke said after he scored a basket and stepped back to the side. Jenny flung the ball up, but it bounced off the rim. "They need an answer by next week."

Leia shot the ball through the hoop and tossed it to Paul. He made the goal. "I'm thinking yes," he said.

Sam stepped forward to take the ball. "I'm thinking we still don't know."

He missed the shot and threw the ball to Luke.

"Where are you going?" Leia asked as she took a long shot, the ball swishing through the net.

Paul made his next basket.

"The Philippines," Luke answered after his dad missed another shot.

Leia gave Paul a high five. "You'd like the Philippines."

"You've been there?" Paul asked.

Back when God was using her life to do something productive.

"Five times. I actually met my husband on my last mission trip."

"Cool." Luke made a basket. "The mission part, not the husband."

"Luke!" Jenny flicked him. "What type of mission?"

"I flew in supplies to some of the remote islands in the north."

Jenny sat down on the lawn chair to tie her tennis shoe. "How many islands are there?"

"Seven thousand—each one beautiful but dangerous."

"I'm there," Luke said as his dad finally made a basket.

Sam tossed the ball to Luke. "We still haven't decided."

Luke's shot bounced off the backboard, and he threw the ball to his mom. She moved back for a three-point shot and missed.

"It's a mission trip, Dad," Luke said.

Leia made another basket. "Avoid the *lechon*."

"What's that?" Paul asked, stepping forward to take his shot.

"Baby pig smothered in liver sauce."

Paul missed the basket.

"Yummy," Luke said.

Leia was in the lead.

The five of them battled for the next half hour, Leia and Paul knocking out their opponents one letter at a time.

"Twenty minutes until the real game." Luke pointed toward the house. "Duke's playing North Carolina."

"You want to watch it with us?" Sam asked.

"You bet."

She missed a shot, then Paul missed a shot. As they neared the end of the game, they had both scored four letters.

When Paul missed his last shot, his brother cheered.

Leia smiled when she shook Paul's hand. He was only a kid, but it still felt good to win.

21

ETHAN PLUNGED INTO THE HEATED SWIMMING POOL, SHOWERING his wife with warm water. When his heels hit the concrete at the bottom, he shot back up through the surface and grinned at her over the edge of the pool.

The hanging lamps around the pool gave a romantic glow to the evening, but Leia's eyes weren't even close to being romantic. She glared back at him, soaked strands of hair glued to her face. Probably not the right time to tell her she was irresistible.

"Very funny," she said as she held up the *Las Vegas Sun.* Water dripped off the newspaper, pooling into a new puddle on the stone patio below her.

"You looked like you needed to wake up."

"I was trying to relax," she said.

"I'm trying to liven things up around here."

She picked up a newsmagazine on the table beside her lounge chair and opened it. "I thought you'd want to rest tonight too."

"What are you reading?" he asked.

"An article on how much money Corporate Direct has lost this month."

"You need to have some fun." He slapped his palm on the surface of the water and shot another stream toward her.

She grabbed her beach towel, flicked him in the head, and then leaned back, flipping a magazine page.

"Any word from Ambassador?" he asked.

She didn't look at him. "Not yet."

"Are you going to call them back?"

"Nope."

"They'll call you?"

"Uh-huh."

He sighed and rolled onto his back. Floating toward the other end of the pool, he looked up at the night sky, the stars shaded gray by the city lights. He preferred the view from the cockpit—deep black space with galaxies flickering white.

The Knapps' dog whined at him from behind the wooden fence that separated their yards. At least someone was making noise. Leia had walled off almost all communication with him, and he couldn't figure out why.

After a month stuck in the house, she'd slowly devolved from a high-strung adventurer to a recluse. She'd stomped out her adrenaline addiction until she wanted nothing more than to be indoors, by herself. No husband necessary.

At first her change was subtle. She'd moped for days after the accident. The doctor had said depression was normal for someone who'd not only been grounded from flying, but also was now isolated in a new city.

He'd tried to take her to church, encourage her to make some new friends, but she'd resisted. At least that much hadn't changed. Leia had always wanted to do things on her own.

She used to hate being in the house, but now it seemed as if she didn't want to leave. And while he'd talked her into joining him by the pool, she was satisfied to sit beside it and watch him swim, lost in her own world. He'd never seen her sit on the sidelines before.

She seemed lost a lot these days. When he was talking to her, her mind wandered, and he wondered where she could possibly be. Her focus was usually razor sharp, honed on getting a job—any job—done in record time.

Even Derek had commented on Leia's absent mind, saying she seemed distracted during his visit. It wouldn't have been any big deal, except Derek rarely observed anything outside his own little world.

Ethan had made up an excuse for his wife, telling him it was probably the pain medication, even though she'd been off the meds for a week. He didn't know why he felt the need to lie to Derek, except he couldn't explain the truth.

He wanted Leia to feel content in their new home. And he wanted her to be satisfied when they had children, enjoying the domestic life as much as his sister thrived on being a wife and a mom. But he didn't want her to shut down.

It was probably no big deal. People change. After she recovered, she'd be back to normal. He'd probably wish she'd mellow again.

He just didn't know what had caused this switch.

He felt a splash behind him, and he jumped as he turned his head. Leia had taken off her brace and waded up to her thighs in the water, her fingers skimming the surface, debating whether to splash him again. He dove and popped out of the water behind her.

She'd complained about gaining weight since her accident, but he thought she looked beautiful in her navy and white swimsuit. He wrapped his arms around her waist and pulled her close to him. Knee injury or not, he could still hold her beside him. Let her know that no matter what happened, he'd never let her go.

He kissed her hair, and she pushed away from him. He didn't like this change either.

"Are you hungry?" she asked.

"Maybe."

"Why don't I make you something to eat?"

He let her go. "Okay."

He watched her pull herself out of the pool on her left leg and wrap the damp beach towel around her suit.

Sprinting up the stairs to the bedroom, it took him only a few minutes to dry off and change into gym shorts. He didn't bother with a shirt.

Before he went back downstairs, he walked into the office, opened up the bottom drawer of his desk, and pulled out a file with their monthly bills. He tucked it under his arm as he turned toward the stairs.

Every week he inputted their expenses into Quicken, so he knew exactly where they were financially. But there was an extra charge that didn't add up this month. It was just a small glitch, but he needed to ask Leia about it.

He sat down on a bar stool in the kitchen as he flipped through the mail in the file. Leia pulled bags of cheese and salami out of the refrigerator and piled the pieces onto a plate. She set a bag of rye crackers on the counter and then grabbed a knife out of the rack with one hand and a green apple with the other.

He looked through the folder a second time. "I can't find our credit card statement."

"I put all the mail in your file."

"It's usually here by now."

She chopped through the apple. "Don't know what to tell you."

"I guess it doesn't matter." He bit into a piece of Colby cheese. "I paid it while I was on the road."

She sliced the apple. "The beauty of online banking."

"We had a weird charge on December thirty-first."

She pointed the knife toward him. "What was it?"

"A cash withdrawal in Black Hawk, Colorado."

Her eyes focused back on the apple. "I can solve that mystery. Julie and I went up there for lunch, and I got some cash."

"That's an odd place to have lunch."

She shrugged. "We couldn't ski because of my leg, and Julie wanted to see a bit of the Old West. Black Hawk was the closest town."

"Good, then." He peeled off a piece of salami and wrapped it around a block of cheese. "Case closed."

It was odd that Leia didn't mention it before. She knew how much he hated those gambling towns. But maybe that's why she didn't say anything.

"So where did you eat?"

"Some little café. They didn't take credit cards."

"I've never been to Black Hawk," he said.

She set the plate of apples in front of him. "It's a tourist trap."

"Didn't Derek say he was in Black Hawk last month?"

"I think so." She cleared her throat. "Small world."

"He told me he couldn't walk two feet without running into a casino."

"That's what it seemed like."

"Highway robbery."

She started slicing another apple. "Nobody made me eat lunch."

"You know what I mean."

"Some people really just gamble for entertainment, Ethan."

"It's a rotten form of entertainment when people get hurt."

"Not everyone is like Brett, honey."

"He destroyed my sister."

"And he was very wrong."

He didn't want to talk about Brett. The very thought of his brother-in-law made his blood boil. Brett and Paige were still trying to mend their rocky marriage ... or at least Paige was.

"We need to talk about our budget," he said.

"Okay." Leia sat down beside him and opened up the folder, leafing through the bills and statements. "What about it?"

"We have to shave five hundred a month off our expenses until you go back to work."

"I thought my income was going straight into our retirement and savings."

He squirmed in his chair. She'd always been too busy to talk about their finances, so he'd created a budget they could both live with. So far, she'd been satisfied with the process, though she went over budget almost every month. Without telling her, he'd padded her portion of their expenses.

"It was, until we bought this house."

"We can't afford it?"

"We can afford it if we cut back a little."

She sat down on the stool beside him. "On what?"

He squirmed. "Satellite TV."

"I'll cancel it," she said.

"What else?"

"I have no idea."

She gathered the bills into a stack and pulled them to her chest. "Why don't you let me handle it?"

He hesitated. "What do you mean?"

"Your checkride's coming up this spring, and you need to study."

"I've got three more months."

She opened one of the files. "I'll be sitting around the house during that time with nothing to do. I can create a new budget and manage our finances, so we don't overspend."

"I don't mind doing it, Leia."

He actually enjoyed managing their money.

"I know, but it will give me something productive to do. Just show me your system, and I'll take it from there."

"I don't know …"

She shrugged. "I'm just trying to help."

He looked down at the paperwork in her arms and back up at her. His checkride for Ambassador Air was at the end of April, and he'd spend the month before cramming for the annual exam. Besides, it would be healthy for Leia to take care of their finances until she recovered. She would know where they stood financially, so they could be a team in their spending and saving. He could check in with her once a month—or once a week—to make sure she was staying on top of it.

"It will take a few hours to show you my system," he said.

She glanced up at the clock—it was a few minutes past eight. "I've turned into a night owl."

He stuck another cracker in his mouth. "Then let's go."

22

THE PHYSICAL THERAPIST'S OFFICE WAS TUCKED BEHIND THE hospital in downtown Vegas. The decor was stark—tan walls with a few posters of southern France. Fabrice was from Nice, and as much as she liked his accent, it didn't distract Leia from the fact that he caused her much pain.

She lay on her stomach, cringing as Fabrice massaged her knee to loosen the scar tissue. It had been three weeks since her surgery, but as far as she could tell, her knee wasn't very motivated to recover.

"Does it still hurt?" he asked when he set her leg back on the pad.

Leia groaned. "Just a little."

"You're improving."

"I'll feel much better when you're not twisting my knee like a corkscrew."

"Stretching, *chérie*, not twisting." He placed an ice pack on her knee. "I'm working out the kinks."

She squeezed the bottom of her shorts as the cold blast shot up her leg. "When can I drive?"

"Not anytime soon."

"An estimate, please?"

"At least eight more weeks."

She groaned.

"Are you getting much rest?"

Of course she hadn't been getting rest, and he knew it. "It's been hard to sleep since I had the surgery."

Anyone could tell by looking at the dark pockets under her red-streaked eyes that she wasn't sleeping. But her knee wasn't keeping her up at night. It was that blasted slot machine. When she lost five hundred dollars last night, she increased her losing limit to eight hundred and changed venues. She lost another three hundred on the new site before she forced herself to turn off the computer and go to bed.

Ethan had never before criticized her appearance, but even he'd commented on her red eyes before he left yesterday.

Neither man should worry about her. She'd be fine in a day or two.

Fabrice took off the ice pack. "Do you need a prescription to help you sleep?"

"No, thanks."

"I'll get you something nonaddictive."

"I don't want anything."

Jenny had told her to take something to sleep as well, but a prescription would make her lethargic when she needed the energy to win. She wouldn't hop off this ride until her streak shot up again. The losses were only a temporary setback.

Once she gained back the money she'd lost, she would be done. Finished. She'd throw away her computer if she had to and get some sleep. Then, when her knee healed, she'd go back to work knowing she'd conquered the slots once and for all.

"Sleep will help you heal faster," Fabrice said as he tightened the immobilizer over her sweats.

"I'll rest today."

"You need your strength."

If he only knew ...

The taxi she'd called was waiting outside. As the driver buzzed through the streets of Henderson, Leia pretended to read the aviation magazine in her lap, but she didn't turn the pages. She was tired of reading about flying and snow skiing and other outdoor adventures. She was ready to be active again. This time around she wouldn't be so picky. She just wanted to do something that challenged her body and her brain. She didn't have to jog. She'd be satisfied with walking around the block or shooting hoops on two legs. The only thing remotely challenging to her these days didn't involve muscle power. She no longer had to push through the burn or concentrate on her technique. All she had to do was push a button or two instead.

The taxi passed a row of colorful casinos that resembled a caravan of gypsy tents. Lights flashed outside each door promising *Loose Slots*. How could anyone make that guarantee? Steady persistence was the only way to win a game. Persistence and a little luck.

Maybe it was time to ditch the computer and try her luck in person. She wanted to clutch the arm of the slot machine in her fingers instead of tapping the mouse over and over like someone sending an SOS. She wanted to watch the paylines swirl until they gave her a match. And, most of all, she wanted to win.

After the pastor at Calvary had talked about God's grace, she'd prayed, asking God to show her if she should stop. If God wanted her to, she'd stop gambling right away, but he hadn't given her a sign.

She'd debated the sin issue in her head and decided that, for her, gambling was a simple escape, not a sin. Other people escaped their problems through video games or movies or books. This was a way for her to enjoy her downtime without going crazy, to enjoy an adrenaline rush without hurting her knee.

If she could, she'd march into a casino right now, but it was bad enough that Derek was harboring her secret. She didn't know many people in Vegas, but what if someone else saw her there?

Her cell phone rang, and she answered it.

"Hey, it's Jenny. Where are you?"

The cab passed another casino. This one was smaller, but the elegant peach paint and white columns made it look like a Southern mansion. "Coming back from physical therapy."

"By yourself?"

"I took a taxi."

"I told you I'd drive you while Ethan was gone."

"I know, but I didn't want to bother you again."

"I want you to bother me," Jenny said. "Are you still planning to attend the church carnival meeting tonight?"

Leia paused. She wasn't sure she wanted to go to church.

"I'll go," she finally said.

"Good. I'll pick you up at five thirty."

WHEN JENNY RANG THE DOORBELL, LEIA WAS STARING DAZED AT THE computer screen, drowning in the abyss. With almost every spin today, she'd lost five or ten dollars. There were no silver credits on the corner of her screen. No flashing victory lights. All she had was twenty dollars left in her online account—the remainder of the five hundred dollars she'd loaned herself after lunch.

She'd lost track of how much she owed on her private credit card. It hadn't seemed important because she planned to win it all back. Just like before.

But with each loss, her balance grew, and she didn't want to find out by how much until she won again. It might shake her resolve.

Jenny rang the bell again, and Leia put the computer to sleep. No sense shutting it down since Ethan wouldn't be home for another day. She'd play again when the meeting was done.

It took her another two minutes to get downstairs on one leg.

Jenny held up her cell phone when Leia opened the door. "I was dialing your number."

"It's a slow day." She pointed at her knee before following Jenny to the Grand Cherokee and climbing into the front seat. She set her crutches on her lap.

"You'll be better in no time," Jenny said as she backed her SUV out of the driveway. "If you're banned from skiing, maybe you can take on a new sport."

"All I want to do is answer the doorbell in under a minute."

"Ever tried ice climbing?"

"That's probably the slowest sport ever created."

Jenny turned onto the street. "It's good to have goals."

"Mine aren't as lofty as they used to be."

"We've got to find you something productive to do until your knee heals."

"I'm fine."

Jenny stopped at a red light and glanced over at her. "I don't know you that well, Leia, but I don't think you're fine."

"I—"

Jenny cut her off. "Honesty is the most important step to healing, my friend. If you're not fine, just say so."

Leia tapped her fingers on the crutch. "I was bored out of my mind right after the accident, but I've learned how to cope at home."

"Coping alone is never a good thing," Jenny said. "I'm sure Misty told you our family's story."

"Misty tends to exaggerate the truth."

"There's not much to exaggerate. We were in crisis, but we were never alone. Our church rallied around us, praying for us, supporting us, showing us God's grace in a very human way. They loved me, and they loved Sam. I'm afraid our story would be much different if they'd left us alone.

"Anyway, I think you'll like this group," Jenny said as she parked the car. "We're all a bit headstrong, but somehow we've managed to come together to form a team."

Leia followed Jenny down a side hall and into a Sunday school room that featured a jungle of brightly colored animals around an ark painted on the walls. There were seven women grouped around a table, and Jenny quickly introduced Leia to them, then started the meeting.

"A quick recap." She clicked her pen against the table. "Just for Leia and the rest of you who don't remember why you're here.

"Calvary is putting on a spring carnival after church services on April twenty-ninth to raise money for our sister church in Indonesia."

She nodded at one of the women who was tapping on her BlackBerry. "That's two months away for those of you who are technologically challenged."

The woman held up her BlackBerry. "Sixty-five days."

"Thank you very much." Jenny laughed. "We'll provide puppets and rides and food to the kids in our community. Our sister church will receive enough money to finish their building."

She spread her stack of papers across the table in front of her and picked one up.

"Now we need to divide the responsibilities and conquer. Caroline—what do you think about overseeing the entertainment?"

In her tailored ivory pantsuit, Caroline looked as glamorous as she had when Leia first met her. "Entertainment is fine as long as I'm not in charge of food."

"I'll take the food," another woman volunteered.

Leia sat back in her chair as the other women plucked up the assignments. She had no idea how to handle the entertainment or food or setup and teardown.

Jenny held up the last paper, and everyone stared at Leia. She didn't say a word as Jenny vouched for her skills. Without hesitation the group unanimously elected her to oversee the final task.

On the drive back home, Jenny thanked her for coming. "It's great to have a real pro on the team."

Leia laughed. "I'm wondering why everyone was so eager to nominate me for the ticket sales."

"You like a challenge, right?"

"Always."

"Good, because the ticket sales were a disaster last year. The person in charge lost a batch of fifty tickets, and then she deleted the Excel chart that tracked the sales off her computer by mistake. We didn't know how many tickets had been sold or who had them."

"Thanks for telling me now."

Jenny smiled. "You still would have wanted the job."

Jenny was right. For the next two months she'd focus on this new task instead of playing games.

23

Six weeks later

THE SUNLIGHT EDGED THROUGH THE WINDOW, CASTING SHADOWS across the desk and turning the burgundy comforter on the bed beside her pink. Leia hung up the telephone and checked off the name of the bookstore from her list. It was the last call she had to make today, and they, along with several schools and the local tourism office, had agreed to sell the church's carnival tickets.

The carnival work had been good for her. The busywork occupied her hands even if it didn't challenge her brain. It kept her mind focused on something other than the call of her computer. But she still thought about winning. A lot.

She opened the file next to the laptop and scribbled a check to pay for trash pickup and stuck the bill into an envelope. Then she paid the electric company.

She rarely felt pain in her knee these days, and she'd started putting weight on her right leg last week. So far, so good. Her appointment with Fabrice was right before lunch, and if she was lucky, he would declare her fit to drive.

She bit into her cold toast, caked with butter and strawberry jam, and relished the creamy spread on her tongue. Brushing the crumbs off her fingers and onto her plaid pajama bottoms, she stuffed the electric bill into the last envelope. Done paying out for today. She'd worn threadbare pajama bottoms along with a white T-shirt all day yesterday and overnight. It wasn't as if anyone came to visit her these days. When Ethan was gone, she couldn't care less how she looked. And even the days he was home, she didn't particularly care.

The only person she saw regularly was Jenny, but even Jenny was too busy at work to take her to physical therapy today.

She ran her crumb-covered fingers through her hair. She didn't want to think about how long it had been since she'd had a shower. Two days? Three? She'd soak in the bathtub for an hour before she saw Jenny and the group of women at the carnival meeting tonight.

She inputted the amounts of the trash and electric bills into their Quicken file and tracked their March expenses. Ethan was right on the mark. They were still five hundred dollars behind budget even though she'd used a thousand of her gambling earnings to pay for groceries and gas for Ethan's car over the past two months. She'd transfer extra money from their savings account to checking to cover her car payment and the water bill.

During the past four years of their marriage, they'd made a down payment on their house, accumulated a decent sum in their 401(k) accounts, and saved eighteen thousand dollars for emergencies. With her out on medical leave, five hundred would chip away at their cushion until she could start adding again to the bottom line.

She threw the stack of paid bills on the bed.

Opening the dictionary on top of the desk, she pulled out the envelope she'd hidden inside and thumbed through the hundred-dollar bills. She still had almost three thousand dollars left from her online blitz—hard cash. She stuck three hundred into her purse to pay for the taxi and a new jacket and their groceries for the week. She'd already told Ethan they could budget easier if they used cash—he just thought the cash was coming from the checking account. He knew nothing about her secret stash.

There was one more bill she needed to check. One she'd been avoiding.

She logged on to the credit card account and typed in her password. The last thing she wanted to do was find out how much she'd lost during her downturn in February, but she needed to pay her bill.

$2,600.

Her fingers froze, her eyes glued to the screen. When had she gambled almost three thousand dollars? It didn't seem possible. She thought she'd spent about a thousand. At most, fifteen hundred.

Twenty-six hundred dollars was a chunk of cash.

The credit card was overdue by a month. She'd have to think of a way to pay it without Ethan finding out. Maybe she could purchase a money order with some of her cash.

At least her winnings still exceeded her losses. She was still over a thousand bucks ahead of the machine.

She reached for her last bite of bread and sponged up the drops of jam from the plate before she ate it. She'd deal with the bill later.

She had two hours to kill before she visited Fabrice. Maybe she could win a few hundred back before her appointment, so her therapist would comment about her upbeat outlook on life instead of the lingering shadows under her eyes.

She could feel the strength building inside her. The drive that needed satisfaction. The need to conquer the next challenge, to succeed. The surge that was about to blow.

In seconds she was back on the Slot Heaven Web site—the one where she'd won almost four grand. Today was a better day. Today she felt like a winner. No game was going to ground her when she was ready to fly.

She added another hundred to her online account, seed money for the big win.

She spun, and the lights flashed. A thousand-dollar bonus popped up on the screen.

Her face warmed. Her hands trembled. This was what she needed to feel alive. The thousand would chip away at the three-thousand-dollar chunk she'd billed to her credit card. Two more thousand and she'd be debt free.

Then she'd stop playing.

She spun again. And again. Her losses slowly chipped away at the thousand she'd gained.

She shook her mouse as if it held a pair of dice and rolled again.

This was ridiculous—her escalations, her crashes, all dependent on a computerized game. Silly is what it was … yet she didn't want to stop.

She heard a honk and stood up to look out the window. A taxi was parked in the driveway, waiting for her. Two hours had passed in a blur.

She pulled a sweatshirt over her T-shirt and replaced her pajama bottoms with jeans.

She trekked down the stairs crutch free, pulling her hair back in a tattered scrunchie and praying that today she could break her convertible out of the garage.

♠ ♥ ♣ ♦

AT THE END OF THE HOUR-LONG THERAPY SESSION, FABRICE squeezed her hand and smiled. "You're doing much better, Leia."

She sighed. It was exactly what she needed to hear.

He washed his hands in the sink and dried them on a green towel. "Aren't you going to ask me?"

She ran her fingers through her stringy hair and smiled. "When can I drive?"

His hands tapped the metal table in a mock drumroll. "I believe it's time."

"No more house arrest?"

"Only a block today. A mile tomorrow. You need to take it slow, and if you feel any pain in your knee, I want you to stop." He stared her down like a teacher who didn't quite trust his student. "Can you handle that?"

"You bet." She stood up. "Flying is next."

"You'll have to take that one up with the doctor."

"You're a miracle worker, Fabrice."

"Take it slow," he repeated as they walked toward the door.

She handed Fabrice the immobilizer. "You can burn this."

Her leg felt good after therapy, though she still wobbled as she walked out of the office into the cool breeze blowing between the hospital buildings. She didn't have time to waste. Not when Fabrice had told her she could start driving again. She was going home and getting into the car and driving a lot farther than a block. Lake Mead. Sunrise Mountain. Maybe even the Valley of Fire. She wasn't particular. Just as long as she could get out of their stuffy house and breathe some fresh wilderness air. Today she was celebrating her freedom.

With a quick wave of her arm, she flagged down a taxi and gave the cab driver her address. She leaned her head back against the gray vinyl seat as they drove toward Henderson. She'd won a thousand bucks this morning. Fabrice had just told her she could drive. It was her lucky day.

The cab flew past the row of gypsylike casinos. Her eyes honed in on the middle casino with its open glass doors and red velvet carpet creating a royal path inside. An invitation to anyone who dared play.

Spinning slots on her computer suddenly seemed passé. She wanted to celebrate her news in style. Besides, in person was the best approach when something needed to be done, and she needed to recover her cash.

Her persistence through life had always paid off. She'd won an all-state title in basketball even when her mother said sports were a waste of time. She'd graduated with honors from college even though she'd hated classroom work. She'd been one of the youngest pilots hired on at Corporate Direct, and she'd tamed her risk taking to obey most of the rules.

If there was one thing her dad had always taught her, it was not to quit when she was down. All her life she had been convinced that nothing could keep her from her goals.

She leaned forward in her seat. "Could you go back?"

The driver glanced back at her in the rearview mirror. "To the physical therapist?"

"No," she paused as she tried to push out the words. "To those casinos."

He gave her a lingering look, one that almost looked sad. But he shouldn't feel sorry for her. She was a winner.

"I thought you wanted to go home."

"I changed my mind."

"Are you sure, lady?"

She could feel the strength rising in her again. "Very."

24

L EIA REFUSED TO MEET THE TAXI DRIVER'S GAZE WHEN SHE PAID him, her eyes focused on the flickering lights inside the casino's glass door. This wasn't Black Hawk. This was Las Vegas—gambling Mecca—a place where people from around the world came to worship. Some of the faithful left as millionaires.

She'd seen the features in the local newspaper, watched the smiling faces on the TV news when someone was awarded a check of massive proportion.

She wasn't asking for massive. She'd be quite satisfied with ten grand or so.

The sign above the door blazed Casa Bonita in white lights. As she stepped toward the red carpet, her heart raced. Her fingers shook. Even her toes trembled inside her tennis shoes.

It was the same feeling she got when she stared down from the top of a black-diamond run. Or when she dodged thunderstorms in her plane. Or when she shot the winning goal.

Fear. Anticipation. The need to seize control.

She stopped for a moment, waiting for the calm before she went inside.

The breeze chilled her face when she stopped. A quiet voice whispered under the wind, offering her freedom if only she'd turn around, promising forgiveness if only she'd acknowledge her sin. It was a simple voice of love that wanted nothing but her.

Right now she didn't want the voice.

Her jaw locked. Her gaze didn't waver. She cut the line to her anchor and sailed through the glass doors. After all, she knew how to play the slots like a pro now. If the players here knew her story, they'd drool with envy. She was one of the few who'd won more than she'd lost. Luck was on her side.

The red-carpet entry led to a sea of deep blue on the casino floor. The place was more formal than Black Hawk. Rich velvet tapestries accented faux windows. Crystal chandeliers dangled from the gold-plated ceiling. The place screamed luxury, but she didn't care about being pampered. She just wanted to conquer the machine.

She moved toward the barred cage of the cashier station, deciding she didn't need to buy a coat after all. Her old jacket would do until she won the jackpot. Then she could buy a closet full of clothes for every season.

She slid her coat money through the open window. The attendant counted the five twenty-dollar bills twice and pushed back a white bucket filled with a hundred dollars in change.

She scanned the casino floor. It was a Wednesday afternoon, but more than half of the slot machines were occupied or spoken for. She strolled up the aisle as if she knew exactly what she was doing and found a winning machine.

The Diamond Breeze was a basic slot machine. One-dollar maximum bet. She glanced at the rules—not much different from those for online slots, except this time she'd pull a silver handle to win.

She sat on the padded stool—comfortable enough to stay for a while yet not cozy enough to fall asleep. That's how she assumed the casino wanted its customers—relaxed but alert. She didn't plan to relax for a second.

She shoved her quarters into the machine as if she were feeding a pet tiger. All she wanted was a little love in return.

The scenery around her blurred. Crowds disappeared. Lights faded to black. It was just her and the machine. And she was going to win.

An hour later, Leia looked down at the plastic bottom of her bucket, her first hundred gone. She picked up her bucket and raced back to the cage to cash in another hundred.

You have to spend money to make money.

Today's investment teetered on incredibly high returns.

When she returned to the stool, a cocktail waitress offered her a free rum and Coke, but she waved the woman away. Nothing was going to distract her from her goal, especially not free drinks. That's what the tourists did when they came to Vegas. They soaked in the comps like kids playing in the sun—distracted by free alcohol and cheap steak and upgraded suites until they got fried.

But she wasn't some wishy-washy tourist. She was hardcore.

The second bucket of coins disappeared even faster than the first, the machine snorting coins like they were crack cocaine.

Leia gripped the lever and squeezed. She *had* to beat this thing. She was falling further and further into the pit, but it wouldn't keep her down. She'd claw her way out if she had to.

The last hundred smoldered in her purse. Grocery money.

This was it. If she lost this money, she'd stop playing and eat ramen noodles for the week.

Someone tapped her on the shoulder, and Leia turned to see a woman with a short black skirt, white shirt, and a tight black cap over her bobbed hair—Brandy was typed in bold letters on her nametag. She smelled as though she'd dipped herself in a pool of coconut milk.

"You need change?" she asked.

Leia reached into her purse and pulled out the last of her cash. "Quarters, please."

Brandy returned minutes later with a new white bucket filled with change. Leia tipped her a dollar before turning back to the machine.

She'd read about slot machine strategy online. Some strategists said you should leave a tight machine after five losses, while others said the longer you stick with a machine, the more likely you are to hit the jackpot. The jackpot on this baby was fifteen grand, and Leia wasn't moving until she took it home.

With a quick prayer, she pulled the lever and watched the payline spin. A diamond popped up in the first box, then a second diamond. She held her breath as the spin ticked down. A red ruby stopped in the third box.

She pressed the button to cash out and steadied her bucket as fifty dollars in change dumped out of the machine. Hopefully this machine would pour out the jackpot after a few more spins.

She spun again and again through wins of two and ten and fifteen dollars and the loss of a hundred fifty more.

Time was not an issue on the casino floor. The lighting stayed the same. The cool temperature never wavered. No one rang an alarm or told her it was time to go home. Her stomach didn't even growl for food.

When her bucket emptied again, she reopened her purse. The cash was gone.

She'd have to use the credit card. She didn't have a choice. She'd already gambled today's winnings plus the three hundred she had left from the money she'd grabbed this morning. She wasn't going home without something to show for her day.

She motioned to Brandy, and the woman scampered to her side.

"Can I use a credit card to get cash?" Leia asked.

"Honey, you can use anything you have including your wedding ring and the equity on your car."

She pushed her credit card toward Brandy. "Can I get a hundred more on this?"

Brandy didn't touch the plastic. "It's no problem, but you've got to go to the cage yourself for the cash. I'll hold your machine until you get back."

As she walked toward the cage, Leia dug her cell phone out of her purse. The screen said she'd missed three calls. She clicked the green button to see who had called. Ethan had called once. Jenny, twice.

She looked down at her watch, and her heart sank. Jenny was supposed to pick her up in ten minutes to go to the spring carnival meeting tonight.

She'd have to make up some excuse for being late.

When she rushed back toward the slot machine, Brandy moved away from the stool.

"I have to go." Leia spouted. "I lost track of time in here."

Brandy nodded down the row of busy machines. "Most people do."

25

IN FRONT OF THE CASINO, THE TAXIS LINED UP LIKE RACE CARS waiting for a green flag. Leia hoped one of the drivers aspired to win the Winston Cup. Speed over safety today. She was willing to brave the danger if it got her home in record time.

She waved down a yellow cab as she dialed Jenny's cell number.

"I was starting to get worried," Jenny said when she answered her phone.

"My physical therapy ran late," Leia lied as a taxi parked beside her. She waited to open the door.

"I thought it was at noon."

"It was, but then I ran a few errands."

"What?"

"Fabrice said I could drive, so I went and bought a coat. Leather."

"That's great, Leia. I can't wait to see your new jacket."

She clutched her chest like the jacket might appear. She should have thought through her story before she dialed the phone. "I actually just ordered it. Should be in the store on Monday."

"I guess I'll see it next week then."

Leia opened the back door, and the driver turned around when she climbed into his car. "Where to, lady?"

Leia shushed the man with one finger. He shrugged as he pushed the meter.

"Who's that?" Jenny asked.

"The TV." She was a rotten liar.

"Did you hear my message?"

"Not yet."

"I called to apologize. I'm running behind tonight, so I'll be about fifteen minutes late."

Finally a break. "Don't worry about it, Jenny. I can drive myself."

"Now what fun would that be?"

"But it's been such a busy day for you."

"Not too busy to pick you up."

"I'd really like to drive, Jenny."

Her friend paused. "No problem. The meeting starts in a half hour."

"I'll see you there."

Leia gave the driver her address, and he rolled his eyes when she told him to book it. She had to arrive at church before Jenny.

ETHAN STROLLED THROUGH THE LOBBY IN THE SOUTH BEACH Marquis—his Miami layover hotel. Behind the reception desk was a tiled mosaic in pinks and blues, an artist's abstract portrayal of an Atlantic sunset. On the other side of the lobby was a crowded restaurant serving a late dinner to several flight crews. He wasn't hungry tonight.

Ethan passed by the restaurant as he dialed home on his cell phone, letting it ring four times before the answering machine picked up. He'd already left two messages, and his wife still hadn't returned his call.

She had a physical therapy appointment this morning. Unless Jenny took her out for a late lunch, she should be at home all afternoon.

He hated it when Leia didn't answer the home or cell phone. He'd called over and over tonight, and she obviously wasn't taking his calls.

A few months ago he would have called an ambulance to check on her if she hadn't called him back in record time. These days she returned his calls at her own leisurely pace. She'd shut down after her accident and never returned.

He walked through a set of sliding glass doors and out into the cool ocean air. The hotel's pristine pool was in front of him, lit up by bucket lamps, and he moved around a row of chaise lounges until he reached a small gate. He opened it.

As he stepped out onto a boardwalk, salty wind from the surf whipped against his face. Leaning down, he took off his leather shoes and rolled up his jeans. He stuffed his socks into the shoes and walked off the boardwalk onto the chilled sand that squashed between his toes.

He was losing his wife, but he didn't know where she'd gone. When he tried to care for her, she thwarted his attempts. When he tried to win her back, she pushed him further away. They'd spent most of their marriage apart—sometimes going for weeks without seeing each other when their schedules didn't mesh. Yet when they were together, it had been an amazing time of playing and praying and camping out in their king-sized bed. There was no place else he'd rather be than at home with Leia.

Even though he saw her three days a week now, they didn't play together anymore. Or pray. Most days she holed up in their room alone as if she was counting the minutes until he left again. She wasn't even interested in being outdoors.

The roar of the waves grew louder as he walked toward the water, the surf breaking off the beach. Lights glowed behind him, rows of them lining Miami's South Beach. He could hear the steel drums of reggae music blaring from a solitary bar down the beach. It was only nine o'clock. The party hadn't started.

As the night progressed, locals and tourists would crowd the beach, the boardwalk lighting up as electric guitars competed against each other and the ocean roar.

He didn't care about the parties. He liked staying in Miami because he got to spend his evenings walking on the beach. Time alone with God.

Cold water trickled over his toes and then raced back out into the sea as he strolled along the sand.

"Please help me find out what's wrong with Leia," he prayed into the darkness.

He stepped on a seashell and reached down to rub his foot. Wisdom is what he needed right now. A Solomon-sized portion.

His personal life was in a free fall, but at least his professional life was intact for the moment. With his checkride three weeks away, he'd spend every hour away from the cockpit poring over his books. A failed checkride could mean a failed career. They couldn't afford for him and Leia both to be out of work.

Yet he didn't know how he was going to win back his distant wife while taking care of their home, maintaining his job, and studying for the exam.

The sound of the steel drums faded. All he heard now was the roar of the waves.

He looked out at the black horizon, wondering how he could win back his wife.

A group of kids walked by him, swinging bottles of beer. Their only stress was probably finding the next party—forget getting to a party on time.

Had his life ever been so uncomplicated? Not that he could remember. He'd spent most of his younger years taking care of Paige while his parents were smuggling Bibles through the Iron Curtain. He'd worried each time they left, wondering if they'd be caught, terrified they wouldn't return.

He'd stressed over Paige's failing marriage to Brett, agonizing for her as Brett's addiction crushed their family. He'd stressed over Leia every day since he met her—wondering how to take care of her when she wanted to be left alone.

In the faint light, he could see a woman walking toward him with a knit sweater and short skirt, swinging her sandals in one hand. He stepped up the beach to let her stroll by him, but she stopped and stared.

"Ethan?"

He squinted. It was a flight attendant who'd flown as a replacement today. He'd been introduced, but he couldn't remember her name.

She stood beside him, water lapping against her ankles, long blonde hair blowing in the wind. Now might be an appropriate time to forget walking and run.

"What are you doing out here all alone?" she asked. He could ask her the same thing, but he didn't like the direction that conversation might head.

"I was craving a little fresh air."

She reached out and brushed his sleeve as if she were cleaning off sand. "You want some company?"

He took a step back. "No, I'm fine. Thanks."

"I don't blame you. It's a good evening to think."

And pray.

She smiled. "Maybe we can get something to eat after you walk."

"I'll see you in the morning," he said.

She scrunched her lips into a pout. "Or a quick drink before bed."

He shook his head as he moved away. The Enemy always sent the most attractive distractions whenever he asked God for help.

He continued his quiet journey down the coast—this time praying for strength.

A half mile down the beach, a new thought occurred to him.

Maybe Leia wasn't just distracted.

Maybe she was having an affair.

26

THE DRIVE HOME FROM THE CASINO TOOK EIGHTEEN LONG MINUTES even though the taxi driver was buzzing around traffic like a worker bee. Leia checked her watch at the top of every minute, counting down the landing. It wouldn't get her home any faster, but if she couldn't drive herself, she could at least clock their time.

If she really had been out shopping, she wouldn't care about being late. But she hadn't been shopping. She'd been gambling.

It was neurotic—this fear that Jenny might find out where she'd been. Completely ludicrous. Thousands of people spent their days inside a casino. It was crazy to plague herself because she'd decided to play the slots.

Maybe she should just come clean. What was the big deal if Jenny found out? She could even ask her not to tell Ethan.

But Jenny couldn't find out. Leia already felt enough guilt without someone heaping on more. Jenny was a godly woman who'd been hurt by gambling. She wouldn't understand. Sam had gone over the top, and she might suspect Leia was on the edge.

Worse, she would think Leia had lost control. But Leia never, ever lost control—of her time, her airplane, her emotions. Her skiing accident didn't count—it was the snowboarder who'd lost it that day. Weather. People. Mechanical failures. She couldn't control those. But she could always control herself.

The taxi pulled into the driveway, and Leia ran inside and back out to pay the man from the twenty-five hundred that remained in her envelope stash. Then she rushed back upstairs, ripped off her clothes that smelled like smoke, and replaced them with a white blouse and tan pants. If only she had time for a shower.

The clock was pushing seven. She'd never make it to the church in five minutes.

Leia opened the garage door, climbed into her Mustang GT convertible, and kissed the wheel. After her meeting tonight, she'd drown the leather in fresh air.

She twisted her back against the seat before starting the ignition. Then she shifted into reverse and hit the pedal. Pain shot up her leg, and she released her foot. Was it supposed to hurt? Fabrice said to start slow, but he hadn't said anything about pain.

She clutched her knee as she backed out of the driveway. She couldn't deal with the pain right now. She needed to beat Jenny to church before her friend asked more questions. If anyone discovered her secret, it would be Jenny. The woman had a way of digging right under the surface to detect land mines.

The church was only three miles away—a little longer than the block Fabrice had allowed her to drive the first time. It was a tiny discrepancy, but it wasn't as though Fabrice were with the FAA. She didn't have to report back to him.

By the time she got to the church, she had to drag her leg out of the car, but she pushed through the pain, limping through the foyer and down the side hall.

She peeked her head into the Sunday school room, and her heart sank when she saw that Jenny had already started the meeting.

She stepped into the room, and Jenny rushed toward her, giving her a hug. When she pulled back, Jenny sneezed, but she didn't say anything about the smoky smell lingering in Leia's hair. Not only did she smell disgusting, Leia knew she looked like trash.

She sat down and tried to act confident in spite of her appearance. Maybe the women wouldn't notice a thing.

"Let's keep going." Jenny nodded toward Caroline. "Can you give us a recap of the entertainment?"

Caroline straightened the collar of her suit, slid her glasses to the rim of her nose, and starting reading from a typed report. "We've secured a ball pit, a giant slide, and a moonwalk. We'll have a puppet show every half hour, clowns, a small petting zoo, and face painting. In the afternoon we'll have a concert featuring several local groups, and we'll draw for door prizes before we shut down for the night. Grand prize is a Disney cruise."

"Good work." Jenny scribbled on her yellow pad. "Do you need me to send out any checks?"

"I'll e-mail you a list of how much we owe each vendor."

"Okay." Jenny turned toward her. "What have you found out, Leia?"

She didn't need notes. "We're selling advance tickets on the church Web site, and the city has offered to link our information on their event calendar. I've talked to a few local grocery stores as well as the Christian bookstores, and they've all agreed to sell tickets for a small commission. The local Christian school has already sold a truckload of tickets to their students, and I've contacted several public schools but don't have an answer yet."

"Great job." Jenny marked the ticket sales item off her agenda and moved on to marketing, facilities, and outreach. Listening to the women, Leia realized she was actually having fun. She was part of a group that wanted to make a difference in the world, connecting with women who weren't content with the status quo.

"Let's plan to meet at least twice a week for the next three weeks," Jenny said as she wrapped up the meeting.

After she prayed, Jenny tugged on her arm, and Leia followed her into the hallway. Leia took her car keys out of her purse and twisted the chain around her finger.

"Are you doing okay?" Jenny whispered.

"I tell you every time you ask that question that I'm fine."

"This time I don't believe you."

"It's been a long day."

Jenny's eyes bore into her like a branding iron. "When was the last time you got a good night's sleep?"

"I sleep every night."

"How about take a shower?"

Leia wanted to tell her it was none of her business, but she wasn't going to drive away her only friend in Henderson. "I didn't have time this morning."

"Do you want me to drive you home?"

Leia shoved her car keys into her pocket. "No."

"Did Ethan change his flight schedule this month?"

Leia nodded. "He'll be working Tuesday through Friday instead of weekends."

"Do you have plans on Friday night?"

"I'm scheduling a shower."

Jenny didn't even laugh. "Why don't you and Ethan come over for dinner? The boys have a party at church."

"That works for us."

"Do you want to check with Ethan?"

"He doesn't have anything."

"Maybe he's planned some sort of secret date night."

She took a step down the hallway. "We'll be there."

The first thing Leia did when she got home was take a long, hot shower. Then she went to bed.

When she fell asleep, she didn't dream about snow skiing or flying or hiking through the woods. She dreamed about the lights and bells and whistles at Casa Bonita.

♠ ♥ ♣ ♦

FIVE HOURS LATER, LEIA WOKE UP. IT WAS STILL PITCH BLACK OUTSIDE, so she shut her eyes, rolled over, and counted diamonds. Sleep wouldn't return. She tossed around the bed for another half hour until she just sat up and stared at the computer beside her.

The online world had lost its draw.

It didn't take long to dress—she tugged on a pair of jeans and a navy pullover. With a quick scoop, she stuffed the cash envelope into her purse, slipped on black Skechers, and shuffled downstairs. As she backed out of the driveway, she pushed the button to open the cloth top of her convertible. Fresh air!

A line of street lamps lit the road in front of her, the houses on both sides still dark.

She was used to driving to the airport before dawn, but 2:45 a.m. was earlier than she normally went to work. Jenny had told her to get a good night's rest, but she couldn't sleep with yesterday's defeat thrashing through her head. Forget going to church. Today she'd show the Diamond Breeze that she was boss.

Parking her car in the casino lot, she took the elevator up to the first floor. The place looked exactly the same as when she had left last night. White lights reflected off the blue carpet. Cocktail waitresses scampered between tables. The same number of people sat at the same machines—a few bracing their chins so they didn't nod off. She wondered if anyone had a clue that it was dark outside.

She wasn't tired anymore. She owned this night, and she was going to make the machine pay for stealing her cash.

The Diamond Breeze sat unoccupied, a lonely cage under the big circus tent. She sat down before anyone else claimed her spot, and she didn't move until Brandy appeared at her side.

The woman smacked her gum in Leia's ear. "I knew you'd be back."

"What are you doing still here?"

"I work fourteen-hour shifts whenever I can."

She handed the woman another hundred.

Brandy counted the cash. "Too bad you didn't stay a little longer last night."

Don't tell me what happened.

"Some guy won five thousand bucks on this machine, ten minutes after you went home."

Why didn't she just punch her in the gut and leave her to wallow in the pain?

"Maybe today will be your lucky day," Brandy said. "Sometimes these machines pay out twice in a row just to mess with everyone's minds."

When Brandy came back with the tokens, Leia hunkered down for the long haul.

27

THE DIAMOND BREEZE DEVOURED FIVE HUNDRED DOLLARS before breakfast. A thousand right after lunch. By dinnertime Leia had spent all of the cash in her envelope. Twenty-four hundred dollars. Two hundred bucks an hour.

Brandy had said good-bye early that morning, telling her not to stay at the casino all day. Leia shooed her advice away with a wave. She'd stay as long as it took to win.

A woman named Patrice took Brandy's place on the casino floor, and she kept Leia supplied with quarters and iced tea. Leia hadn't taken a sip of the tea in hours. She'd barely heard the chimes that blared in competition around her or felt the intensity of the flashing lights.

It was just her and the machine that had become her worst enemy ... and her best friend.

Patrice eyed the number of coins left in Leia's white bucket. "Don't you want something to eat?"

Leia clutched the bucket. This time she wanted the slots to refill her bucket instead of the cage. "What time is it?"

Patrice glanced at her watch. "Five o'clock."

Leia pushed her heels against the machine. She'd been playing for more than twelve hours without one significant gain. Her measly wins didn't even come close to covering her losses. A tourniquet wouldn't stop the bleeding.

She had to win it back. And in order to do it, she had to win big.

"I'm not hungry," Leia said. She didn't have time for food.

Patrice leaned against the stool next to her. "Have you eaten anything since you got here?"

She shook her head.

"I'm bringing you a cheeseburger and fries. On the house."

Leia couldn't argue with something on the house—though it was hardly free. If she counted the money she lost yesterday, the burger cost her almost three thousand bucks.

"You sure you don't want anything stronger to drink?" Patrice pointed toward the tea.

"I don't drink alcohol."

"It's on the house too."

"Still don't drink it."

When Patrice left for the kitchen, Leia stared at the slot machine. White and silver diamonds glittered across the top, the silver arm sparkling in the light. Her palm was glued to the metal; her arm ached from milking the handle.

What was she doing here? She'd spent all of her cash, lost in the shadow of a jackpot, trapped by a possible win. But she wasn't winning. She'd lost everything she'd come with; her luck had dried up.

But she couldn't leave this machine. Not to go to another game. Not to go home. Someone would step in and steal all her cash, and she wasn't going to let that happen. It was a matter of principle now. She wouldn't let this thing break her.

"Here you go," Patrice said as she handed Leia the burger and fries and a fresh glass of tea.

Leia set the tea on the small pullout tray, steadied the plate in her lap, and took a bite of the burger. She took a second bite for the protein even though she didn't taste it. It would give her strength. The longer she stayed in the room, the more the lights around her turned gray. Sounds silenced. Smells disappeared. All she could see were the colors on the box in front of her. All she wanted to taste was the sweet thrill of a win. Relish in the smell of victory.

Her cell phone rang, and she reached toward her purse. A security guard appeared like magic at her side before she even looked at the screen.

"You need to turn that off, ma'am." He stayed two feet away from her as he spoke, probably for the benefit of the security cameras. Nothing like being on TV.

"I won't talk on it."

"Doesn't matter. House rules."

She glanced at the caller ID before she shut it down. It was Ethan.

He'd kill her if he knew where she was … and that she was almost three thousand in the hole. Make that six thousand with her credit card debt.

She shoved up the sleeve of her sweatshirt and looked at the date on her watch. Today was April 5. Ethan would be back in the morning. She had to finish her game, collect her winnings, and beat him home.

When she reached back down into her bucket, her knuckles scraped the plastic as she scooped up the last fistful of coins. One at a time she plunged them into the machine and spun until all of her cash was gone. A total loss. She waved at Patrice.

"Can you reserve my machine?" she asked as she jumped off the stool.

"Of course."

Leia fled toward the cage, her credit card out of her purse before the attendant asked what she needed. Cash. She needed five hundred more dollars in cash.

She couldn't think about what she was doing. The implications were too steep for her to face. She needed to stick with her goal. Drive for the win. Beat the machine and then flee this place.

She signed the credit card receipt for her personal account. She'd conquer this mess, and Ethan would never know the difference.

She lost track of how many times she returned to the cage during the next twelve hours. The night passed in a blur of spinning diamonds, emeralds, and rubies. She was lost in her own world, alone in the crowded room.

Hours later she felt a tap on her shoulder. She sniffed coconut before she turned around.

Brandy greeted her with a wide smile above her freshly ironed shirt. "You're still here?"

Leia needed another shower. Her fingers felt greasy. Her breath was rancid. "I thought you went home."

"I did. Twenty-four hours ago."

Leia pointed at the machine. "I can't beat this thing."

Brandy leaned in toward her. "Of course you can't. It's a slot machine."

"I thought if I played long enough."

Brandy shuffled her feet and moved close, taking Leia's watery tea off the tray.

"Go home," she whispered. "Surely someone is looking for you."

Her husband.

Ethan would wonder where she'd gone.

28

E THAN PULLED INTO THEIR DRIVEWAY EXHAUSTED. IT WAS ONLY noon, but he had been up since 4:30 a.m., flying from Miami to Baltimore, then back to Las Vegas to end the trip. He'd crisscrossed the country five times in the past four days: the cities, airports, and hotels all blurring together like black ink spilled across a map.

Some pilots got off work and went home to run family businesses, or they jetted to Maui or New York City to play. Not him. By the end of his workweek, he was ready to hunker down for a few restful days at home, preferably with his wife. Since they got married, they'd worked hard to coordinate their flight schedules even if it meant spending holidays in the air. They'd decided that the important thing was to spend as much time as possible together as a couple—and someday soon, as a family.

After a long trip he liked to dream about a houseful of munchkins greeting him with giant hugs and kisses. His own welcome committee every time he came home.

He was more than ready to add a kid to the mix, but they couldn't start a family if he and Leia didn't get a few things straightened out.

First of all, she had to stop ignoring his calls. He was already worried sick about her. When he couldn't get hold of her from the road, it put him over the edge.

He couldn't stop thinking about what was wrong with his wife. The threat of an affair hung over him like a bulging thunderhead that hadn't produced rain. But every time the word entered his brain, he blocked it. There was no way Leia would cheat on him. Everything had been fine between them until her accident. Her evasiveness was just a glitch, a kink to knead out after she healed.

But why had she stopped taking his calls? Why didn't she want to talk anymore? Or even go play when he was home?

She'd gone from an overachiever searching for the next big wave to someone content with paddling in the shallows. Someone he didn't know. Her willpower seemed depleted; her nervous energy had turned into a strange calm.

She wasn't interested in anything except being by herself—a hermit of her own making. Every day she had progressed physically, but emotionally she'd fled.

He wanted his wife back.

He reached up to open the garage door, but before he punched the opener, someone shouted his name. Misty dashed across the rocky lawn to his left, her red hair blowing in the breeze.

He rolled down his window. "Good morning."

She glanced down at her watch. "More like afternoon, isn't it?"

Whatever. He was too tired to argue.

"What's up?" he asked.

"I was looking for that wife of yours."

Leia would hang him for offering but ... "Do you want to come inside?"

She arched an eyebrow as though he'd propositioned her. That's not what he meant.

"To see Leia," he added.

She didn't attempt to stifle her grin. "I've been knocking and knocking all morning but can't get a soul to come to the door. I was getting worried."

He didn't tell her that Leia probably wouldn't answer if Misty knocked for the next three days.

"I'm sure she's fine."

"She went tearing out of here so fast yesterday that it scared me."

He gripped the steering wheel. "Tearing out?"

"I heard her car race down the street at three in the morning. Thought maybe she'd gotten sick or something."

"Her car?"

"Yep. That's what had me worried. I didn't think she was driving."

"Maybe someone was just making a U-turn."

"Red convertible. Top down."

He reached up and pressed the garage door opener. Misty glanced inside the empty door and then back at him, tilting her head like a parent who'd caught their child with both hands in the cookie jar. Except he hadn't done anything wrong.

He let his foot off the brake. "She probably just ran out for groceries."

Why did he care what Misty Knapp thought? This was between him and Leia, and it was about to get hot.

He rolled up his window and drove inside.

SOMEONE TAPPED ON LEIA'S WINDOW. SHE GROANED, RUBBING HER sore eyes. It wasn't time to get up. It couldn't be. She felt as if she'd been run over by a truck.

Another tap.

Her eyelids were too heavy to even lift, to say nothing about her arms and legs. She'd sleep another hour or two until she heard her alarm.

The tap turned into a pound—or was that the pain in her head?

The noise wouldn't stop.

Couldn't Ethan answer the door? Didn't he know how exhausted she was? She reached over to shake him, but her hand hit a wall.

She bolted straight up, her hair brushing across the vinyl convertible top.

Where am I?

In a parking lot. The casino parking lot! She hadn't even made it home.

She whipped her eyes toward the window, slowly recognizing the woman knocking on the glass.

Long dark hair and a sleek body that rivaled J-Lo's. Danna something, from Misty's gossip group. The Guatemalan beauty queen.

It was too late to run. She certainly couldn't pretend she hadn't been here. Resigning herself to the inevitable, she turned the key in the ignition and rolled down the window.

"I thought I recognized you," Danna said. "You okay?"

"Long night."

"You didn't strike me as the party type."

"I was just getting out of the house for a few hours."

"Sure." Danna dug in her purse for a stick of gum and handed it to her through the window. "Can I get you something to drink? Black coffee, maybe? My husband owns this little joint, so I can conjure up anything you want."

Secrecy. Anonymity. *How about locking your mouth shut and throwing away the key?*

It was too late for that. This gossip was way too sweet. For Misty's next playgroup, she'd be dessert, supersized.

"Don't worry," Danna said, as if she were reading her mind. "What happens at the Casa Bonita stays at the Casa Bonita."

Leia felt sick. "Thanks."

"Can you drive?"

"You bet."

Danna waved as she headed toward an unmarked door. Leia started the engine.

Her right knee screamed when she hit the pedal. She should stop and stretch it, but it was too late to think about it. She had to get home.

Maybe Ethan's flight had been delayed this morning. It happened all the time—sometimes he didn't even get home until the next day. If she had any luck left, this would be one of those days.

She turned on her cell phone with one hand as she steered with the other. Eight missed calls, probably all from her husband. She held the phone up to her ear to listen to Ethan's three messages. In the first two he sounded worried, begging her to call him back the second she checked her voice mail.

But his last message sounded much different. This time he was mad.

"Where are you?" he demanded. "I'm home, and there's no note or anything to tell me where you've gone. C'mon, Leia. Call me back."

What was she thinking? Her life was out of control, her husband on the verge of a heart attack, and it was all her fault.

She'd lost a lot of money in the past twenty-four hours. A couple of months' worth of salary. Maybe more.

She hated herself for losing.

The noose was tightening around her neck. She could feel it slowly strangling her with every loss. Ethan would never forgive her if he found out she'd thrown away their hard-earned cash, shoving it into some machine as if it would devour her if she didn't feed it first.

She'd become a junkie, and there was no place to detox.

29

ETHAN SHOUTED LEIA'S NAME AS HE STOMPED INTO THE house. Of course she wasn't home, but he wanted to give her the last strand of the benefit of his doubts that were compounding by the second.

Why was she leaving in the middle of the night? Who was she going to see? How long had she been escaping like this? Was this the reason she was exhausted whenever he came home? He thought she was bored, but maybe she was too tired to spend time with him. She'd kept herself entertained after all.

Leia had gained weight since January, her toned muscles turning soft. And she'd stopped caring about simple things like taking a shower or brushing her hair or wearing something other than pajamas for the day. She'd never been particular about clothes, but she'd always been neat, whether she wore gym clothes or her pilot's uniform. Didn't someone who was having an affair dress up instead of down?

He grabbed a stack of mail off the kitchen counter and searched through it, no real idea what he was looking for. Proof, maybe. Evidence that his wife was cheating on him. He wanted answers, but at the same time he was afraid to discover the truth.

He threw the mail on the floor and picked up the phone. Who had Leia called before she left?

He punched in *69 to check the number of the last incoming call, and then he dialed it. The phone rang twice before a man answered.

"This is Sam."

Ethan slammed his fist on the counter. Who the heck was Sam?

He wanted to throw this guy against the wall, show him what happened when anyone messed around with Ethan Carlisle's wife.

"Hello?" the man said.

Ethan wondered what this guy had. Money? Power? Too much time on his hands?

"I'm looking for my wife," he growled.

The man paused. "And your wife is?"

A class act. Didn't this man know he was ruining lives?

"Leia Carlisle."

"Oh, sure. Hold on a sec."

Ethan braced himself as he waited for her. How dare Leia do this to him? He wanted to blast her. Tell her never to come home again. He wouldn't live with a woman who'd committed the ultimate marital sin.

Would God really want him to forgive this? An affair?

Four years of marriage wasted. He'd never have guessed that this woman he loved would cheat on him. The woman he'd cared for when she was sick. The woman he had brought roses to on every anniversary and birthday. The woman he had prayed for every day they were apart.

"This is Jenny," a woman said into the phone.

"Who?"

"Jenny Frazer. Is this Ethan?"

Jenny Frazer—Leia's new friend. The only person Leia seemed to enjoy these days.

He sighed. Leia had called Jenny before she left the house.

"I'm looking for Leia."

"I don't know where she is."

"I thought …" he stuttered.

"Sam said you sounded a little upset."

Sam was Jenny's husband?

"I just got back from a trip, and Leia's car isn't here."

"She's probably just out enjoying her newfound freedom."

"What freedom?"

Jenny hesitated. "Driving."

"When did she start driving?"

"Her therapist told her she could start driving short distances at her appointment this week."

Thanks for telling me, Leia.

"Does six o'clock still work for you tonight?" Jenny asked.

"For what?"

"I guess you haven't talked to Leia today."

How could he talk to her? She was ignoring his calls.

"Nope."

"Sam and I invited you guys over for dinner, and Leia thought tonight would work."

If she decided to return from wherever it was she disappeared to.

"Okay."

"Don't worry, Ethan. I'm sure she'll be home soon."

He hung the phone up on the kitchen receiver, pulled out a glass, and filled it with water. Why had he allowed himself to jump to the conclusion that Leia was having an affair? Why had he allowed himself to doubt her love? To doubt their marriage? His wife was keeping an awful lot of things to herself lately. She'd never been a great communicator about her feelings, but she was rigorous about keeping him informed. Information was critical in the cockpit—with the information you had, you made life-and-death decisions. He didn't have enough facts to make a decision right now.

Maybe he needed to gather a little more information before he made a judgment call.

What he was looking for exactly, he didn't know. He opened a kitchen drawer and rummaged through it. Nothing unusual. The junk drawer had the typical paper clips, receipts, phone numbers on scrap pieces of papers. He sorted through the papers, but there was nothing odd. Telephone numbers for Jenny, the electric company, and Leia's physical therapist—Fabrice something. The French guy.

He held the therapist's number in his hand.

Was there something going on between her and Fabrice?

Now he was being paranoid. The idea of her having an affair actu-ally seemed a little silly. He was driving himself crazy with all these doubts.

Leia was resting, recovering. She deserved a break after working her tail off her entire life. She needed a vacation from her lifetime of achievement. And he wanted her to have a vacation, but when she dis-appeared, all he could do was worry. He moved upstairs with deliberation—on a quest now. He was determined to find some sort of answer before his wife came home. He didn't know what—a note, a receipt, a rung in the ladder that would lead him to the truth.

He practically tiptoed up the stairs and into the office, feeling like a thief in his own house, stealing information before his own wife found out what he was doing. He sat down at the desk and pulled a three-ring binder off the bookshelf beside it. Flipping through the pages, he stopped at February's credit card statement and read through the charges to see if there was anything unusual. Groceries. Haircut. Gas. His one emergency run to Starbucks after a late flight into San Jose. Nothing strange.

He turned to the telephone bill and skimmed through the long-distance numbers. Mostly calls to Denver—him calling his sister, Leia calling Julie.

With a tap, he turned on the computer and opened her e-mail.

He'd never looked through her personal files. He'd never had a rea-son to check before, but he was doing this for her own good. For their own good.

The self-talk didn't comfort him. He felt like a crook.

At the top of her inbox was a chatty e-mail from a Denver friend. He only read a few lines and moved on. Any more and he'd lock himself up for trespassing. He passed over the spam—solicitations to buy Viagra, to win a free vacation, and to gamble online. Junk.

He opened up her trash folder, but her old e-mail had been deleted.

Maybe this whole thing was all in his head. The anxiety about his checkride was messing with his mind.

He had just opened up their Quicken file to check the state of their finances when he heard the garage door open. He quickly closed down the computer and headed toward the door.

"I need wisdom, Lord," he prayed again.

He braced himself before he walked downstairs. A vortex whirled in front of him, threatening his marriage and his sanity. But it was too late to turn back. No matter what happened, he still needed to fly.

30

L EIA RACED UP THE STREET AND INTO THE DRIVEWAY AS THOUGH the convertible's tailpipe were on fire. She'd run into the house, act surprised to see Ethan—what was he doing home so soon? She'd say she'd thought she'd beat him home.

She cleared her throat as she practiced the words out loud. She could make them sound believable—couldn't she? Calm her voice. Flash a cute smile. Kiss him on the cheek. Women did this kind of stuff every day. If only she had a hint of female charm, that special allure that some women have, she could pull it off.

But the second she opened the garage door, she stopped and sat idling in the car. She couldn't do the charm thing. She'd never learned the art of diverting a man's attention with a look and a grin. If only she could call her mom. Until she went to prison, Sondra Vaughn had been a master at diversion.

Tapping her fingers against the steering wheel, she took a deep breath. This was it. The last time she'd ever return from a casino. She'd cut her losses and somehow manage to pay back what she'd lost—without Ethan finding out. If she sliced a few personal expenses out of their budget, she could make it work. She'd skip some meals, cancel their satellite TV like Ethan suggested. She'd get a cheap dial-up for the computer and suspend their magazine subscriptions—when they were working, neither of them had time to read anyway.

She'd climb out of this hole she'd fallen into and be free. No matter how much she wanted to win, it wasn't worth it to come home frazzled like this. She'd played her game, and she'd lost. It was no big deal. People lost money gambling every day and moved on with their lives. She needed to let it go.

She had an amazing husband to live for. A God who loved her in spite of her weakness. She could do this one simple thing. She could be strong.

She'd tell Ethan she'd gone out to lunch with Jenny. It was easy enough. He would be fine. She would be fine. They'd move on with their life, and she could forget about these last two miserable days. At least until she braved a peek at the credit card statement. She'd wait a few weeks before she looked.

She practiced the words. "I'm so sorry, Ethan. Jenny and I lost track of time."

Where had they gone to lunch? What had she eaten? And why did she smell like smoke?

These obvious questions needed good answers. Simple explanations that were solid enough to ward off the scrutiny she knew she would have to face inside.

She should drive around the block until she pieced her scattered plan into a presentation. Something that even she could make believable.

Shifting into reverse, she glanced into her rearview mirror. Clear for takeoff. As her foot hit the pedal, she looked back at the garage and saw her husband, standing beside his car with his arms crossed, his jaw locked into a scowl.

Not exactly the greeting he usually gave her when she came home.

She turned off the ignition and slid out of the car.

Ethan didn't move toward her. He didn't even hold out his arms for a hug. He flicked his fingers toward the convertible. "Welcome home."

What was she going to say?

"I'm sorry, Ethan."

He made a grunting noise. "I left three messages, and you still didn't call me back. Not a voice mail or even a note to tell me you were gone."

Leia looked over and saw Misty peeking out from behind her curtains. She stepped into the garage.

"I was planning to be home by noon."

"Glad to know I made your list."

She shook her head. This was going all wrong. "I should have called you back."

"Why didn't you?"

The garage felt hot even in the winter. "I got distracted. I was with Jenny."

"That's funny. I just talked to Jenny, and she didn't have a clue where you were."

"Last night," she retorted. *Or was it two nights ago?* "I was with her at the carnival meeting when you called. This morning I took a drive."

"Where?"

"Around town."

"And your phone didn't ring?"

"I forgot to turn it on. I don't get many calls these days."

"I call you every day, Leia. Sometimes three or four times when you don't bother letting me know if you're still alive."

She stepped toward the open door behind him. "Our neighbors are listening."

"They're watching too." He followed her into the family room, but neither of them sat down. "Misty said she watched you race out of here a couple of nights ago."

Her fingers squeezed the ribbing on the couch. She hadn't even begun to think of a story to cover her early morning flight. It figured that Misty would be watching. She'd probably hacked into her computer too, following every move of her gambling career.

How long had it taken Danna to call her with the good news that Leia had crashed and burned?

"Leia?"

"It was actually morning, and I didn't fly."

"She said it was 3:00 a.m."

She braced herself against the wall. She was too tired to think. "I wanted to get out of the house, Ethan. Fabrice told me I could start driving, and I couldn't wait until daylight to go."

"Did you go see him?"

"Who?"

"Fabrice."

"Why would I go …" She stopped talking as he stepped toward her.

"I want to know if you're having an affair."

She gasped. Is that what he thought? That she was sleeping around? She almost wanted to laugh. If he knew the current status of their finances, he might think an affair was an improvement.

"I can't believe you'd think I was cheating on you!"

"Something is going on, Leia, and I want to know what. If you don't give me an answer, I'm setting up an appointment with a counselor at Jenny's church, and we can go see him together."

She'd created an awful, spiraling, out-of-control mess. It was her fault that her wonderful husband was plagued by doubt. He was right to question her. She'd escaped to a place where he didn't belong. Of course he thought she was having an affair. She'd left a trail of doubt behind her. A trail that led nowhere nice.

She sank into the couch, the soft folds enveloping her body. Sleep would clear her mind.

"It's been the hardest three months of my life, Ethan. I've felt trapped, useless, and I've taken it out on you. I'm sorry." She rested her head on a pillow, her eyes locking with his. "I'm not having an affair, honey. I'm trying to find my way back to who I am."

He hesitated as if he wasn't sure whether he should believe her.

He had to believe her. The only card she had left was the truth.

"You have to start calling me back," he said.

"I will."

He sat down on the coffee table in front of her. "I'm not kidding."

She wanted to say something sarcastic like "make me," but she wanted to keep her marriage intact even more.

"I'll call."

"You're scaring me, Leia. I don't know what's been going on with you."

"It will pass."

He managed a smile. "Have you heard anything yet from Ambassador?"

"No."

"You really should call them."

She nodded. "I will."

"Is there anything else I can do to help you?"

Do you have an extra ten grand stashed in the Caymans?

"Forgive me," she said.

He reached out to her this time, and she leaned over to give him a hug.

31

E THAN KNOCKED ON SAM AND JENNY'S FRONT DOOR AT SIX o'clock. When Jenny answered, she wrapped both him and Leia in her arms and squeezed tight before she let them breathe again. Her curly hair was pulled back in a headband, and she wore a red turtleneck with flared jeans.

She tugged them inside. "You found her?"

He wished he hadn't called this morning. Wished he hadn't been so cruel to her and her husband on the phone—mad and desperate and pathetic rolled into one.

"I did." He cleared his throat. "Apparently she had just escaped for a few hours."

"Since when did I need you two to babysit me?" Leia joked as she took off her jacket.

"Babysit?" Jenny laughed. "We're your biggest fans."

The front room reminded Ethan of a classic Western flick. A painting of an angry grizzly hung on the long wall that climbed past the beamed loft. An afghan was tossed over a brushed leather couch, and the wooden coffee table was studded with silver long-horn pulls. A flickering gas fireplace added heat to the already stifling room. He wiped the sweat off his forehead before it stung his eyes.

"Are you hungry?" Jenny asked him.

"Starving."

A man strode under an arched entry and into the living room, his gait as steady as his smile.

"I hear we have company." Sam reached out to shake his hand. "Of course, we already met via phone."

Ethan cringed. "It's been a rough day."

Sam pointed him into the kitchen, leaving the women to talk about a collage of photos on ghost towns. Sam's eyes scanned back toward the living room like a nervous spy about to make a drop, his easy smile grim.

He leaned in toward Ethan and whispered. "Heard you tell Jenny you were starving."

"I am."

"If you tell my wife you're hungry, you'll have to eat her food."

"But—"

"Put on your game face. Stomach a few bites. After dinner I'll break open the bag of chocolate chip cookies and beef jerky I have stashed in my den."

Ethan sniffed Swiss cheese and what smelled like lemon chicken. "It's that bad?"

Jenny walked into the kitchen. "What are you two boys talking about?"

Sam winked at him, the smile crawling back to his eyes. "Dinner."

They ate in the sunroom overlooking a golf course and a pristine pond with three token mallards swimming around lily pads and marsh grass. Jenny brought out a platter of baked sea bass covered in spices, followed by a cheesy squash casserole, and arranged them on the table beside a fresh salad and a basket of rolls.

She spooned a large helping of casserole onto a plate and handed it to Ethan. "I hope you don't mind my trying out new recipes on you. I love to cook, but I don't spend much time in the kitchen these days. Sam always insists on getting takeout."

"It saves her a lot of time." Sam grabbed two dinner rolls. "We're both so busy at the store."

"Everything looks wonderful," Leia said.

Jenny passed the sea bass to Ethan, and it smelled delicious. Maybe Sam just didn't like seafood. He looked more like a steak-and-potatoes kind of guy.

Ethan selected a small portion of the fish and moved it to his plate beside the casserole. He'd make Sam happy for the moment and then take another serving or two as the evening progressed.

Jenny reached for his hand, and Sam blessed the meal so enthusiastically that he wondered if the man had been joking about the quality of his wife's meals. Anyway, how bad could the fish be? Ethan liked his seafood baked, broiled, fried, blackened, and steamed.

With knife and fork in hand, Ethan tried to cut through the fish, but his knife slid off the meat. He clutched the utensil and carved.

So the fish was a little overdone. No problem. It smelled great, and he hadn't been lying when he said he was starving.

He put the bite in his mouth and tasted the fish ... or was it fire?

He forced his throat to swallow as he gave Jenny a weak thumbs-up.

The thing on his plate wasn't sea bass. It was an overripe lemon slathered with vinegar and doused in hot sauce. An embarrassment to the whole ocean community.

After a bite of the casserole, he decided the squash tasted even worse.

Sam didn't say a word, but Ethan met his amused eyes. The guy was dying to laugh. At least Sam had warned him.

Good thing he'd also told him about the beef jerky.

"You have a beautiful home," Ethan said. Maybe if he talked, his hostess wouldn't notice he'd stopped eating.

"We've been blessed," Jenny said as she took a bite. Apparently, she thought this stuff tasted good.

He grabbed a white dinner roll from the basket and tasted it. He'd never been so thankful for store-bought bread. "I'd love to live on a golf course."

Sam laughed. "The irony is we don't even golf. That sliver of a pond you see through the window was the only water view we could afford."

"How long have you lived here?" Ethan took another tiny bite of fish followed by a gulp of his too-sweet tea.

Sam put down his fork. "Do you know our story?"

Ethan shook his head, but out of the corner of his eye, he saw Leia nod. Sam probably figured out the talking secret a long time ago to avoid having to eat his wife's food.

"Eight years ago we lost our home." He hesitated as he met Jenny's eye. "We lost everything actually. I had a good job, a decent income, but I spent my paychecks on blackjack."

Ethan shoved his food to one side of the plate. He didn't want to hear this. Sam seemed like such a nice guy. A smart guy. Smart people don't throw away all their money on cards.

"When my paychecks were gone, I spent our retirement and savings until I had lost it all."

"Didn't Jenny know what was going on?" Leia asked.

Ethan glanced over at his wife. Her voice sounded strained.

"She knew something was wrong, but I became a pro at covering my tracks. Amazing how many meetings and weekend trips you have to make when you're a businessman."

Ethan gazed around the table until his eyes rested on Jenny. She was smiling at her husband as if he'd hung the moon. How could she love a man who'd wrecked their family? How could any woman do that? Ethan had asked his sister that question a hundred times.

"And you decided to stay in Vegas?" Ethan managed another bite of fish.

"I finally got help. It was either that or lose my wife and kids."

"What kind of help?" Leia asked.

"Our church reminded me of what was important, and Gamblers Anonymous helped me overcome my addiction. I discovered that my gambling was an emotional and spiritual problem, not a financial issue."

"A spiritual problem?" Ethan asked.

Sam nodded. "It wasn't until I admitted I was too weak to stop gambling on my own that God demonstrated his strength."

Ethan squeezed the handle of his fork. It wasn't like someone was standing over Sam's head with a gun, making him empty his pockets onto a card table. His wife and boys were the victims in this situation, not him. He'd almost ruined their lives over a stupid game and then had the audacity to blame it on an addiction. An addiction can't be controlled ... but gambling? Anyone can choose to get up from a poker table and walk out the door.

"Is Gamblers Anonymous like Alcoholics Anonymous?" Leia asked.

Why couldn't his wife just change the subject? Ask Jenny how she made this awful sea bass or something?

"Exactly." Sam grabbed another roll. "Compulsive gambling can never be cured, so I still go to meetings every week, though I haven't gambled in years. GA has got more than a hundred groups in Nevada alone."

Unbelievable.

"Enough about that," Jenny said. Ethan wanted to give her another hug—until she offered dessert. "Who wants my special apple pie?"

Leia nodded. Sam just said, "No."

Ethan rubbed his stomach and flashed his best kid grin. "I don't have an inch of room left."

"But you hardly touched your food."

He waited for Sam to come to his rescue, but the man just gulped down a tiny bite of the concoction that Jenny called food.

"It was delicious, but I'm stuffed."

"I thought you said you were hungry."

Famished. "I guess I'll take a tiny slice."

She grinned in triumph as she served him the pie.

When he took a bite, he pretended he was eating chocolate chip cookies in the den.

32

IN THE BATHROOM, LEIA SLIPPED ON HER PURPLE SATIN PAJAMAS and stared at her image in the long mirror. They were the baggiest pajamas she owned, the only ones that fit these days. She'd gained fifteen pounds since the accident. Even though she'd practically stopped eating when she camped out at the casinos, she binged on junk food while Ethan was home. And working out was as negotiable as making meals, showering, or even taking her pills. They all seemed like a waste of time.

Now that she could put weight on her knee, Fabrice told her she needed to exercise again, even if it was as simple as walking around the block or lifting weights. But she was too tired to tone her body.

When the men had rushed off to the den after dinner earlier that evening, Jenny had asked if she could pray for her. Ten minutes later Jenny was done praying, but Leia didn't feel any better. God's presence had left her. His peace was gone. It was as though he'd blown away in the desert wind.

She walked into the bedroom and climbed into bed beside Ethan. Her husband was reading his Bible, and she peeked over his shoulder at the book of James.

Dear brothers and sisters, whenever trouble comes
your way, let it be an opportunity for joy. For when
your faith is tested, your endurance has a chance to
grow.

She leaned back against the pillow and closed her eyes. Joy? If only it were that easy ...

Ethan reached over and squeezed her hand.

She looked over at him. "What are you doing tomorrow?"

"Cramming for my checkride."

"What about Sunday?"

"Cramming. And the same thing on Monday too."

"It will all be behind you in three weeks."

He pulled the covers over his shorts. "Three weeks and three days."

She smiled. "But who's counting?"

"Why don't you go take it for me?"

"Gladly." She stretched her legs. "Did you have fun tonight?"

He propped his pillow next to her shoulder. "Why didn't you tell me Sam had a gambling problem?"

"He doesn't have a problem anymore."

"You should have at least alerted me to it before the man brought it up. I didn't know what to say."

"I didn't think it was that big a deal." She squirmed. "He's obviously recovered."

"Not a big deal? After what Brett did to our family?"

"Sam's not the same as Brett." She took a deep breath. "Sam quit when he realized he had a problem."

Ethan changed the subject. "I wonder what Sam and Jenny's house looked like before he threw it all away."

Leia crossed her arms on her chest. Her husband would never understand that some people weren't as strong and moral and perfect as he. Even after they were saved, not everyone achieved the Ethan Carlisle standard of perfection.

"He didn't try to throw it away, Ethan. He didn't *want* to hurt his wife and kids."

"He may say he didn't want to, but he was being selfish."

"Like my mom …" The words slipped out of her mouth, and she clasped her fingers over her lips. She hadn't meant that. Her mother was a different story. Her mother had hurt her!

Ethan sat up and looked in her eyes. "That's not what I meant."

"Sure you did."

"I'm talking about Sam, not your mother. She obviously has some sort of illness." He was poor at backpedaling.

"She can't seem to stop herself either." She sighed. Since when had she started defending her mother?

"Have you talked to her lately?"

"She called a few weeks ago from prison."

"When did she go back in?"

"In January. She tried to swipe a couple of scarves from Macy's."

Ethan took her hand in his. "Why don't you tell me these things, honey?"

"I just did."

"Yeah, but I have to pry information out of you."

She shrugged. "I don't like to talk about her."

"It's not just your mom. You're being so secretive these days."

And it was hard work. The lies strung together other networks of lies until she couldn't keep them straight. The tangled web of deceit.

She didn't want to talk about her mother or her secrets. "I thought you liked Sam."

"I did." He hesitated. "Until I found out about the gambling."

Hence the problem with the truth. When it was discovered, all respect was lost. What would Ethan do if he found out her secret?

She shuddered.

"Are you cold?" He put his arm around her, and she rested her head against his chest. His skin felt warm against her neck, his chin resting on her hair. She should be satisfied, content. But she wasn't. She used to love spending time with Ethan, but now all she wanted was to sit in a casino and play. She didn't even miss the old days.

"We've got an amazing future together, Mrs. Carlisle."

"You think?"

"I know." He held her face in his hands. "This house is just the beginning. We'll buy a cabin someday. Maybe even a lodge. We'll have a couple of kids. Get a dog to keep everyone entertained. It'll be perfect."

"Not everything works out perfectly, Ethan."

"God is taking care of us, Leia."

She was hardly still in God's hands.

"You know I love you, don't you?" he asked softly.

She knew what that meant, and she wasn't interested. She pulled the sheet up to her chin. "And I'm grateful for you."

"Do you know you're beautiful?" he whispered.

"I'm overweight and out of shape, Ethan."

"You're stunning."

A rush of heat flushed her face.

"I can't believe you don't remember our anniversary night at Le Rivage."

A candlelit table. The best food she'd ever tasted. A view of New York's harbor. "I remember."

He grinned. "After dinner, by the docks."

She'd forgotten. "Oh …"

He kissed her gently, and she surrendered.

LEIA DIDN'T WAIT UNTIL THE GARAGE DOOR CLOSED BEHIND ETHAN on Tuesday before she hopped into her convertible. She'd promised herself that she wouldn't go back to a casino, but that was before she tried to pay off some of her credit card balance online. She owed twelve thousand dollars! She didn't know when she'd blazed through that much cash, but it was somewhere between the computer and the casino. Her gambling debt was fast approaching the amount in their bank account. And she was supposed to be saving money!

Ethan had spent his three days at home worried about her condition. She wished her husband wouldn't stress; she was stressing enough for both of them. She was going to get out of this mess. She'd fallen into a rut—that was all. It was a simple matter of climbing back out. When she won big, she'd pay off her debt in a lump sum and treat them to a vacation in Santa Barbara.

As she drove down the street, she decided she was going to leave Brandy and Patrice and the Diamond Breeze behind. Danna's casino was a money pit. She needed to find a new place near the Strip. Not on the Strip exactly—but a casino nearby that would have to pay out to keep the tourists from venturing off to the more swanky places along the Boulevard.

A little gambling strategy—that's what she needed. The key was not to get caught up in the losses. She'd already made that mistake.

She drove around the Strip for a half hour before she honed in on her new stomping ground: the Regal Palace. The entrance looked like a palace with marble columns, stone arches, and a bronze statue of a mermaid spouting water into the air.

After she parked in a deck under the casino, she strutted toward the elevator. She knew the drill now. Stroll with confidence to the cage. Get your bucket of quarters. Find your machine. And no matter how tired or hungry or sick you feel—plant yourself on a stool and play until the slot paid off.

She stepped out of the elevator into an extravagant lobby with a blown glass chandelier shimmering above. In front of her was a clear tunnel enclosed in water, and as she walked through it, tropical fish played in the coral around her.

The tunnel led to a golden bridge and wide doors that opened up onto the casino floor.

She stepped into the casino and looked around the room. Stone towers anchored the corners of the floor—she could almost hear the prince calling for Rapunzel to let down her hair. Pictures of noble men and women were displayed over an antique fireplace, and the subdued light of electric candles shone from bronze sconces along the wall. Jazz music played softly behind the bells and whistles of winning machines.

She'd arrived at a palace of luxury. But even better than the atmosphere was the knowledge that no one she knew would find her here.

She waited in the short line in front of the cage as she eyed the rows of slot machines. This casino didn't have nickel or quarter slots.

The betting minimum was a dollar a spin, rewarded with much larger payouts than those at Casa Bonita. With a little persistence she could take home a jackpot.

There were only two seats left on the row of machines … she'd wait a couple of minutes to see if a hot seat opened up. Like the man who'd stolen her big win from the Diamond Breeze, she could use the power of someone else's dollar to make a win.

With two hundred silver dollars secured in a bucket under one arm, she watched the long row of slots until an elderly woman stepped down from one of the stools, shaking her head. Leia beelined toward her machine before someone else decided it was ripe for picking.

This slot was called Pirate's Cache. A little cheesy, but it had a button to spin the paylines instead of an arm. She rubbed her sore elbow and slipped a handful of dollars into the slots before she pushed the button to start the game.

Sitting inside the stately palace walls, she hunted treasure until her money was gone.

33

L EIA'S FOOT TAPPED THE TILE AS SHE WAITED IN FRONT OF THE
cage for the cashier to give her the next two hundred in cash. It
shouldn't take more than five minutes to run a credit card. She'd
already been here for almost ten.

The floor attendant wouldn't hold the Pirate's Cache for much
longer—the woman had snapped at her, telling her to be back soon or
her machine was history. She didn't get it—they should be happy that
she was spending her money. She'd flooded this casino with cash. If
they gave the attendant a cut of what Leia had spent, the woman
wouldn't be so grumpy.

After dealing with the snubs from the royalty at the Regal Palace all day,
Brandy and Patrice seemed like her best friends, the Casa Bonita her home.

If the attendant didn't hang tough, someone else would swoop in
and win her jackpot. She'd tip her an extra dollar if the woman managed
to wait long enough for Leia to return with a fresh batch of change.

The cashier returned to his seat; he was a scrawny guy with acne
splotching his nose and forehead.

"I can't give you any more cash." He slid her credit card back
through the tray. "Your card's been declined."

"What?" She leaned toward the window. "I have a fifteen-thousand-dollar limit."

"I tried three times."

"It can't be …"

She'd only been here at the Regal Palace for a few hours—or maybe ten or twelve. Even so, she couldn't have spent another three thousand already.

She glanced back toward her machine. The attendant had moved a few steps away from her stool. Leia couldn't use her other credit card. Ethan was probably checking that balance online every day.

He shouldn't have given her the responsibility of handling their finances. He should have locked all their money in a vault and hid the key.

She turned her head one more time, and the attendant was gone.

"Will you take a check?" she asked the cashier.

"Not out-of-state."

"From Henderson."

"Sure. Just make it out to cash."

She wrote it for $250 and rushed back to her seat.

The bucket felt heavy on her lap. It was their grocery money, their electricity payment, their telephone bill.

What is wrong with me?

Her teeth clenched as she stared at the blinking yellow and white lights around the screen.

Life was crashing around her, and no one cared. Not even God. If only he would let her win just one jackpot, she could pay back the money she'd borrowed and move on with her life. If he could move mountains, surely he could loosen up a slot machine. He could take away this burden from her shoulders, free her from this trap.

She couldn't do it on her own.

♠ ♥ ♣ ♦

THE NEXT MORNING LEIA DROVE HOME EVEN THOUGH THE PIRATE'S Cache had sucked every bit of energy from her brain and every extra cent from her purse. She'd cashed checks until she'd drained their account.

Not only had she spent their grocery money, but she'd thrown away the payment for their car and their house. She could use money from their savings to pay these bills, but if she pulled much more out of the bank, Ethan would take back their finances. Then she'd never be able to recoup what she'd lost.

She sat in the driveway and stared at their house. She needed money. She'd already dipped into their savings, and the government wouldn't let her raid her retirement account. Even if she borrowed some from the 401(k), it would be weeks before the money arrived. She needed money now. But what would she tell Ethan about her car?

Her cell phone rang beside her, and it was him.

She'd have to borrow more cash.

"Hey, honey," she answered, a poor attempt at sounding alert.

"Are you out?"

She checked her watch. It was 10:00 a.m. "Running a few errands. How's the trip?"

"Rough flight out of Dulles last night."

"So what's it like—flying?"

"Just a few more months, Leia, and you'll be back in the cockpit."

She let his words sink in, but the excitement wasn't there. Where had her familiar "fly or die" urge gone?

"Can't wait," she mustered.

"I just wanted to check on you," he said. "Glad you're able to get out of the house."

"Me too."

"Don't spend too much," he quipped.

Right.

When he hung up, she plucked her personal credit card out of her purse and called the account information number. Clicking through the automated phone system, she finally got a live operator on the line and gave her the card's account number.

The woman typed in her information.

"What can I do for you, Ms. Carlisle?"

"I want to increase my credit limit."

The woman paused. "You've incurred ten thousand dollars in expenses during the past week."

So?

"That's right. I'd like to apply for five thousand more."

"Just one moment." She placed Leia on hold.

She tapped her fingers on the steering wheel as she listened to the elevator music. Misty pulled out of her driveway and waved as she drove past Leia's car.

The operator came back on the line. "I have my supervisor on the phone to speak with you."

Supervisor? She was only asking for a few more dollars—not the gold at Fort Knox.

"How are you today, Ms. Carlisle?"

"Just great. Thanks."

"My associate tells me that you are requesting an increase in your credit limit."

"A small one."

The woman paused before she answered. "I want you to know you're a valued customer, but at this time, we can't increase the limit."

Who writes these scripts?

"I'd settle for a thousand more."

"If you pay your minimum payments on time for the next three months, we can reevaluate your request."

"But I need the cash right now."

"I'm sorry, ma'am, but we can't consider extending your credit until August first."

"You're a credit card company! You're supposed to extend credit."

"Call us back in three months."

Leia disconnected the phone without saying good-bye.

Her head sunk to the steering wheel. How was she going to get cash?

Her eyes rose to look back at their home. They'd put a decent down payment on this place—maybe she could get a little back out of it to help her out of this rut.

Suddenly she didn't feel tired anymore.

She climbed out of her car and raced toward the door and up the stairs. When she reached the office, she pulled the financial binder off the top of the desk. The mortgage company information was at the right spot—filed under the Home Loan tab.

She flipped through the entire binder. Everything was perfectly filed. Not a bill out of place. Ethan had perfected his system, his financial plan. He just couldn't predict all the unknowns ... like her stupid trip to Black Hawk. If she could turn back time, she never would have gone to Colorado. Never skied that weekend. And certainly never gone to a casino. She'd been playing defense every since.

It was time to get back on the offense. Drive toward an open path. Take a clear shot at the goal. Get her life back under her control.

She ran her finger down the loan statement as she picked up the phone. Then she called.

"I'm interested in applying for a home equity loan," she said after she gave the man her loan number, address, and mother's maiden name.

"No problem," he said. "Could I ask what you're planning to use the money for?"

"Improving the house," she fudged. "Adding another bathroom and retiling the kitchen."

She heard him tapping on his keyboard.

"How much do you want?"

She sat down on the bed. Should she go high? Low? She needed enough to pay off her credit card with a little extra to invest so she could get back the money she'd drained out of their checking account and replace the money she'd drawn from savings.

"Twenty thousand."

"That shouldn't be a problem," he said. "You can download an application from our Web site and fax it in."

"My husband's out of town right now."

"No problem. We just need one signature."

She almost cheered. "How long will it take to get the cash?"

"About a week. It will take three business days for us to approve and process the loan, and then we'll send you the check."

She hoped she could wait that long.

34

ETHAN RAN HIS FINGERS THROUGH HIS HAIR AS HE REREAD THE overview paragraph in his flight manual about hydraulic power and its two parts: the mechanical linkage and the hydraulic systems. His checkride started in less than two weeks. April 29 had been etched in his calendar and his brain for a year.

He made a note on his pad about the actuators powering the hydraulic pressure and then leaned back from the kitchen table. Hydraulics—a miracle of modern times. The only way a commercial pilot could fly a large and complex piece of equipment.

He took a sip of cold coffee.

After a grueling hour of questions last year, he'd hesitated when the instructor asked him to describe the hydraulic system. This year he'd be prepared.

He rubbed his temples, forming the response in his mind. "A 737 operates on three thousand pounds of hydraulic pressure," he rehearsed. "The hydraulic systems consist of actuators that are powered by the hydraulic pressure generated by pumps. Servo valves control the movement of these actuators as they convert this hydraulic pressure into control surface movement."

He turned the page to memorize the makeup of the mechanism that links the cockpit controls with the hydraulic systems, a complex series of rods, pulleys, and cables.

"You ready to eat?" Leia asked over his shoulder.

"In a sec." He scribbled another note on his pad.

He usually passed the open-book portion of his checkride without a problem, and if he stayed calm, he'd speed through the hour-long oral exam with only a few minor errors. He spent so many weeks cramming facts and numbers into his head that answers poured out when he opened his mouth.

The examination was a headache, but he didn't dread it. Not like the simulator ride. The sim made him lose sleep. It was four intense hours on high alert—averting disasters caused by engine fires, rejected takeoffs, stalling, emergency descents, cargo fires, and radio failure. On his last sim ride, he almost bought the farm when he lost power in both engines at thirty-seven thousand feet. But he donned his oxygen mask and performed the emergency descent procedure until he restarted an engine at thirteen thousand feet. Better in the simulator than in the air, but he'd had nightmares for a month after the checkride.

He looked up from his book. "Something smells good."

"We're going simple for lunch today," she said.

He drained his coffee mug. "I'm all for simple."

She lifted a plate over his head, and he cleared a portion of the table for her to set it down. He looked at the meal in front of him and turned back toward her.

"What is this?"

"Macaroni and cheese with some sliced tomatoes."

He stuck his fork in the orange noodles. "Boxed macaroni?"

She shrugged. "I'm trying to cut back on expenses."

"A few cuts, honey. We don't have to starve."

"We're not starving. Plenty of people eat macaroni and cheese every day."

"Yeah," he snorted, "if they're two."

"I'll make something more nutritious for dinner."

He took a bite of the macaroni. It didn't taste any better now than it did when he'd tried it as a kid.

He pulled his credit card out of his wallet. "Maybe we should order pizza."

Leia looked as if she was about to cry. "I'm just trying to help."

He put the card back in his wallet. When this checkride was finished, he'd start cooking again. He'd allocated plenty of money in their budget for decent meals. Not gourmet, but something healthy that wasn't out of a blue cardboard box.

He met her eye. "Are we running low on cash in the checking account?"

She turned away, walking behind the kitchen counter to serve herself a bowl of macaroni. "A little."

"Don't worry about it," he said. "We can pull a few hundred from savings if we need to. Do you want me to do that?"

"No," Leia said. "I can manage."

He looked back down at his book, circling the pullout that listed navigation equipment. "I don't mind helping."

"You study." She kissed his hair. "I'll transfer the cash."

LEIA SQUIRMED AS SHE SAT AT THE DESK BESIDE THE BED AND checked the balance on their savings account. They had fourteen thousand dollars left.

If Ethan didn't get something decent to eat, he'd be checking on all their funds. She transferred five hundred dollars from their savings account to checking. Then she added five hundred more just in case.

That left them with a thirteen-thousand-dollar cushion before they got the money from the home equity loan.

Outside the bedroom window, she watched the mail truck pull up in front of the house. She pushed back her chair and hurried toward the stairs.

"I'm going to get the mail," Ethan yelled up to her.

She looked down at him from the loft. "I'll get it."

He opened the front door. "I need a break."

She watched the back of his head as he rushed out the door. She was tempted to run and tackle him, but that was hardly subtle. She moved down the stairs and outside, sitting on their porch swing as he opened the mailbox.

He thumbed through the letters as he strolled back toward the porch. Then he handed her the small stack. "For you—a book of coupons, some credit card offer, and a statement from the mortgage company."

Her fingers trembled as she took the mail. "Great."

He leaned back against the windowsill. "What are you going to do this afternoon?"

"I'll make a grocery run to get us some food for dinner and maybe go to the mall and window-shop, so you can study in a quiet house."

"You don't have to leave for me."

She stood up and kissed his cheek. "Sure I do."

Leia's first stop was the bank. When she walked into the lobby, she saw Allison sorting money behind the counter—Misty's competition for homecoming queen. She looked around for another open window, but Allison waved her forward. "It's nice to see you again, Ms. Carlisle."

"You too," she mumbled as she passed her the check from the mortgage company.

Allison deposited the loan into their checking account—a temporary move until she paid off her credit card debt. Then Leia requested five hundred dollars in cash for groceries and expenses and asked Allison to transfer four thousand dollars back into their savings account to cover what she'd taken out for household expenses.

If Ethan checked it, the seventeen thousand dollars would appear intact. She'd become a master of illusion.

"Have you considered overdraft protection?" Allison asked.

"My husband usually handles our banking."

Allison handed her a pamphlet. "We could set it up so the money would transfer from your savings account if you don't have the funds in your account to cover a check."

Leia skimmed the literature. It wouldn't cost her a cent, and it would protect their checking if she made any mistakes while trying to juggle their accounts. If Ethan knew how complicated their finances had become, even he would think this was a smart move.

"Can I add it right now?" she asked.

"Sure." Allison wrote her account number on a form and slid it across the counter. "It's effective immediately."

Leia filled in her address and signed it.

Next stop was the grocery store. She loaded her cart with romaine lettuce, fresh strawberries, rosemary, green beans, ingredients for a cheesecake, and a fresh cut of tenderloin. Their dinner would keep Ethan from guessing the state of their finances.

After she checked out, she walked past a lineup of video slot machines against the wall. The flashing lights on the video screens made the front of the grocery store look like a carnival without the rides. She leaned into one of the games and then glanced over her shoulder. No one was looking her way right now, but everyone who bought groceries would pass her on the way to their car.

She hiked the bag of groceries up on her hip. Jenny probably shopped at this store. And Misty. That's all she needed, a little more fuel for the gossip fire.

Focusing her eyes on the sliding glass doors, she marched toward the front of the store, climbed into her convertible, and sped out of the parking lot. Her destination was the mall, but when she passed the white lights at Casa Bonita, she tapped the brakes.

She'd been terrified that Danna had told Misty about her escapades, but Misty hadn't shoved down her front door, salivating with the news. Maybe her secret really was safe here.

She U-turned back toward the casino, parked the car, and set the alarm on her watch for an hour. This was much better than the mall.

She won a hundred bucks on the slots and still made it home in time to grill rosemary steaks for dinner.

35

LEIA STOOD IN FRONT OF THE BATHROOM MIRROR AND BRUSHED her teeth, her body wrapped in a towel after her shower. The house was quiet—Ethan had left for Miami before she got out of bed.

Depending on doctor's orders, it might only be a matter of weeks before she'd be working again, leaving the house before dawn to go to the airport instead of a casino. This afternoon Dr. Rosenthal was checking on the progress of her knee. If all went well, she'd make the June schedule.

She reached for the blow-dryer and switched it to high.

Before she got back in the cockpit, she had to wrap up her business in Las Vegas. Even though she'd be home for seven-day stretches when she went back to work, today was the end of her gambling spree. Once and for all.

She turned off the blow-dryer and stepped back from the mirror. A wave of nausea swept through her, and she sat down on the toilet, taking deep breaths until it subsided. Strange. She'd been off pain medication for weeks.

She gulped down a glass of water and moved into the bedroom, dressing in jeans and a T-shirt before pulling her damp hair back into a band.

A better strategy was what she needed to win. It was time to move up the ranks. She sat down in front of the computer and surfed through several gambling technique sites, studying advanced slot machine strategies for an hour. One expert she read said to skip the quarter and even the dollar slot machines. The five-dollar or higher machines had the highest percentage payout range. His recommendation—bet the maximum amount at the higher-stakes slots to get a big return.

Maybe that was her problem. She wasn't betting enough for a solid win. Her five- and ten-dollar wins didn't amount to much.

She turned off the computer and walked down to the car.

The road between her house and Casa Bonita was practically grooved from all her travel. Danna had managed to keep her secret, and unlike the Palace downtown, attendants like Brandy and Patrice would never let someone else steal her machine.

When she arrived on the casino floor, she walked three rows past the Diamond Breeze and settled on a new stool. The Next Millennium was a coinless video machine sitting under twinkling yellow and pink lights. Five paylines. Five-dollar minimum bet. Twenty-five-dollar max. She could feed her hundred-dollar deposit directly into the machine. No need to refill her bucket with change. She read the directions—at the end of her game, she'd print a voucher, and the cashier would give her hard cash at the cage.

"You've given up on the Diamond Breeze?" Patrice asked behind her.

Leia's eyes stayed focused on the video screen. "It needed a break."

"Long Island tea?"

Leia turned. "Very funny."

"One iced tea." Patrice smiled. "On the house."

Leia set her watch alarm for 3:30 p.m., so she'd have a half hour to drive to the doctor's office for her appointment. She slid five twenty-dollar bills into the machine and pressed the button for the maximum bet across all the paylines.

She pushed the button to spin.

Stars, planets, and pyramids whirled across the screen just as they did in the older slot machines, but these icons moved in 3-D. A galaxy of lights twirled and bowed toward her when she won thirty bucks.

An hour slipped by as she slid crisp bills into the Next Millennium. After she had used the cash left over from the five hundred she'd extracted at the bank, she wrote a check for another thousand.

On her next spin someone pulled up a stool beside her and sat down, his breath warming her neck. Her eyes didn't leave the video screen, but she knew who was sitting beside her by the lime scent in his cologne.

"What are you doing here?" She pushed the red button under her fingertips. The lines spun, and triple moons made a diagonal line across the screen. The credit meter blinked $385.

Derek flicked the screen. "Not bad."

She bet five bucks on each of the paylines and spun. "When did you decide to come back to Vegas?"

"Last night."

She lost fifteen of the dollars and bet again.

"So …" He scooted closer to her, but she didn't budge. "I get this call from a friend of mine who said she's worried about your gambling. Thought I might be able to help."

"Does this friend happen to be married?"

"A minor inconvenience."

Thanks, Danna. So much for whatever happens at the Casa Bonita stays at the Casa Bonita.

His nose was in her hair. "How can I help?"

She pushed him away.

"Be careful." He pointed to the ceiling. "Security's watching."

She placed another bet. "Pretty sure they're more worried about you than me."

He nodded to the icons spinning on the screen. "I thought Black Hawk was a fluke."

"It was."

"And yet here you are."

The alarm on her watch beeped, and she hit the button to turn it off.

"It's none of your business, Derek."

He squeezed her knee. "When my best friend's wife is in trouble, it's my business."

She batted his hand away, nausea washing through her again. "Don't you have somebody else to screw?"

The elderly man at the next slot machine jumped, eyeing them from the corner of his eye.

"I think about other things than sex, Leia."

She choked. "Flying and beer maybe."

"All good things."

She bet twenty-five dollars and spun. "You wasted your time coming here for me."

He stood, the corners of his mouth curling in a smirk, and whispered, "I didn't come here for you."

And then he was gone. At least she thought he was. She didn't turn around to watch him walk away.

How dare Danna blab her secret! Concerned? Right. She probably couldn't keep a secret if someone paid her.

The video machine blinked at her, the stars soliciting more cash.

She stood up and waved toward Patrice. It was only a matter of time before Derek told Ethan about her gambling. She had to win back the money she'd lost, and she had to do it fast.

"Leaving already?" the attendant asked.

"Where are the higher-stakes slots?"

Patrice bit the edge of her lip. "Are you ...?"

Leia didn't let her finish. "Yes."

She pointed to the other end of the room. "There's a row of twenty-dollar machines over there. All video."

Leia's feet hit the carpet as Patrice stepped away.

"Could I have something else to drink?" Leia asked.

Patrice turned to face her again. "Sure. Another tea?"

"No." Leia paused. "A rum and Coke."

The attendant put her hand on her hip. "You don't drink alcohol."

Leia took a step toward the twenty-dollar slots. "I'm starting today."

As Leia downed her second rum and Coke, the chills from Derek's visit started to subside. How dare he show up at the casino and taunt her. She could do whatever she wanted. If she spent all her money on gambling, it was none of his business. And it was none of Ethan's business what she did with her free time.

She slid two fifty-dollar bills into the video machine. After she lost it, she fed it a hundred dollars more.

Her winnings were higher at the twenty-dollar machine, but so were her losses. The machine gobbled up the dollars without chewing, much less savoring the taste.

Maybe the only way to get out of this rut was to be even more daring, to try something new.

Derek had won her money back playing blackjack in Colorado. If she could fly an airplane, she could easily learn how to play a simple game of cards. The problem with the slots was that she had no real control over her destiny. She could play and play, but it was all based on luck. The slots weren't getting her money back.

Patrice handed her another drink.

She desperately needed the money back.

She played until the hundred dollars was gone, and then she put her elbows on her legs and propped her head up. Another two thousand bucks down the drain.

In one swoop she picked up her glass and guzzled the drink.

Her stomach gurgled, and she shot up. Clutching her purse, she raced toward the bathroom and started to lock herself into a stall.

But she didn't have time to turn the lock. She leaned over the toilet and gagged, her body purging itself of the rum.

She wiped her mouth with toilet paper and threw up again.

"Are you okay?" someone asked from the next stall.

She stood up and checked her watch. It was five o'clock. She'd missed her doctor's appointment by an hour.

After she gagged one last time, she told her neighbor she'd be fine.

36

Ethan glanced out the window at the East River from his hotel room in Queens. It was the apex of spring, but he couldn't see a single tree. No cherry blossoms or green leaves— just a strip of water dammed in by concrete and the busy New York skyline.

He'd flown into LaGuardia at seven tonight, and he wouldn't fly out for twelve hours. When he had a layover in New York, he usually took a long walk along the river, but tonight he needed to exercise his brain instead of his legs. Two hours to study and maybe a half hour to swim laps, a meager attempt to relax his racing mind before he tried to sleep.

His checkride was two weeks away, and he'd only plodded a quarter of the way through the study manuals. He still had to memorize hundreds of pages of airplane systems and maintenance procedures and Federal Aviation Administration regulations before he could even think about going to Denver for the test.

Someone pounded on his door. "Room service!"

Ethan opened the door, and the server wheeled in a silver platter. He smoothed a white tablecloth over the room's small round table and set a china plate with his meal along with a pink carnation in a clear vase. A lot of hoopla for a cheeseburger.

Ethan signed the receipt and followed the server out into the hall to the soda machine. It was ridiculous to pay a dollar and a half for a can of Mountain Dew, but it was cheaper to buy it from the machine than pay three bucks for someone to deliver it.

Locking the door to his room, he sat down on the leather chair beside the table. He bit into the pricey burger and leaned back to enjoy it. One benefit of being an airline pilot was the daily food stipend. He rarely used the extra money to treat himself with room service, but tonight he needed to stay in his room and work. Nothing helped ease the pain of having to study like a decent meal that didn't involve boxed macaroni and cheese.

He flipped to the fifth chapter in his flight operations manual and then shut it. Before he got lost in his work, he wanted to check his e-mail.

Opening his laptop, he clicked the Internet icon and typed in the password he had been given at the front desk to connect with the hotel's high-speed network. Then he checked his e-mail.

Derek had sent him a quick note saying he was on leave for two weeks and might come to Vegas if Ethan wanted to go out some night. He'd e-mail him back later.

He took a sip of his soda as he trashed their spam. The last message was from his mortgage company, and he almost deleted it—every few weeks they sent him offers on rates and home equity loans. But the subject line caught his eye.

Late payment.

He took another swig and set down his drink before he opened the message.

Dear Mr. Carlisle,

This is a courtesy message to remind you that your mortgage payment is overdue.

He choked, wiping the soda off his mouth with his sleeve.

We have extended your grace period, but we must
receive your payment by April 20, or we will assess
a late charge. As you know, late mortgage payments can seriously affect your credit rating, so we
appreciate your prompt action to correct this over-
sight.

He leaned back in the chair, clutching the can of soda. Overdue? He stood up in front of the desk and paced the floor. He'd specifically told Leia they had to pay their mortgage by the first of each month. How could she have forgotten to pay for their house?

He hovered back over the computer and typed in the URL and password to check the total in their savings account. $17,000. The bottom line hadn't changed since he'd checked it last. At least Leia had managed to pay the rest of their bills out of the money he deposited into checking. They could pull funds from this account to pay the mortgage.

He rapped his fingers on the keyboard and then reached down to pull his credit card out of his wallet. If Leia had missed the house payment, she might have forgotten to pay the credit card too. He typed in their account info, and the statement popped up.

The charges looked normal. She'd paid the bill online on April 8, cutting the payment close, but at least it was paid two days before it was due.

He'd never tested the fifteen-day grace period on their mortgage payment, but right now he was grateful it worked. Even more grateful the company had notified him.

He picked up his phone and dialed his wife's cell. He was shocked when she actually answered.

"Are you home?" he asked.

"Just pulled into the driveway."

He cleared his throat. "I got an e-mail from our mortgage company today."

She didn't respond.

"We're over fifteen days late on our house payment."

"Oh no," she said, but she didn't sound upset. She sounded relieved.

"What happened, Leia?"

"I've been so busy that I forgot."

"Busy?"

"Okay, not so busy, I just forgot."

"Do we have enough money in our checking to cover it?"

"Yes."

"Good. Just give me the account number for our checking account, and I'll transfer the money from here."

"I'll handle it," she said.

He clenched his wallet in his hand. "Let me do it, Leia."

"It's my responsibility right now. I'll take care of it."

"Leia—"

"I'll do it."

His shoulders tensed. He couldn't force her to give him the number over the phone, but ... if he didn't change the track of this conversation, he'd say something he regretted.

He slapped the wallet against the bed. "How was the doctor's visit?"

"He had to reschedule."

He logged out of the credit card site. "Why?"

"I don't know."

He closed the laptop and reopened the flight manual on his desk. If he was going to focus on his work, he had to calm down.

"You're studying tonight?" she asked.

He was trying to. "Yep."

"I'll let you go." She paused. "I love you."

He propped his feet up on the bed. "I love you, too."

"I'm sorry about the mortgage," she said.

"You'll pay it, right?"

She grunted. "Before I eat dinner."

He said good night and hung up the phone.

In twelve days he'd be done with his checkride, and when he wrapped up that project, he'd recover their family finances. Giving Leia the responsibility hadn't relieved him from worrying about their money. In fact, he worried about it a lot more when it was out of his hands.

Leia would be starting back to work again soon anyway, and she would probably want to return the books to him. If she didn't, he'd wrestle them away.

He read the bullet point on the page in front of him. The first in a long list of Ambassador's procedures for loading cargo. The words blurred, and he read it again.

He had to get his focus back on these books, or he was going to fail this ride.

37

A FTER SHE SAID GOOD-BYE TO ETHAN, LEIA POUNDED HER CELL phone on the steering wheel. How could she have forgotten to pay their mortgage? It wasn't as though it was complicated to pay a bill. Not nearly as hard as keeping track of what she owed.

If she lost her focus, Ethan would reclaim their finances and discover her disaster. She needed to repair the damage before she could give it back to him. If only there were a standard operating procedure for this type of emergency. Her engines had stalled, and she was free-falling … with no place to land.

At least the mortgage company hadn't e-mailed Ethan about their loan.

She pulled her car into the garage and shut the door. As she stepped out onto the cement floor, a pain raced up her leg. Great. Her knee was swelling. She limped into the house and grabbed an ice pack out of the freezer. Sitting down on a stool, she placed the ice over her pants leg and let the cold numb the throbbing.

The answering machine on the counter was blinking, and she hit the play button.

The first message was from Dr. Rosenthal's office, reminding her that she'd missed her checkup and that she'd be billed for the appointment even though she didn't show.

She wrung her hands, frustrated at getting so easily distracted from the goal. Seeing Dr. Rosenthal was the last major hurdle to getting back into the cockpit. One she couldn't afford to mess up.

She dialed the doctor's number, and when the receptionist answered, she apologized three times for missing her appointment, blaming it on problems with her calendar. The woman rescheduled the appointment for the following Saturday. Another nine days to wait for the doctor's green light to fly.

Then Leia listened to the second message—from their bank. The woman said it was a courtesy call to let them know there was unusual activity on their checking account. She wanted to confirm that Mr. and Mrs. Carlisle were aware of the transactions.

Leia hit the delete button. Mrs. Carlisle was perfectly aware of it.

She limped over to the couch and slumped down, staring at the cream-colored flecks on the ceiling. Her slide had turned into an avalanche—clearing the grass, rocks, and trees along the way. How could she stop it before the crash?

It was impossible to keep track of where she'd pulled money from and where she'd patched it with a Band-Aid. There were holes in every one of their accounts, blood gushing everywhere.

When the swelling in her knee subsided, she walked upstairs to the computer and typed in their account information for the checking account. Today she'd spent more than three thousand dollars on the slots. Another surge of nausea passed through her and was gone.

She transferred part of the home equity loan she'd deposited to pay for their mortgage—one hole plugged for the moment. Then she opened up the account for her personal credit card. Interest and overdue payments had kicked the balance up to $15,812. She transferred the minimum due from the checking account. She'd come up with an answer for Ethan when he asked about the strange transaction. In August the credit card company would have to give her more money if she needed it.

But she wouldn't need more money in August. Her spending rave had to end long before then.

If only there was someone she could talk to …

Ethan wouldn't understand. Julie would tell her it was no big deal. Jenny would overreact after what had happened to Sam. And if she called Paige, Paige would tell Ethan.

The only people who knew she was gambling were Derek and Danna … and, of course, Brandy and Patrice. Hardly the people to give her good advice.

She stared at the computer screen for a moment before typing in the name of her mother's current home. The contact information popped up on the screen.

She picked up the phone and dialed, asking the operator for the warden.

"Warden May's office," a woman answered.

"I'd like to speak with my mother."

"Does she work here?"

"No. She … lives there."

"Is she an inmate?"

"She's a temporary guest."

The woman chuckled. "Aren't we all?"

"Could I talk to her, please?"

"Inmates aren't allowed to receive phone calls."

"I know, but I wondered if you could make an exception."

"I'm not the one to make exceptions." She paused. "But I can try to get her the message that you called."

"Sondra Vaughn is her name. You can tell her I'm at home."

"I'll try, hon. It's sweet of you to call."

Leia hung up the phone. Sweet? Hardly. She hadn't called her mother in years.

She eyed the computer screen and surfed until she found a Web site that detailed the game of blackjack. If Derek could win at cards, so could she.

She already knew the basics from college days. The goal—to accumulate twenty-one points without going bust. Easy enough.

She read down the strategy list. Surrendering bets. Splitting pairs. Doubling down.

Using instructions from the site, she created a strategy chart of number combinations to determine when she should split, double, and split with doubling. Blackjack wasn't going to be a soothing escape like the slot machines, but she needed to edge back into reality. And she needed to win.

With her chart in one hand, she went downstairs and set a teapot on the stove, turning the burner to high. She crunched a packet of ramen noodles, ripped it open, and sprinkled the noodles along with a packet of seasoning into a bowl. When the pot whistled, she poured hot water over the spicy noodles and ate dinner as she memorized the combinations.

The telephone rang, and she answered it.

The operator repeated the lines about a collect call. This time Leia didn't hesitate to accept.

"That was fast," she said when her mother came on the line.

"Olivia's a friend of mine."

"How are you doing?"

"I'm taking a pottery class. Helps pass the time." She paused. "Are you okay?"

Leia stirred the soupy noodles. "No."

"What happened?"

"Are you still in therapy?" Leia asked.

"Yes."

"And it's helping?"

"It seems to be, but I won't really know until they release me."

"What does your therapist say?"

"That only a Higher Power can restore me to my normal life. I'm begging God to give me the strength to overcome this."

"Is he?"

"He's given me people to help me until I'm released. The hardest step for me was to admit I was powerless to stop shoplifting by myself."

Leia stood up and looked through the sliding glass door to the swimming pool. Therapists always boiled things down into nice, neat packages. Life was so much more complicated than that.

She believed in God, but he hadn't helped her get out of this mess. Besides, she wasn't powerless to stop gambling. She could stop anytime. She just wanted to dig her way out of debt before she quit for good.

"What's going on, Leia?"

Leia cleared her throat. "I'm trying to help a friend."

"You can't force someone with a compulsive disorder to get help. They have to decide on their own that they have a problem."

Leia picked up her bowl and walked toward the sink. "How would she know if she has a problem?"

"When she can't stop drinking or gambling or shoplifting even when she really wants to. Even if it's destroying her life. I never wanted to shoplift. I never needed the things I took. But I couldn't seem to help myself."

"And now?"

"Now I know that Someone greater than me is going to help me overcome it."

She poured the noodles down the disposal. "It sounds too simple ..."

"Maybe for God, but it's really hard for me to put my trust in him. I want to conquer this on my own."

An operator interrupted to say they had a minute left.

"I'm praying for you," Sondra said. "And your friend."

"Thanks, Mom."

"I know you and I are very different, yet there are things about us that are the same."

If she only knew ...

"No matter what's going on, I want you to know that I love you."

When Leia's eyes filled with tears, she quickly blinked them away. "I love you, too."

38

ETHAN OPENED THE SLIDING GLASS DOOR ON HIS HOTEL ROOM IN San Diego and spread his manuals and laptop on the balcony's wrought-iron table. Sunshine warmed his skin as he sat down on the padded seat dressed only in a T-shirt and shorts. It was so much better than being bundled up in chilly New York.

He took a sip of his iced mocha and admired his clear view—a strip of sandy beach along the Pacific to his right and waves crashing through a cluster of rocks on the left.

The espresso drink was an indulgence, but the combo of a caffeine-and-sugar jolt would supply the energy he needed to study another three hours. He hated cramming for his checkride like this, but he had no choice. In the past, he'd studied at home while Leia was out of town. When they were both at home, it was difficult to focus on memorizing the mounds of material.

He opened his laptop to check his e-mail account before he started working.

The first message was from the mortgage company—a receipt that their payment had been received. At least Leia had rescued their credit history for the month. One less thing for him to worry about.

He deleted several pieces of spam and clicked on an e-mail message from Eva Dellman.

> Sondra wanted to talk to you directly, but she can't place collect calls to cell phones, and she didn't want to try you at home. Leia called her yesterday, and Sondra's worried. She wouldn't tell me anything specific, but she asked me to e-mail you to let you know that she's praying for you both. If there's anything else she can do, to help Leia, please e-mail me, and I'll let her know.

Ethan read the message again.

Leia called her mother? That was a good sign ... wasn't it?

He'd never actually met Leia's mom, but he'd heard plenty about her. On the day he and Leia married, Sondra was serving the end of a three-month jail sentence at an Ohio state prison. Ethan tried to convince Leia to postpone their wedding until her mother was out on parole, but she refused. He assumed she was embarrassed that her mother was a convict, but now he realized that it was anger instead of embarrassment that had severed their relationship. She was bitter about her mother's weakness for shoplifting and her apparent lack of grief after Leia's dad died.

He'd tried for years to negotiate a reconciliation between the two of them, but Leia always refused to discuss it. Ever since he met her, Leia had denied the fact that her mother was a convict. Practically denied the fact that she even had a mom. The whole situation was messy, and neither woman would bridge the gap. Having family was a privilege that he tried to make Leia understand, but she only wanted to talk about her dad. She had plenty of good things to say about him. Leia, he realized, was a textbook daddy's girl.

Even Sondra recognized there was a problem with Leia, though Leia had yet to admit she had issues, and he didn't have a clue as to what they were. She'd never given any indication that she had problems with stealing like Sondra or any other vice. Her only real compulsion was the cockpit, and even when she was flying, she thrived on staying in control.

He opened his manual.

He and Leia both needed all the prayer they could get.

AFTER SHE TOOK A SHOWER ON THURSDAY MORNING, LEIA DRESSED in black pants and a matching jacket. There'd be no casino hopping for her this morning. She had work to do on Calvary's spring carnival, and Derek would probably be back at Casa Bonita anyway, hardly hiding his fling with the owner's wife. The guy lived a little too dangerously.

She marched out of the house with her head high and a briefcase filled with carnival tickets.

It took two hours to distribute the last batch of tickets to the stores that had requested more and to the local Christian school whose students had already sold three hundred. If they ran out of those, they'd have to wait and buy tickets on-site for ten bucks.

At noon she met Jenny and the other committee members at Carrabba's. When Jenny said the church was paying for lunch, Leia ordered the sea scallops—a couple of steps up from her new ramen noodles diet.

Before the meal arrived, Jenny launched the women into a round-robin discussion. She started with marketing and moved to entertainment, food, and ticket sales. Everything was in place for the event.

"I distributed the last of the tickets this morning," Leia told the group when she had finished eating a second wheat roll. "We've sold almost five hundred tickets at eight dollars each. I'm hoping we'll sell at least a hundred more by next weekend."

"Fantastic." Jenny sipped her water. "That's twice as many as we had sold by this time last year."

"And we'll have at least a hundred more people buy tickets the day of the carnival," Caroline said.

"Next week is going to be busy, busy for all of us, and Alicia's home with the flu," Jenny continued. "Leia, could you be the point person for vendor questions until she's better?"

Leia smiled as she picked up her third roll and broke off a piece. "I'm always happy to talk food."

"Good. We need to make sure they have everything they need to be ready by eleven on Sunday. The rest of us need to meet at the gates by nine."

The server arrived with a large platter and served each woman her plate. Leia sniffed the buttery sauce of the sea scallops before she took a bite. She closed her eyes for an instant as she relished the taste. Heavenly.

Jenny ate a bite of her eggplant Parmesan. "We've got six deacons lined up to be security guards, and they'll be roaming the grounds to check on safety issues."

"I can help with security," Leia volunteered.

"I'd like you to stay with the ticket sales," Jenny said. "Make sure there aren't any problems with the money."

AFTER LEIA HAD FINISHED A FUDGE BROWNIE TOPPED WITH CHOCOLATE mousse, she drove back to Casa Bonita. Derek wouldn't intimidate her. Just because he was fooling around with Danna didn't mean Leia had to stay away from the casino. It was her territory.

She waved at Brandy as she passed through the noisy row of slots. She was on to bigger things, using brainpower to beat the system. She passed the black sign for the one-dollar table and sat down at the stool beside the red sign—five-buck minimum bets. She set a hundred-dollar bill on the table, and the dealer nodded toward her, exchanging the cash for twenty chips. She slid two of the chips into the felt betting box and stacked the rest in front of her.

So far, so good.

The dealer dealt her a six and a five. His upcard was a five.

According to the strategy chart she'd memorized, she should double down. She placed two more chips beside her initial bet. The dealer slid a card under her bet, and she waited for the two other players to finish their rounds.

The dealer turned over his next card, a ten, and drew one more.

Leia fidgeted with her hands under the table while she waited for the dealer to flip his third card. The seven busted his hand.

Her latest card was a nine, so he matched her bet with four red chips.

She left all eight chips in the betting box. If she was going to win her money back like Derek, she had to think big, risk big.

She glanced around the room and saw Derek Barton's dark hair and brown jacket two tables down from hers; Danna was talking to an attendant behind him. Derek turned his head, and his eyes caught hers. Leia stared back at him, but neither of them waved. When Danna touched his shoulder, he broke their stare.

The dealer dealt her two kings, and she focused her eyes back on the cards, waving her fingers across them to stand. He gave himself two more cards, adding a two and a seven to his double sixes. Twenty-one points.

In a smooth swoop, he took her forty dollars in chips along with the rest of the chips on the table.

She took a deep breath and rolled her shoulders. One loss. No big deal.

She started to put four chips on the table but held back two of them. The dealer dealt, and she grinned when she turned over an ace and a queen. Blackjack.

The dealer added three chips to her two. She shouldn't have let the last loss spook her. If she had bet four chips, she'd be looking at sixty bucks right now.

She added two more chips to the five she had in the box and lost them when she went bust with twenty-three points.

In the next four hours, Leia managed to break even. Winning chips, losing them, and then winning them back again. When she felt like she'd mastered the science of the game, she moved to the next table. A green sign hung above—twenty-five-dollar minimum bets.

She lost three hundred dollars in the first half hour, and then she gained five hundred. But by dinnertime she'd fed the dealer hundreds of dollars in cash for new chips, with no clue as to how much she'd lost.

When the dealer scooped up her last pile of chips, she didn't buy more. Instead she headed back to the slot machines, slipping back into the buzz.

39

LEIA FLIPPED THROUGH THE PAGES OF *FITNESS* AS SHE WAITED IN the lobby of Dr. Rosenthal's office. The photos and articles that used to intrigue her now read like a torture manual. Killer abs. Sculpted quads. What were those? Her muscles had turned into jelly during her four-month hiatus from exercise.

She scarfed down the last bite of a glazed doughnut that she'd bought in a drive-through on her way to the doctor's office. She'd been inhaling junk the past few days—munching through the chips and chocolate bars that her husband had bought for "brain food."

Ethan had to take a few days off work to study, but the only time she saw him was when he came to bed at one or two in the morning. He sequestered himself in the office, poring over his manuals for three days. The man was going to be able to fly the 767 and 777 along with the 737 after he finished studying. While she was packing on the pounds, he had lost weight this month, stressing out calories through every pore.

She stressed before checkrides too, but nothing like her husband. Even though the anxiety tormented him up for weeks beforehand, he'd never failed a ride.

Her cell phone rang, and when she answered it, Jenny asked her if she could meet with two more vendors today—hot dogs and snow cones. She'd already talked waffles, ice cream, french fries, and Italian sausage this week. She could add a couple more food groups to the list.

Jenny hung up before Leia said good-bye. The woman was going to kill herself over a carnival.

Leia stood up to get another magazine but collapsed back down in her seat before she took a step. That nauseous feeling was back in her gut. If she moved a muscle, she was going to throw up again.

She leaned her head back against the wallpaper and rested until the feeling went away. Then she picked up *Better Homes & Gardens*.

It wasn't the doughnuts that were making her sick. It was a truck-load of Casa Bonita–induced stress. She'd dumped another four thousand dollars into the pit last week. Between the blackjack tables and the slot machines, the casino had sucked her dry.

The cash from the home equity loan was gone, and she hadn't paid a cent down on her credit card balance. She'd tried to get another home equity line of credit, but the loan officer had taken the stance of the credit card company, denying her request before she applied.

"Leia Carlisle?" the nurse called from the hallway.

She set down the magazine and followed the woman back into the warm examination room. Someone needed to turn up the air-conditioning.

When the nurse left the room, Leia slipped out of her jeans and into a pair of shorts. Then she sat on the table and waited.

In just a few more weeks, she'd be back in the cockpit—cruising across the country at thirty thousand feet. She hadn't gone four months without entering a cockpit since she was in high school. She closed her eyes and imagined herself back in the captain's seat—dim orange, red, blue, and white backlights across the control panel. Dials, throttles, and knobs.

She'd never thought about it before, but the cockpit's instrument panel resembled a slot machine … except that the cockpit's stakes were much higher.

"Hello, Leia," Dr. Rosenthal said when he opened the door. "How's that knee?"

"Much better."

He rolled up his stool beside her and examined it.

"Has it been swelling?"

"Only a couple of times. I iced it."

"When was the last time it swelled?"

She considered fudging the truth, but if the doctor caught her in a lie, he might punish her by keeping her off the line. "Last week."

He gently lifted her leg and bent it to check the range of motion.

"Is it sore?"

"A little."

"I'm going to give you some antibiotics in case it's an infection." He made a note in her chart. "Are you still going to the physical therapist?"

"Once a week."

"Good."

She scooted to the edge of the table. "When can I go back to work?"

"In about four weeks."

Her heart raced. "Really?"

"Possibly more if you have an infection, but overall your knee's looking good. The next few weeks are critical to your recovery." He closed the chart. "I don't want you to do any high-impact exercise until the end of the summer, but it would helpful if you could swim and walk regularly to speed the healing."

Another surge of nausea hit her, and she clutched her stomach. She couldn't throw up right now.

Dr. Rosenthal leaned toward her. "What's wrong?"

"Just a little sick to my stomach."

"Have you been feeling nauseous for a while?"

"Just this past week."

He reopened the chart and flipped through it. "Have you had a fever?"

"I haven't felt warm."

"Sore throat? Muscle aches?"

"No."

"Any chance you could be pregnant?"

A knot blocked her throat. *Pregnant? Oh God, please. No.*

Her nausea was the stress-related anxiety from the gambling.

"I don't think so," she muttered.

"Do you have a gynecologist?" he asked.

She shook her head. "We just moved here."

"Let me send out a blood sample for a few tests." The doctor wrote something on her chart. "My nurse will call you with the results."

Her legs were frozen on the table. "Okay."

"Unless your knee flares up again, I'll see you again in four weeks."

LEIA HARDLY REMEMBERED THE WOMAN PRICKING HER ARM TO TAKE blood. There wasn't anything wrong with her body, and she certainly wasn't pregnant. Just the suggestion of pregnancy would make her vomit again. It was the massive losses that were making her sick—she just couldn't tell that to the doctor.

In another month she'd be back in the cockpit, and she could start earning back some of what she'd lost.

Climbing into her car, she checked her watch and drove toward the church. She was fifteen minutes behind schedule, but the vendors usually arrived late anyway.

She turned on the radio, and an announcer started reading the day's news. She tuned out the words until she heard him say, "Corporate Direct." She turned up the volume.

"Bankrupt Corporate Direct announced this morning that it will shut down on May 1 after ten years in operation. Based out of Denver, this private jet charter company has been struggling to stay afloat over the past year. Corporate Direct employs eight hundred people to fly personal and group charters across North America."

Employed eight hundred people.

Leia whipped the car around at the next U-turn. Hot dogs and snow cones were the least of her concerns.

40

Spring snow fell outside the window of Denver's Soho Café as Ethan pored over his study materials while he ate a fried-egg sandwich for breakfast. He sipped his third cup of coffee with extra sugar as he rubbed his temples. The persistent ache wouldn't go away. He'd crammed so much information into his brain that adding to it actually hurt.

Ready or not, his checkride started in two hours. The only thing consistent about these rides was the schedule. Today was packed with recurrent training on safety issues—watching videos of recent accidents, operating aircraft doors, reviewing ditching supplies like rafts and radios, and listening to updates on new rules and equipment. Easy enough except that he didn't know how he was supposed to learn anything new before the actual exam.

Tomorrow was a simulator refresher to practice emergency procedures like fires and engine failures since—thankfully—he hadn't had to perform any of those procedures during the year.

And then there was the third day. The day he dreaded. Before lunch he'd take an hour-long oral exam that included solving complicated weight and balance problems. After lunch was a four-hour sim ride followed by a half-hour debriefing. And just for fun, a Federal Aviation Administration inspector might appear unannounced to observe the checkride. As if the day wasn't stressful enough without the involvement of the FAA.

He ate the last bite of his sandwich, but the food didn't relieve his stress.

"Can I get you anything else?" the server asked.

He pushed away the coffee mug. "I'm done."

She tore off the handwritten bill from her pad and handed it to him. "That'll be five eighty."

He traded the bill for his credit card and waited while she walked to the register to ring it up.

In three days life would go back to normal.

When he finished his checkride, he and Leia should go somewhere to celebrate. Maybe they could put aside their financial worries for a week and go to Santa Barbara like she wanted. Or he could surprise her with a couple of days in Cancún. The doctor might not let her scuba dive, but they could snorkel and swim.

Even though she'd forgotten to pay their mortgage, Leia had been careful with their spending the past few months. They could splurge on a nice getaway, a much-needed trip to revive their relationship.

He looked up at the server, chatting away with a manager at the register. He checked his watch. Couldn't they talk after he'd signed the receipt? He needed to get back to the hotel for a final study session before he went to the training center.

Drumming his fingers on the table, he stared at the server until she met his eye. Then she strolled back to the table.

"I'm sorry, Mr. Carlisle." She slid the plastic card across the table. "But your credit card company won't accept this charge."

"What do you mean?"

"Your card's probably maxed out."

"There's no way."

She shrugged. "You'll have to take it up with them."

He opened up his wallet and handed her seven dollars before he picked up his flight bag and walked back toward his hotel. They had a ten-thousand-dollar limit on their credit card—last time he'd checked the balance was $750. The company was probably having technical difficulties—unless their card had been stolen.

He sighed as he pulled out his credit card and dialed the customer service number on the back. He didn't need this hassle today.

As he read off his account information, the woman searched for his records.

"How can I help you?" she asked.

"I couldn't use my credit card at a restaurant today."

She paused. "That's because the expenses have exceeded the credit limit on this account."

"But I have a ten-thousand-dollar limit."

"And your account is at $10,185."

"There's no way."

She clicked on her computer keys. "Almost nine thousand of these charges were incurred yesterday in cash advances."

"Someone must have stolen my number."

"There's a Leia Carlisle listed on this account as well," she said.

"Leia's my wife."

"Did she use the card yesterday?"

"She couldn't possibly have spent nine thousand dollars."

"I'll put a note on your account, but you might want to talk to her before you report the card missing."

Ethan stormed into the hotel as he dialed Leia's phone number. When he got her voice mail, he told her to call him right back.

If their credit card was maxed out, what about the rest of their funds?

He had twenty minutes before he had to report in at the training center. Stopping at the public computer in the hotel's lobby, he keyed in the account information to check their savings account.

The bottom line punched him in the gut: $0.00.

He closed his eyes.

Where had all their money gone?

♠ ♥ ♣ ♦

LEIA WOKE UP IN THE FRONT SEAT OF HER CAR, HER EYES BURNING when she tried to open them. Her clothes reeked of smoke and sweat. She tried to lift her head, but a searing pain shot through her neck. When her head collapsed back against the leather seat, her cough turned the pain into a deep throb.

With her eyes crunched shut, the memories from the night before flashed through her mind. Horrible memories. If only it had been a nightmare. The loss of her job. The loss of their cash.

She'd spent the night in the casino, one final attempt to win back her gold. Brandy had brought her a drink to calm her nerves. And then another. She relaxed as she drained their checking account on the twenty-dollar slot machines. When that was gone, she spent their savings on blackjack. She moved to the hundred-dollar slots in a last-ditch effort to recover her losses, playing until she maxed out their personal credit card. Then she pawned her wedding ring.

As the night turned into early morning, she'd stripped them clean.

She pushed open the car door, throwing up on the cement.

Last night she hadn't cared about losing the money, hadn't cared about Ethan finding out that she'd emptied their savings account. All she wanted to do was win.

The parking garage's gray cement walls closed in around her. Wiping her mouth with a Kleenex, she turned the ignition to pump cool air into the car.

She closed her eyes. How had she gotten to this place? She'd always been the strong one. The fighter who wouldn't quit. The sprinter who ran, walked, or crawled until she reached the finish line. The risk taker who flew vintage planes and bumped down moguls and skydived at ten thousand feet.

But when she had jumped out of the airplane this time, her chute didn't open. All of Ethan's careful planning for the future had been demolished with the swing of her wrecking ball. She was like the Grinch who stole Christmas, except that there was no way to give Ethan his presents back. She'd already dumped them over the cliff.

She clutched her gut, but she didn't throw up again.

It was over. There was nothing left to gamble.

Nothing except her car.

She glanced around at the black interior. Maybe all hope hadn't been lost. Maybe she could use her car as collateral to take back a few thousand in cash, and then she'd buy it back.

The pain in her neck ached. If she lost her convertible, she'd have to call someone for help.

And who would she call? Danna? Derek? Jenny?

Leia slammed her fists on her legs. Jenny! She was supposed to be at the spring carnival in three hours.

She eyed the sinking needle on her gas gauge. She didn't even have enough money left to fill up the tank.

She prayed she could make it home.

41

LEIA PROPPED HERSELF UP AT A CARDBOARD TABLE BEHIND CALVARY Church, attempting to smile at the crowds that passed through the gate and onto the grassy field that had been transformed into the spring carnival. She'd slept another hour when she got home and somehow managed to shower, brush her teeth, and throw on a sleeveless shirt and capri pants.

A garden of daffodils and tulips had sprouted at the back of the brick church building on her left. To her right was a ball pit, a dunking machine, and a puppet theater, along with a sea of striped tents, trailers, and hundreds of kids roaming the grounds with a few dazed-looking adults in the droves. At least today's record attendance was a success.

Jenny had called yesterday afternoon, upset that Leia had missed the meeting with the vendors. She lied to Jenny yet again, saying her knee had flared up after her doctor's appointment. She took some medicine when she got home and fell asleep before she called the vendor to cancel.

Jenny may have been quick to forgive her, but Leia couldn't forgive herself. She was a rotten friend.

Jenny dropped a leather folder on the ticket table beside her. "How's it going?"

She wanted to say "awful." She'd lost her job, drained their bank accounts, demolished Ethan's trust, and destroyed their future.

Her life was a disaster.

Instead she pointed to the locked steel box in front of her. Her left hand felt naked without her wedding ring. "We've sold another hundred tickets."

"Excellent." Jenny pointed to the sky with her walkie-talkie. "Thank God for beautiful weather."

Leia tapped her fingers against the sides of her metal folding chair. She didn't check the weather this morning. She hadn't even had time to eat breakfast or grab her cell phone in her race out the door.

"High of eighty-five," Jenny said. "Makes me actually glad to live in Vegas this time of year."

Jenny motioned to someone on the facilities team and asked him to set up an umbrella over the ticket table.

"Denver's getting pounded today," Jenny said as she helped the man prop the umbrella over the table.

Leia could kick herself for not checking the Weather Channel. "How much snow are they supposed to get?"

"A foot dumped last night along I-70, and they're supposed to get another ten inches today."

If only she'd been snowed in last night. At home. She wouldn't have spent the night shoveling money into the casino. She clutched the seam of her pants. In the late-night hours she'd lost more than she'd lost in the last month of gambling. She'd gone for broke—and succeeded.

A man stopped at the table and bought two tickets for him and his son.

"Isn't Ethan in Denver right now?" Jenny asked.

Leia nodded. "He started his checkride this morning."

"He's not going anywhere for a few days."

"The training center's right next to the hotel."

Jenny leaned in toward the table. "Are you feeling okay?"

"No problems."

"If your knee starts aching again, I'll have someone replace you, so you can go home."

"Don't worry about me, Jenny."

Caroline tapped Jenny on the shoulder. "We have a lost child."

Leia and Jenny both looked down at a little girl clutching Caroline's hand. Her curly dark hair was pulled back in a purple band, and her brown eyes were filled with tears.

"Her name is Alexandra," Caroline said.

Jenny took the girl's shaking hand. "Hello, Alexandra."

The girl didn't smile.

Caroline pointed toward an orange awning. "I have to get back to the doughnut shop. They just lost power."

"No problem," Jenny said. "She can stay with me."

Jenny's walkie-talkie crackled. "Earl calling Jenny."

Jenny held her finger up to Caroline. "Just a sec."

She pushed the button on the walkie-talkie. "This is Jenny."

"The ball pit's starting to deflate."

"I'll be right there." Jenny shook her head. "This has turned into a circus."

Jenny looked down at Alexandra. "Would you like to walk with me, honey? We can look for your mommy."

Alexandra burst into tears at the mention of her mommy.

Leia tapped the empty chair beside her. "She can wait here with me until we find her mom."

Jenny's eyebrows shot up. "Are you sure?"

The girl stopped crying, eyeing Caroline and Jenny and then Leia.

Leia winked at the child. "We'll talk about girl stuff."

Alexandra let go of Jenny's hand and hopped onto the chair. Leia shooed the two women away as she sold tickets to another family.

Alexandra crossed her hands on the table just like Leia.

"How old are you, Alexandra?" Leia asked as she put another stack of bills into the lockbox.

"Five." Tears filled her eyes again. "Mommy calls me Allie."

"That sounds a lot like my name. I'm Leia."

"You look sad, Miss Leia."

Leia sat back in her chair. "Why do you say that?"

Allie shrugged. "I can just tell."

"I guess I am a little sad. I had a rough night."

Allie rested her head on her hands. "I'm having a rough day."

Leia reached over and squeezed her arm. "We'll find your mom soon."

"Why'd you have a hard night?" Allie asked.

"I lost a few things I needed."

Allie nodded as though she understood. "Just like I lost my mommy."

"Something like that."

"Maybe you'll find what you lost pretty soon."

"I hope so."

Leia fiddled with the lock on the moneybox. What a pathetic life she led! She hadn't really talked to her husband in months, yet here she was consulting with a five-year-old. Like little Allie needed another burden.

A woman with twin toddlers in a stroller walked up to the table, and Leia handed Allie three tickets. "Why don't I take the money while you hand out the tickets?"

"Really?"

"Yep. I could use an assistant."

Allie smiled. "I'm a good assis ... assistant."

"Chief assistant."

"A good chief assistant."

Leia smiled back at her as she handed her a stack of tickets. "That's what I thought."

For the next fifteen minutes Leia took money, and Allie distributed tickets. As they worked, the girl explained why the sky is blue and where her daddy lived and how her Sunday school teacher chewed gum when she talked. She was getting ready to tell Leia about her Barbie birthday party when someone called her name.

"Allie!" A woman with dark bangs dangling over her eyes yelled again, rushing up to the table and throwing her arms around the little girl. "Where did you go?"

"To the bathroom."

The woman was crying as she scolded her daughter. "You know you are not allowed to go to the bathroom without telling me first. I couldn't find you anywhere."

Allie's lower lip quivered. "I'm sorry, Mommy."

The woman gave Allie a kiss. "I'm so glad I found you."

Allie pointed at her. "I'm Miss Leia's chief assistant."

"I'm Diane." The woman pushed back her hair and reached out her trembling hand to shake Leia's. "Thank you for taking care of her."

"You've got a sweet little girl."

"She's my miracle baby." Diane smiled. "God works in mysterious ways."

Leia looked down at Allie holding her mommy's hand. "Indeed he does."

♠ ♥ ♣ ♦

THE LAST VENDOR TO SHUT DOWN FOR THE NIGHT WAS THE COTTON candy maker. Kids had stood in line for forty-five minutes to consume their final sugar rush before bed.

Popcorn bags and crumpled napkins littered the grassy paths between the vendors. It would still be light for an hour, but the carnival workers looked like they needed to go to bed before the children.

When the last parent pulled her crying child through the gate, Leia packed up the ticket table. Jenny collapsed in Allie's seat, dropping a bag beside Leia before her head fell into her arms.

"Are we done yet?" she asked.

Leia picked up the bag and clutched it in her fist. "Just when you think it's all over, it's time to clean up."

Jenny groaned. "Why did I do this again?"

"To help a very needy church in Indonesia."

"Can you tell me that a couple hundred times tonight?"

"You did an awesome job today. Everyone had a blast."

A group of volunteers walked through the gates with trash bags, working their way from the entrance back through the field.

"Why don't you let me handle the cleanup?" Leia asked. "You go home and crash."

Jenny lifted her head two inches before she let it sink back down. "I'm here till the end."

"The best leaders take breaks."

"I'll take a long break tomorrow." Jenny picked up her head and eyed the box under Leia's other hand. "Did you count the money yet?"

"I was waiting for you."

Jenny pointed at the cash bag. "That's the money from the dunking machine and all the other games."

"Great."

Jenny tapped the box. "Let's see what we made."

Leia let go of the box long enough to pull the key out of her pocket, but she didn't unlock it. "We should probably count the cash inside."

Jenny groaned. "I don't want to move."

"It's a church carnival, Jenny. We might as well flash 'naive' in red lights."

"You're right." Jenny pushed herself up. "Better safe than sorry."

Leia handed Jenny the key as she grabbed the moneybox. They walked to the sanctuary, and Jenny pulled out another set of keys to unlock the church office. When they stepped inside, Jenny locked the door.

Leia unloaded the first stack of cash from the box, counted it, and then handed it to Jenny to recount.

"Sam to Jenny."

She lifted the walkie-talkie to her mouth and pushed the button. "Hi, honey."

"Doesn't the church own a leaf blower?"

"In the utility shed. Why?"

"I'm going to blow some of this mess into a trash pile."

"Very ingenious of you, sweetheart."

"You married an ingenious kind of a guy."

Someone else's voice came on the speaker. "You know this is a public channel, don't you?"

"Quit eavesdropping, Earl," Sam said.

Leia counted the last stack and waited for Jenny to verify the amount.

"I counted $438," Jenny said as she stood up.

"I got $432."

"Are you sure?"

"I'm not sure of anything right now."

Jenny sat back down and recounted the cash. "You're right. It's $432."

Leia noted the number on the paper.

"For a grand total of …?" Jenny asked.

Leia punched the numbers into a calculator. "$6,880 today."

She added the amount from the tickets sold before the event. "$11,680 total."

Jenny clapped her hands. "Fantastic!"

The walkie-talkie crackled again. "Earl to Jenny."

"Yes, Earl."

"We need you back over here by the slide."

"What's wrong?"

"Apparently, a kid or two thought it'd be fun to stick wads of chewed gum on every step. The rental company wants to talk to you."

She sighed. "We'll clean it with Goo Gone."

"They'd still like to have a word."

"I'll be right there."

Jenny reached into a filing cabinet, pulled out a padded moneybag, and handed it to Leia. "The cash goes in here."

Leia stuffed the money into the bag as Jenny wrote the total on a money slip. Then Jenny sealed the bag.

"Could you drop this off at the bank for me?"

Leia waved the bag away. "Shouldn't you do it?"

"I have no idea when I'll get out of here."

"You could do it in the morning."

Jenny pushed the envelope toward her again, and Leia curled her fingers around the edge. "It's easy—all you have to do is drop it into the deposit box."

"Maybe Caroline can take it when she leaves—"

"No," Jenny cut her off. "I need you to handle it."

"But ..." Leia protested. It was too late. Jenny had already walked out the door.

42

THE FUEL LIGHT ON LEIA'S DASHBOARD BLINKED EMPTY AS THE needle on her gas gauge dipped into the red. If she didn't stop for gas now, she'd be stranded on the side of the street, and she didn't have money for a taxi ride home.

She passed by Henderson Savings & Loan on the right and pulled into the gas station, turning off the ignition after she parked by a pump. With a quick tug on the ashtray, she dug through a stack of receipts to the spare change collecting in the bottom. She counted the nickels and dimes—a total of $1.46. Barely enough to get her home.

She searched through her purse, but there was nothing left in her wallet.

She crushed her head against the steering wheel. What had she been thinking? Obviously, she hadn't been thinking, or she wouldn't have spent all their money. Forget gas. What were they going to do for food? Ethan didn't get paid again until next Friday. All they had left in the house were a few bags of ramen noodles.

She stared out the window at the lights of a 757 preparing to land at McCarran. If she couldn't keep gas in her car, what was going to happen when she went back on the line? Mistakes like running low on fuel would take down both her and her equipment.

She shuddered at the thought.

The blue and white deposit envelope sat on the passenger seat beside her with enough money to fill up a parking lot of gas tanks. All she needed was a couple of bucks. She could explain to Jenny that she'd run out of gas and cash before she made it to the bank. It would be easy to reimburse a few dollars to the carnival fund. No big deal. She'd call Jenny tonight and apologize before the bank called her to say that someone had tampered with the deposit.

She ripped open the envelope, took out four dollars, and stuffed it into her pocket along with a dollar in change from the ashtray. Then she got out of the car and put five bucks worth of gas in the tank. That would last her a few days if she didn't drive far.

She glanced around the dimly lit station. Only one other woman was pumping gas into her vehicle. There was an old Chevy parked by the car wash, and two men were smoking cigarettes on the sidewalk. Not exactly the safest place to leave thousands in cash.

Tucking the envelope under her arm, she walked toward the station.

A bell chimed when she opened the glass door. Flashing orange and yellow bulbs lit the dark hallway by the entrance like candles on a Halloween cake. She glanced down the row of black machines—slots, video blackjack, and video poker. There was nothing fancy about this place. No lush carpet or chandeliers or attendants serving free drinks. Grease stained the floor, and the room smelled like motor oil and car exhaust.

Leia walked past the machines to the front counter stacked with rows of gum, candy, and magazines. She handed the cashier the money to pay for her gas, praying that Jenny would understand. They were only four bucks down, and she would pay her back.

She marched out to the car and climbed in. Maybe she could replace the money before she went to the bank. She could at least try to get four dollars in cash. Ethan probably had a stash of spare change someplace in the house. She'd drained everything else. She might as well borrow from that too.

She gunned the convertible out of the station's driveway. Instead of going back to the bank, she raced through the Water District and turned left into her neighborhood. She locked the car door, but she didn't close the garage door as she ran into the house, the envelope resting on the front seat of the car. For some reason leaving the door up made her feel better—like she wasn't trying to sneak around with the church's money.

Inside the house she tugged out the kitchen drawers, rummaging for spare change, but there was nothing in the kitchen. So she moved to the living room, pulling out the drawers in the hutch, riddling through stacks of cloth napkins they never used, antique napkins rings, the telephone book, and a stack of faux leather coasters on the floor.

There wasn't even a penny hidden in their junk. Maybe Ethan had some change upstairs. She needed less than what it would cost to buy one of his mocha drinks at the airport.

She bolted up to the office, searching through the drawers that held paper clips and pens and rubber bands. At the back of the top drawer, she found a dollar bill.

In the bedroom she emptied Ethan's nightstand and dresser. There was no money left on her side.

She opened the window seat and tossed out the stash of extra pillows, searching for some sort of jar or moneybox. There was nothing there.

Moving into the bathroom, she opened the closet, throwing towels and bottles of medicine on the floor. If Ethan was hiding money from her, it would be in a place she'd least expect. She sat down on the edge of the bathtub, her sandals resting on the carpet of bottles and cotton balls and washcloths scattered across the tile. Where was Ethan keeping his extra cash?

Maybe in his tool chest.

She ran back downstairs and turned on the garage light. She picked through his tools for a money jar, and then opened the lid on the red metal chest. When she tipped the box, nails and screws poured out onto the workbench. Then she emptied the stack of drawers underneath.

Nothing.

She leaned back against the hood of her car, her stomach in knots.

She'd spent thousands of dollars last night, and now she couldn't find just a few more.

"Yoo-hoo!" she heard Misty call.

Her neighbor peeked her head around the side of the garage. She was wearing a bright blue scarf around her neck, a striped blouse, and tight jeans.

Leia clutched her elbows to steady her shaking hands. "Hey, Misty."

"You okay?"

"We're fine."

"I saw the garage door open, and it got me worried since it was dark. Thought you might be in trouble or something."

She stepped into the lit garage and walked around Leia's car.

"You can never be too careful these days. Someone got robbed over in Summerlin because they left their door open for the night. A thief traipsed right into their house while they slept and stole their TV."

Misty eyed the clutter on the bench and floor. "Do you need a nail or something? My husband has gobs of stuff."

"I need three bucks," Leia said.

"What?"

"I owe someone money, and I can't find three dollars in this entire house."

"Oh … okay then." Misty looked for a minute as if she might run, but she took a step toward Leia instead. "Well, that's an easy problem to solve."

"It's much harder than it seems."

Misty dug in her pocket and pulled out cash. She unrolled a five-dollar bill as she walked toward her.

Leia shook her head as she eyed the bill. "I can't take your money."

"Sure you can. It's just five dollars."

"I only need three more."

"Get yourself a cup of coffee or something."

Leia reached for the money. "I'll pay you back."

"No problem." Misty eyed the mess around the workbench. "You might want to clean this up before Ethan comes home. My husband would have a heart attack if I messed with his cave."

Leia didn't care what Ethan thought right at that moment. "I appreciate the loan."

"I'm hosting a Mary Kay party next weekend." Misty started to back out of the garage as though she was in a hurry. "You should come."

Like she had money to spend on makeup.

"I can't."

"Okay, well … 'bye then." Misty stepped out of the garage and disappeared.

Apparently asking for money was the only way to get rid of their neighbor.

She walked back into the house and grabbed the purse that she'd flung on the counter. She lifted her cell phone from the cradle and glanced at the screen—six new messages. She stuffed the phone into her purse. She couldn't listen to Ethan's voice right now.

Climbing into the car, she backed out of the driveway and sped toward the bank. She'd be rid of the cash envelope in minutes, and then she could deal with her own money problems. One burning issue at a time.

She drove past a row of art galleries, cafés, and casinos, pressing the money in her palm against the steering wheel. Her destination: Henderson Savings & Loan.

She braked at a light and looked over at the gas station. She could see the lights of the video machines through the window.

Misty had suggested coffee, but it wouldn't hurt to play the two extra bucks. Besides, she needed one-dollar bills for the bank envelope. The machine would give her the change.

With a quick turn, she pulled into the gas station.

She'd bet the two dollars to make an extra three to pay Misty back. One blackjack was all she needed to make everyone happy.

She rushed through the front entrance, clutching the cash envelope close to her side. Her sandal slid on a candy bar wrapper, and she swore as she caught herself on the edge of a machine before she hit the floor. Why couldn't anything be simple these days?

She unwrinkled the five-dollar bill and inserted it into the blackjack machine. She bet two dollars, and with a few clicks, she beat the dealer. The video game matched her bet.

Maybe she should have ditched the blackjack table in the casino and gone straight for a machine. She could use her brain without the pressure of having a dealer critique her every move.

All she needed was one more dollar to pay back Misty, and she'd be done for the day.

She bet another dollar and pressed the button. The machine dealt her a ten and a three. She clicked for a hit, but the dealt card was a jack. Bust!

She took a deep breath. No problem. She was back where she started. She bet another dollar and won. She was never going to get anywhere going back and forth.

She bet two dollars on the next hand. One win and she'd collect her money, run to the bank, and then go home and wait until she had to face Ethan's wrath.

She had two more days before she had to tell her husband that she'd annihilated their savings ... and then some.

She couldn't think about it right now.

The machine dealt her two threes. She split them and played two hands. One hand won. One went bust. A wash.

Her palms were sweating now. Adrenaline coursed through her veins. She bet two dollars on another hand. The dealer's hand was a blackjack, so she added an eight to her five and two. Another hit. She clicked again. A nine. Bust.

She bet three more dollars. The odds were that she'd win this round with Misty's money, and then she'd leave.

An ace, a five, and a king.

She stood on sixteen points, but the dealer had twenty. The three dollars disappeared with the flash of a light.

She had two dollars left from Misty's five plus her dollar from the desk. She needed one dollar back to take the full deposit to the bank. One measly dollar.

She bet three dollars for a quick win.

Blackjack! She won three dollars. The rush warmed her like a mug of hot tea. The win was nothing compared to what she owed, but it didn't matter. It was still a win.

The red light blinked five dollars—money available for her to bet.

She was back to her original number. She looked around her—she was the only one playing in the dark hall. She should cash out now.

But she'd sipped the elixir, and she craved more. She longed to feel the rush again. Savor the high. Just like the hours when she had been cranking out money online.

She fingered the padded envelope under her arm.

Maybe she could win back more than a few dollars. Maybe this was the opportunity for her to win back some of what she'd lost overnight. She'd spend a few more dollars and see how it went. Twenty bucks was all she would risk. If she lost it, she'd replace it somehow. Jenny would understand.

She glanced out the window behind her. For an instant it felt like someone from church was watching over her shoulder.

It shouldn't matter. She wasn't doing anything wrong—she was only borrowing the money. She'd pay it right back.

She pulled a twenty-dollar bill from the pack, slid it into the slot, and waited for the machine to ding.

Ready to play!

Her heart started pumping, blood rushing to meet the risk.

When she won thirty dollars, she screamed inside. Maybe this was it! Her time for a jackpot.

But she'd have to risk more to succeed.

She pulled over a stool from the next machine and sat down. Then she pulled fifty more dollars out of her bag.

43

With her eyes glued to the video monitor in front of her, Leia stuck her hand inside the bank envelope. Her fingers searched for another handful of cash, but there was nothing left. Her gaze raced to the envelope in her lap. She opened it wide and shook it upside down.

She couldn't possibly have spent it all.

She stuck her hand inside again, poking and probing the plastic as if it had consumed sixty-nine hundred dollars. She felt under her legs and looked down at the muddy floor around her stool to see if some of the cash had fallen to the floor. Nothing.

She glanced back up at the video screen, the credit meter displaying a giant zero.

The carnival money was gone. She'd lost it all—to a blackjack machine!

A wail escaped her lips, and she clutched her mouth. The envelope slid from her lap to the floor. Jenny never should have trusted her with so much cash. She couldn't be trusted with seven dollars. Forget seven thousand. Her friend had handed her the keys to a vault and then left the bank.

She braced herself against the cold sides of the machine, her arms trembling. Maybe this was all a nightmare. A bad nightmare. She'd wake up in the morning and rush the envelope filled with carnival profits to the bank.

The bell on the station's door rang, fresh air drifting down the rancid hallway.

It wasn't a nightmare. She'd stolen the new building from the Indonesian church.

She moaned, brushing her hair out of her face. No one would believe her story—that she'd only meant to borrow the money. They'd think she was a thief. A criminal. And Calvary would put her in jail for embezzling. Jail!

They couldn't lock her up. She'd go crazy in prison.

Her mouth felt as dry as the desert, and the lights swirled around her head. She'd fought it as hard as she could, but she'd still become her mom.

"Are you okay, lady?"

She turned to see the cashier standing over her, his tiny eyes boring into hers, scared rather than concerned.

She shook the blackjack machine until the speakers buzzed back at her. It was the thief, not her. The machine had stolen the church's money.

"Lady?"

She shook harder. "Give it back."

The bell on the door rang again, and she watched a family walk through the door, laughing as if they believed Las Vegas was a fun town. Entertainment only sucked in the unsuspecting. Vegas was all about despair.

"I think you better leave," the cashier whispered.

"No!"

She couldn't leave. The church's money was right here. Right in front of her. Jenny had given it to her, trusted her to take care of it. She wasn't going anywhere until she got it back.

She grabbed the cashier's arm and squeezed. "Can I borrow a few bucks?"

"You need to go."

She dug her nails into his skin. "Just ten dollars."

He pried her fingers off him, stepping back. "I'm calling the police."

"Please!" she yelled as he rushed toward the counter.

When he held up the phone, she slid off the stool, her nails scraping across the machine one last time. Dazed, she picked up the envelope, wiped off the dirt, and moved toward the door.

She couldn't think about what she had just done. It would kill her.

Her convertible was parked crooked by the sidewalk. She fumbled for her keys in her pants pocket and reached down to unlock the door, but it was already open. She hadn't even bothered to lock it; she was only supposed to be inside the station for a minute or two.

How long had it been? Three hours? Four? How long did it take to feed sixty-nine hundred dollars to a video machine?

She stuck the key in the ignition. Her stomach felt like it was about to erupt, so she rolled down the window until the cool air soothed the wave.

She didn't even have a job to help her pay it back. Forget the knee injury. That was an easy hurdle. No company would hire a convict to fly their plane. She wouldn't even be able to tow banners.

If only the desert wind could blow her away from here. Some place far from the bank and the church and the Clark County justice system. Some place where she could be content without milking a slot machine or hurting the people she loved.

But before she went anywhere, she needed to get the church's money back.

She leaned back on the headrest, her body begging her to sleep.

She'd rest when this was over.

Her mother said the first step to her recovery was admitting she was powerless.

She opened her eyes and looked out at the light poles towering over the gas station, saturating the darkness with artificial light.

Okay, she was powerless to stop this thing. Gambling had consumed her mind, blackened her soul. But her weakness wasn't Jenny's problem or Ethan's. She'd done the damage. She might not have power over gambling, but she had the power to make it right.

She turned on the car, and the clock flashed 3:38 a.m. Las Vegas prime time. There was only one person who could help her, and she knew exactly where he was.

♠ ♥ ♣ ♦

THE DRIVE TO CASA BONITA ONLY TOOK FIFTEEN MINUTES. LEIA walked onto the gaudy elevator and couldn't help staring at herself in the mirrors that were glued to every side. Her hair was greasy and wind-blown from the carnival, her mascara smeared, her capris wrinkled. Her face was blotched with red, and dark shadows bulged under her eyes. She'd lost control.

The doors opened on the casino floor, and she pushed herself for-ward in spite of the awful throbbing in her gut. She couldn't stop her pounding heart or her sweat-drenched forehead, but she willed her feet to walk. She'd run out of options. There was only one way left to recover the money.

She had to keep moving ahead.

She ignored the lure of the flashing lights and jangling coins as she crossed through a row of slot machines. She didn't have any money left to gamble.

"Hey, Leia!" Patrice called out to her.

She didn't wave back at the attendant. These people weren't her friends. They'd sucked her dry—not caring about her or anyone else they destroyed as long as they got their cash.

She rounded the end of the row and perused the layout of black-jack tables, searching for his dark hair. She'd never thought she'd be looking for him, but she had no choice today. If she couldn't find him now, she'd wait.

She was pushing through a crowd around the roulette table when she heard his laugh. The same one she'd heard four months ago in Black Hawk—the same day she was banned from snow skiing and took the long plunge down the dangerous slope of gambling instead. She should have heeded the warnings. The hundreds of danger signs. But she ignored every caution light, every red flag, until she hunted the forbidden fruit right off the side of a cliff.

Derek was sitting with two other men at a table. No women crowded around him for the moment. Danna must be playing her own cards under the table.

"Are you winning?" Leia whispered.

"Leia Vaughn." He met her eye, a slow grin slinking across his face. "What do you want?"

"I need your help."

He turned his cards, displaying twenty-one. "Of course you do."

He slowly gathered his chips into a neat stack and nodded to the dealer. Then he took her hand.

She pulled away from him. "Your girlfriend might see you."

He grabbed her hand again. "Fuel for the fire."

"I need a drink first."

Derek walked up to the bar and ordered a shot of tequila. She guzzled the fiery liquid like it was Kool-Aid.

She shivered as he led her out a side door and into a long hallway painted a muddy yellow. His fingers felt like snakeskin against her hand.

It didn't matter what she did to herself. Someone like her shouldn't be allowed to walk free. She deserved jail, but the church in Indonesia needed their money before they locked her away.

Derek opened a plain door on the side of the hall and pulled her inside. She reached for the light switch and flipped it on—a crowded janitor's closet filled with racks of toilet paper and cleaning supplies, brooms, and mop buckets.

She didn't want to be there. Especially not with him. But this wasn't the time for her to be weak in her resolve. The repulsiveness would pass if she maintained her strength. It wasn't about her anymore.

She cleared her throat. "This is your hangout?"

"Only when we can't go to Danna's room."

"Very chic."

He pulled her to him. "I've been waiting for this for a long time."

She pushed him back. It was too warm in there. "We have to negotiate."

"I'll help you win back whatever you lost."

"I've lost over seventy thousand dollars."

He whistled as she watched the look on his eyes in the dim light. Pleasure replaced the shock.

He brushed her hair back from her ear. "Two thousand to start."

"Ten."

He untucked his shirt, and she cringed. She had to do this. For the church in Indonesia. For Ethan. For their future.

"Seven."

"Okay," she whispered. Seven thousand at a time. Ten times. Maybe she could pay back the church before they even knew the money was gone. "How do I know you're lucky enough to win it back?"

"Luck has nothing to do with it." His hand was on her thigh. "I have an eye for it."

She braced herself against the metal racks. "You count the cards?"

He didn't say anything.

"That's illegal."

"It's not."

"But ..."

"The casinos can't do anything if they don't know."

"Seven thousand," she repeated.

He grabbed her face and kissed her lips so hard she tasted blood on her tongue. Then he ripped her shirt, and she gasped, clinching her eyes shut so she couldn't see him.

Ethan's gentle face appeared in the darkness. He'd been so good to her, so kind. But instead of caring for him, she'd hurt him over and over. She didn't deserve his love or Jenny's or God's. They could never forgive her. And they shouldn't forgive her. She was trash.

Derek pressed himself against her, and her stomach rumbled. She tried to stop it, but the tequila erupted inside her. She leaned over and threw up in a bucket.

Derek leaped back as if he had been stung. His arm clutched a shelf of toilet paper as he stared at her in horror.

She wiped her mouth off on her arm. "I can't do this."

Not even to help the church.

She pushed open the door and sprinted down the hallway. She had to get out of there.

"Leia!" Derek called, but she wasn't going back.

She could hear his footsteps beating the floor behind her until she heard someone else in the hallway.

"Excuse me, sir," a new voice commanded.

Derek's steps stopped, and she turned around. A security guard had his arm.

"The boss would like to talk to you."

She ran out the side door.

She had one more card left to play, and she wouldn't fail. She'd ride the golden parachute out of her mess.

44

ETHAN'S HEAD POUNDED WHEN HE HUNG UP THE PHONE FROM HIS
6:00 a.m. wake-up call on Monday morning. He hadn't been asleep
when the desk clerk called—in fact, he hadn't slept much all night. He
opened up the breakfast menu on the nightstand and thumbed through
the laminated pages.

He'd survived the first and second days of his checkride. The
instructor pounded so many new regulations and safety procedures
into his head that he didn't have room to think about his depleted savings account during the past two days. Or, at least, he hadn't allowed
himself to think about it. One bad slipup during his checkride could
send him down the slope of unemployment; and whatever trouble Leia
had gotten into, losing his job would only hurt the situation.

Yet, even though he wouldn't let himself think about it during the
day, he couldn't stop thinking at night. He'd stared out the window for
hours last night, watching the frosty snowflakes fall against the backdrop of the city lights. He had called Leia's cell phone and their home
phone over and over, but she never picked up.

He dug his wallet out of his pants pocket and counted the cash.
Ambassador Air footed the hotel bill and paid him for his time, but he

paid for food on this trip. He'd planned to put the expenses on his credit card.

Yet he needed a decent meal to get him through the stressful day. He picked up the phone beside the bed, called room service, and ordered a small pot of coffee and a ham and cheese omelet. The attendant said someone would deliver his breakfast in twenty minutes.

He threw on a T-shirt and called Leia's cell phone again. He didn't expect her to answer, but he'd keep trying until someone picked up. If she'd left him, he'd find out when he got home. The burning questions in his mind were—who did she flee with, and how much had she taken?

He hung up the phone and walked into the bathroom to brush his teeth. Today he needed to focus on his sim ride. Even if his marriage was crumbling, he needed to be confident when he walked into the cockpit. Alert in spite of his lack of sleep. Exhaustion was no excuse.

As a pilot he couldn't allow personal issues to affect his performance. When crisis struck at thirty thousand feet, he didn't have the luxury of consulting an expert or second-guessing his decisions. There was no time to stop and analyze a problem when he was in the air. He had to make a decision and stick with it. The decisions he made in the sim today could save lives when he was back on the line. He refused to let his marital problems shake his drive.

He turned on the showerhead, waiting until the spray turned hot. As he soaked in the water, his muscles relaxed, and he prayed for his wife. He didn't know where she was or what she'd done, but he'd taken a vow to love, honor, and cherish her for the rest of his life. With God as his strength, he was sticking to his vows.

When he finished his shower, he tried her cell phone again.

LEIA IGNORED HER RINGING PHONE ON THE CAR SEAT BESIDE HER AS she fled Casa Bonita's parking garage. She had to get out of this awful city, miles and miles away from the devastating trail she'd plowed. She'd become an expert at destruction.

She sped through Henderson and into the desert wasteland, past dusty basins painted with cactus and creosote bush and orange-tinted sandstone. The sun crept over the mountains beside her, coloring the ridges a brilliant pink.

It was a new day. Time for a change—fresh beginnings for some people, endings for others.

It was over for her. She'd destroyed too many lives. An accident was the ace in her hand. She'd avoid jail. Ethan would collect her life insurance. The policy would cover what she'd lost, including the money for Indonesia, and he could start fresh with someone who loved and respected and deserved him. Someone who didn't flush their hard-earned money down the sewer and then steal to feed her addiction.

She shivered as she veered right onto a narrow side road and turned into the pullout where she and Ethan had lunched—before her life had spun out of control.

She parked the car and leaned her head back to watch the yellow streaks reflecting off Lake Mead below her. The lake's dark ripples turned purple and red.

She couldn't go to prison. She went crazy just being confined at home. Spending a year in a jail cell would be her death sentence. She'd bypass a judge and render her own verdict.

There was nothing left for her in this life anyway. She'd lost everything she and Ethan had worked for. Maybe God, in his mercy, would still welcome her home. She cringed. Or maybe not. She'd been a terrible witness of Christ's love.

She shifted the car back into drive. Maybe God wasn't even listening to her anymore.

The images of the slot machines flashed in her mind, calling to her even as she stood on the brink.

She could never break free. The game had consumed her.

"I'm sorry, Ethan," she whispered. This was the only way to make it right for him. She'd already gone too far down this dark road alone. No turning back. She eyed the break in the guardrail. Her escape route. With enough speed she'd clear the rocky field on the other side and hit the water in seconds.

She slammed the gas pedal to the floor and sped toward the rail. The wheels jumped the curb, and for an instant it felt like she was flying. She closed her eyes for the plunge.

Her head smashed into the steering wheel, but she didn't fall. Rubbing her forehead, she hit the gas pedal again. No response.

She opened her eyes to look down at the fuel gauge.

Empty.

She didn't even have enough luck left to commit suicide!

Pulling herself out of the car, she walked to the front of the car. She'd hit a rock. Without gas, she wasn't going anywhere.

She glanced toward the cliff. She'd have to jump. If she didn't hit water ... the stony shoreline would free her from her sins.

She sat down in the car, her feet dangling out the side. The jolt from banging into the rock made her lose her nerve for the moment. If she didn't jump now, she might change her mind, and then Ethan would have to clean up her mess. He had enough to deal with without visiting his wife in the penitentiary.

She eyed the cell phone on the seat beside her and picked it up. She wanted to hear Ethan's voice one last time....

His first message sounded strained at the beginning; then he was mad. He knew their credit card was maxed out, their savings gone. And he wanted to know why.

She sighed. Ethan deserved some sort of note to say she loved him, but the life insurance company would call her bluff. Even with the wrecked car, they still might give him the money. And he might even grieve until he learned what she'd done.

The next message was from the nurse at the doctor's office. She asked that Leia call her right back.

Leia deleted the message and waited for the next one.

It was the nurse again. She said she hated to leave this kind of news on voice mail, but Leia should know as soon as possible that she was pregnant.

Leia gasped.

Pregnant? She pressed her hands against her forehead before slapping the steering wheel. The doctor had guessed right. She'd been the only one in denial.

She fled the car and the phone, bolting toward the edge of the cliff. She couldn't think. Not about consequences. Or the baby. Or the future. She just had to jump. Jumping would make her forget everything.

She jammed her eyes shut and leaned forward into the air.

Allie's dark hair and brown eyes stared back at her in the darkness. She could almost feel the girl squeezing her hand.

You look sad, Miss Leia.

She jerked herself back from the edge, collapsing on a rock.

Ethan would never have to know she was pregnant, but she knew. Her life was expendable, but the life growing inside her was innocent. The baby didn't have a choice.

She couldn't kill her unborn child.

She dropped her head to her hands, the heels of her sandals grinding the red dirt on the ground.

What was she going to do?

Sleep. She'd slept only two or three hours in the past forty-eight. A little rest might clear her head.

She sank down to the dirt, the lake breeze blowing across her arms. In seconds she was gone.

45

LEIA RUBBED HER EYES, AND THE RAW PAIN SHE FELT WHEN SHE touched the right side of her face jolted her awake. She glanced down at her pink arm. Sunburn. Her mouth was parched, her head pounded, and her neck ached from sleeping on a bed of rocks.

She blinked several times at the lake below her before she realized where she was. She brushed her hands across her face and felt the bump on her forehead. She'd almost gone over the cliff.

She propped herself up on the dirt and pulled her knees close to her chest as she looked out over the water, the Western sky tugging the sun toward the horizon.

She'd slept most of the day. The rest sharpened her mind, but it didn't alleviate the impact of what she'd done. She'd failed the church and Ethan and Jenny. She'd failed her mom and her dad. She'd never be able to recover her losses, and it was too late for redemption. Her life was just beginning to unravel.

She'd spend a year or two in prison. Ethan would divorce her. Her baby would spend his first year without a mom, and if Ethan fought her for custody, it might be longer than a year. And she'd never be able to fly commercially again.

She eyed the steep cliff in front of her. A single jump would terminate her problems in seconds. She could escape all the repercussions from her gambling spree in the deep waters of Lake Mead.

Her body trembled at the thought. She might escape facing Jenny and Ethan, but if she jumped off that cliff, she'd soon be facing God.

God doesn't let us go.

The pastor's words rushed back to her. He'd said that God wouldn't stop loving her even when she sinned; he was waiting for her to return to him.

She'd ignored God's voice long enough. He had sought her. Rescued her over and over. Loved her in spite of her weaknesses. Yet just as she'd done with Ethan, she'd ignored her heavenly Father.

She'd chosen the game over God.

"Please forgive me," she whispered to the breeze.

He was there. She could feel his presence in the mountains and the cactus and the ripples on the lake. He was God of the boats that sailed below and Lord of the vast blue sky above. He was even the God of Sin City.

She'd tried to stifle his voice. Yet here he was in the light. For months she'd hidden in the darkness.

Why had she run from him? She'd tried to handle this problem all by herself. Win back her losses and stop gambling on her own. Needing someone meant failure, so she had pretended she didn't need God or anyone else.

You're my child.

Tears rushed into her eyes, spilling down her cheeks. She wiped the tears with the back of her hand, but she couldn't stop the flow. The torrent streamed down her face so fast that she quit trying to wipe it away. Salt filled her dry mouth, burning her cracked lips as she tasted her pain. She'd hurt the people she loved. And she'd hurt herself.

She leaned over and sobbed, the desert ground soaking in her grief. She cried until her tears dried up.

The cliff was two steps in front of her. She planted her fists into the parched dirt and scooted back.

She wouldn't kill herself or her baby. She stood up and walked back to her car. The front tires were shredded; the right side of the hood crunched from hitting a rock. And she'd probably blown the suspension as she forced the car over the curb and through the rocky field.

She opened the door and took a sip of the bottled water she had stored underneath the passenger seat. Then she tried to start the engine. Still dead. She'd need a wrecker to pull her out of this mess anyway. She'd planted her battered convertible behind the metal guardrail and a row of scrubby brush.

She was tired of running.

Her dad had always confronted a problem head-on. It was her mother who ran away. With God's help she'd face her problems like her dad had done. No more living in denial.

She picked up her cell phone and dialed the Frazers' home number.

"Jenny ..." she whispered when her friend answered the phone.

"Leia!"

Jenny covered the phone and shouted for Sam.

"Where are you?" she asked.

"At Lake Mead."

"I called the bank this morning, and they never got the deposit envelope."

"I know." Leia closed her eyes. God—it hurt to ask. "I need help."

"What happened?"

"I'm in trouble."

"Okay." Something crashed in the background.

"I ran out of gas."

Jenny probably had a hundred questions: What are you doing out at Lake Mead? Where is the church's cash? And why don't you have any gas?

"That's an easy problem to fix," Jenny said instead. "I'm on my way."

"Thank you," Leia whispered. "I'm off Lakeshore Road. Near Las Vegas Bay."

"Don't move."

"I'll walk to the main road so you can see me."

Leia slipped her cell phone into her pocket, grabbed the bottle of water from the front seat, and took a blanket from the trunk. She wrapped the blanket over her head and around her sunburned arms as she hiked out to the main road. Then she sat on a rock and waited.

♠ ♥ ♣ ♦

IT TOOK JENNY AN HOUR TO FIND HER. WHEN SHE PULLED THE CAR off the road, Leia didn't move from the rock. Her friend opened the door and slammed it shut before walking toward her. She stared for a moment at Leia's sunburn and the bump on her forehead. Then she handed her an icy bottle of water and sat down on a rock next to her, waiting for Leia to speak.

Leia took a long sip of water, trying to form the words in her mind. What had Sam said when he told her about his addiction?

She chose the simplest route.

"I have a gambling problem."

Jenny's gaze veered off Leia's face and then snapped back. "How bad is it?"

Leia wrapped her fingers around the cold bottle. "I've spent our savings and then took out several large loans to cover my losses."

"Does Ethan know about this?"

"No."

Jenny sighed. "The money for Indonesia?"

"Gone." Leia choked on the word. "I only meant to borrow a few dollars for gas, but when I saw the video blackjack machines in the station ... I never meant to spend it."

"That money was for a new church building."

"I'm so sorry."

Jenny kicked the dirt with her tennis shoe.

"Leia ..." She stopped and looked out at the lake. "So where do you go from here?"

"I'll pay back the church. I don't care how long it takes me."

"There are consequences for stealing."

She dropped her head. "I know. I'm prepared to go to jail."

Jenny grabbed her hand and began to pray. "Lord, you are a God of mercy and grace. I beg you to help my dear friend right now. I know you will forgive her for what she has done, but I ask that you take the pain out of her heart and grant her the freedom that can only be found in you. Show her that with your help, she has the freedom and power to break free from gambling and be reconciled with you and her husband.

"I pray that you will give both her and Ethan strength to face the coming days and that you will surround her with your angels as she breaks free from the powerful hold of this addiction. Please be strong even when she is weak."

When Jenny finished her prayer, she hugged Leia's neck. And for an instant, Leia wondered if this is what it was like to have a mom.

"I need to get help," Leia said when Jenny let go of her.

"Good. I know exactly where you can find it." Jenny stood up. "But first I brought a couple gallons of gas for your car."

"My car's not going anywhere."

Jenny's concerned eyes probed deeper into hers. "What did you do?"

Leia shrugged as she stood up and walked to Jenny's truck. She got inside and pointed down the remote trail.

When they turned into the pullout, Jenny gasped at the sight of the convertible on the other side of the barrier.

"Leia?"

"I wasn't thinking clearly last night."

Jenny grabbed her cell phone. "I'm calling Ethan."

Leia nodded her consent even though Jenny didn't ask for it. Better that Jenny talk to him before she did. "He's taking his checkride in Denver."

Jenny dialed 4-1-1 and requested the phone number to the training center.

Leia slipped out of the truck when they connected Jenny to Denver. She couldn't stand to hear her tell Ethan what had happened, couldn't bear to hear the anguish in his voice.

46

A HUGE THUNDERHEAD WAS BUILDING TO ETHAN'S RIGHT, PAINTING yellow and red cells of precipitation across the radar. Level two and level three echoes.

He radioed air traffic control, and the controller gave him immediate permission to deviate from the flight plan and vector twenty miles around the storm. He turned right thirty degrees.

Rain pelted the cockpit window. Flashes of lightning lit the gray clouds. He couldn't see the ground, but Tucson was thirty-five thousand feet below. In forty-five minutes, he would be landing at San Diego International. At least he hoped he'd land this bird.

A bell rang in the cockpit as the red fire light blinked on the center console. Engine number two.

Ethan took a deep breath. Since they'd taken off from Houston an hour ago, the captain had passed out; and while the captain was incapacitated, Ethan had lost the left half of the hydraulics system.

He was on his own.

Ethan reached down and pulled the alarming T-handle to close the fuel valves to the engine. Then he twisted the handle clockwise to discharge the agent, but the warning bell didn't stop dinging in his ear.

His sweaty palms soaked the handle as he twisted the handle counterclockwise.

The alarm stopped.

He switched his brain to autopilot. This is what he was trained to do. He reached up to the fuel panel and configured the system, balancing the fuel with a single engine. Then he started the auxiliary power unit. Backup pneumatics and electricity—on.

Next he had to find an airport nearby that could accommodate a 737-400.

He switched to the emergency frequency of 121.5 megahertz and called air traffic control.

"Albuquerque Center, this is Ambassador Air 863." He tried to steady his voice. "We are declaring an emergency and requesting vectors and an immediate landing at Tucson."

The controller replied. "Roger, you are in radar contact. We will vector you for a landing at Tucson."

His mind ran through the list of procedures he'd memorized. He had to make decisions about foaming, fire equipment, and the thunderhead that still threatened the plane.

He pressed the microphone to speak with the flight attendant in charge. "This is Ethan. We have lost an engine and will be landing in Tucson. You have fifteen minutes to prepare the cabin for an emergency landing."

Another warning bell went off in the cockpit; another red fire light blinked. Engine number one.

Fires in both engines!

A woman's voice sounded overhead, but he didn't register what she said.

Ethan gripped the T-handle and yanked it right. How was he supposed to land at Tucson without an engine?

The woman's voice interrupted his crisis mode as she repeated: "Urgent call for Ethan Carlisle."

His heart was racing too fast, his mind too focused on the task to digest the words. When the alarm didn't stop, he pulled the handle up and twisted it again.

The flight instructor behind Ethan leaned forward. "Can it wait thirty minutes?"

"It's a family emergency."

Ethan was still squeezing the T-handle when the gray clouds outside the cockpit turned black, and the bell silenced. For an instant he thought he'd crashed the plane.

He slowly let go of the handle and clenched his fists, reminding himself that he was in a simulator. It would take awhile before his pounding heart remembered they were safe on the ground.

The sim shuddered and beeped as it repositioned and lowered back to the floor.

A family emergency? Not until the doors opened in the back of the simulator did the woman's words process in Ethan's mind. He was back to reality now. This wasn't a drill.

He climbed over his seat and rushed out the back. Someone handed him a phone number, and he dialed it on his cell phone.

Red lights flashed around the simulator bay. The fiberglass sims looked like a team of horses bucking and bowing in a ring.

A woman answered his call, but he didn't recognize her voice.

"This is Ethan Carlisle."

"It's Jenny."

Why was Jenny Frazer calling him in the middle of his checkride?

"Where's Leia?" he demanded.

"She's outside my car."

"I need to talk to her."

"You need to come home."

If only it were that easy. "I can't, Jenny. I'm right in the middle of my annual checkride."

"Postpone it."

"I can only do that if there's a crisis."

"Leia tried to …" Jenny's voice cracked. "She tried to drive her car off a cliff this morning."

His back slumped against the concrete wall. "Suicide?"

"I'll let her tell you the story when you come home."

He caught the eye of the flight instructor staring at him. "I'll be back as soon as I can."

Ethan's shaky fingers could barely hit the button to disconnect the call.

He would have believed that Leia had run away—she'd lived the last few months like a trapped animal, biding her time, plotting an escape. He would even have believed that she'd had an affair. But kill herself? His wife would be the last person who'd succumb to suicide. She'd always been in charge of every step, every emotion. She'd climb a mountain with her injured knee before she attempted suicide.

He looked down at the phone in his hands before stuffing it back in his pocket.

How dare she do this to him! To herself! The depression must have taken over. He'd hire a counselor. Get her medication. Lock her up in a hospital. Whatever it took to get her well.

But what if it was his fault? What if he had done something to drive her to the brink? He didn't know how many angry messages he'd left this weekend about their bank account.

Losing his money didn't compare with losing his wife.

He marched over to the instructor. "I'm going to have to reschedule this ride, Chuck."

The instructor studied him as if he was trying to figure out whether Ethan was finagling his way out of a crash landing. Ethan wished it were that simple.

"What's going on?" Chuck asked.

Ethan hesitated. How do you tell someone the woman you love tried to kill herself? "My wife has a medical emergency."

"Didn't you tell me your wife worked for Corporate Direct?"

He didn't have time for chitchat. "She still works for them."

"Not anymore." Chuck wrote something on his tablet. "They announced Saturday that they're shutting down."

Would she kill herself over her job?

"I have to go home."

Chuck handed him a sheet of paper with the rescheduled date. "We'll postpone it for two weeks."

Ethan jogged back to his hotel, snow caking his shoes and the bottom of his pants. If he hurried, he might be able to catch the 5:30 p.m. flight home.

Before he took the elevator up to his room, he checked out at the front desk. The clerk handed him a bill for his food expenses.

"Would you like me to put this on your credit card?" The clerk held up his registration with the card number.

"Yes …" he started. "No."

He pulled out his wallet and handed her a twenty. "I'll pay cash."

As she printed his receipt, he counted what was left in his wallet. Fifteen dollars until he got home.

Ten minutes later he was packed and back downstairs, waiting in the lobby for the shuttle. The first flight left in an hour—hardly enough time to get into Denver International Airport and through security. He looked through the window at the snow piled up in the parking lot. Forecasters had predicted six inches, but Denver had accumulated over a foot this afternoon. Hopefully the weather hadn't backed up the flights.

He checked his watch. If he ran through the airport, he could be home in three hours.

But when he got home, he wasn't sure what he'd say to his wife.

47

LEIA STARED AT CASA BONITA'S FLASHING LIGHTS AS JENNY passed the casino on the way to her house. When Leia had left home last night, she had thought she would never see Henderson again. She had thought her trip out of town would be her last.

Yet here she was riding back through downtown. Life still moving around her as though nothing had changed. As though her secret hadn't been revealed.

It would take months—if not years—to sort out the consequences.

Jenny parked the car in the driveway, and Leia climbed out, following her friend up the stairs to a guest bedroom. Jenny pointed to the queen-size bed, and Leia collapsed on top of the comforter.

The room was warm, cozy. Jenny closed the blinds as Leia succumbed to sleep

When she woke up, Leia stretched her arms and her legs. Then she opened her eyes and sat up. It was still light outside.

Her face hurt from the sunburn, but the rest of her body felt rested. Even the nausea was gone.

The green numbers on the clock beside her bed read 10:04. She glanced back at the window. Why wasn't it dark?

Then it hit her. She had slept all night.

She slid her bare feet off the edge of the bed and onto the soft carpet. Her sandals were aligned perfectly by the door. Jenny must have slipped them off after she fell asleep.

She twisted the blinds open and gazed out at the blue comfort of the sky. She quietly thanked God for the gift of light.

At the side of the room was a small guest bath. She moved slowly across the room, relishing the peace that washed her body. And then she stopped.

She may feel refreshed, but her life would never be the same. While she wasn't peering over the edge of a cliff anymore, she was still about to hit the rocks below. God help her! All she could do was try to hold on to the pieces of her life as she fell.

Jenny now knew her secret, and it was up to her to decide what to do with the information. If she wanted, she could punish her for delving into the industry that had taken her husband down, but it didn't seem like Jenny was intent on destroying her. She'd opened her arms with a heart full of grace even when she knew what Leia had done with the church's money. And she'd rescued her from herself.

Her fingers trembled as she stared at her blotchy face in the mirror; the purple bump on her forehead looked like a third eye.

She had never shown anyone that kind of grace. She'd even turned away from her mother the first time she'd been jailed for shoplifting, condemning her sin without searching her heart. Could she ever forgive her mother for what she had done? If she couldn't forgive her own mother, how could she ask someone like Jenny to forgive her yet again?

Leia gently rinsed her sunburned face and hands in the sink and scrubbed her teeth with the brush and toothpaste that Jenny had left on the counter alongside a bottle of aloe vera. Then she slathered the gel on her face before combing her fingers through her hair.

She pushed her hair behind her ears. She was in desperate need of a good cut. An inch or two off the back and layers on top. She stepped back from the mirror. How absurd. Yesterday morning she was willing to kill herself, but this morning she was worrying about her hair.

Someone knocked on the bedroom door, and she walked across the room to open it.

"I thought I heard you," Jenny said. In her hands she held a wooden TV tray with French toast, bacon, and a large glass of orange juice. "I thought you might be hungry."

"Famished."

"Good," Jenny said as she set the tray down on the oak desk in the corner. "Ethan couldn't fly out of Denver last night because of weather, but he's hoping to catch a flight this morning."

She'd forgotten that she had to face Ethan today.

"Why don't you eat and take a shower?" Jenny handed her a clean T-shirt and black leggings. "After you're done, there are a few people Sam and I would like you to meet."

A knot clenched her stomach. "Who?"

"Come on downstairs when you're finished getting ready."

She sat down by the desk and poured maple syrup on the French toast. The bread was burnt, the bacon rubbery, but she was so hungry she didn't care. She hadn't eaten anything since the doughnut at the doctor's office on Saturday. Or did she have a bagel on Sunday?

The shot of tequila didn't count.

Jenny wanted her to meet with a group. Probably tell them about her weakness for gambling.

When she was done eating, she climbed into the shower and let the warm water soak her arms and back. Then she shampooed her hair, twice, before she stepped back out onto the tile and sponged the water off her burnt arms.

What was Ethan going to say to her when he arrived? She couldn't blame him if he'd rally behind the church's cry for justice. Her chest tightened under the towel. What would they do to her when they found out about her sin?

She stopped breathing for an instant.

She'd face the consequences—even if it meant going to jail.

She picked up the blow-dryer and blew her hair dry before dressing in the baggy clothes.

The clean fabric felt good on her skin.

When she descended the staircase, she saw four people sitting in the living room that overlooked the pond. They were talking so intently that they didn't hear her steps. She cleared her throat.

Jenny hopped up from the couch and raced over to her.

"Where are your boys?" Leia asked.

"At school."

She nodded toward Sam. "Shouldn't you or Sam be at the store?"

"We hired a new employee to help us man the shop."

Jenny pointed to an overstuffed chair, and Leia moved toward it. Before she sat down, Sam gave her a giant hug.

She looked to her right and saw Caroline dressed in a cream corduroy blazer with brass buttons and a long brown skirt. To her left was a man she'd never seen before, fortyish with a gray-flecked sweater and glasses.

Jenny didn't sit down. "I'll put on a pot of coffee while you chat."

Leia almost grabbed her, begging her not to leave her alone, but she was frozen to the seat. If this was an inquisition, she was defenseless. Yet, if she was going to get help, she'd have to stop demanding her own terms.

"You know Caroline Coffer," Sam said, and Leia shook her head. "This is Andy. He's an associate pastor at Calvary Church.

"You already know my story," Sam continued. "But Caroline and Andy wanted to tell you their stories."

Caroline has a story?

"I'll start," Caroline said, and Leia turned. Caroline's long hair was swept back, and she looked the way she always did—like the perfect professional. In control.

"Did you know I was divorced?" Caroline asked.

Leia shook her head.

"I was married for eight years to the owner of Coffer Steaks. My husband was an intense businessman, and I admired his drive from the day I met him at a friend's party. I already had my MBA and was working my way up the corporate ladder at another franchise. We got married a year later, and I helped Duncan manage the steakhouses by overseeing the accounting and payroll department. Business was good. Revenues up. Neither of us saw any harm in spending some of the money to play cards."

Caroline brushed her hand over her hair, and several strands fell out of the clip. "Duncan was a high roller at several casinos, and I'd tag along with him on weekends to watch him play Texas hold 'em. Once he started playing, he'd forget I existed, so I decided that I would one-up him and excel at an even harder poker game. I read strategy books, took a class, and the next time I went with him to the casino, he didn't even notice me leave to play seven-card stud. I was the only woman at the tables and felt very proud of my new abilities even if Duncan didn't notice."

Caroline tugged on her long hair. "Have you ever played stud?"

"No."

"It's a complex game that a lot of poker players avoid because it can be humiliating, but I liked the strategy of the game. To get good at stud, you have to play a lot."

"And you did," Leia said. A statement, not a question.

"I could play the game, but even if I played well, it didn't mean I'd win. If you gamble long enough, you always lose."

Jenny returned with a tray and set four mugs, a black carafe, a pitcher of milk, and a bowl of sugar cubes on the coffee table. Then she retreated back to the kitchen. No one reached for a mug.

"I found out that Duncan was having an affair with one of the company's vice presidents, but instead of confronting him, I decided to spend his money. Every night he went out with his girlfriend, I spent his fortune on cards. I was happy to lose.

"It only took two weeks for me to become addicted. By that point I was past revenge. In order to survive the end of my marriage, I needed the escape of gambling, the feeling of being in control.

"When our personal funds ran out, I started drawing cash from the business."

"And Duncan didn't know?" Leia asked.

Caroline reached down and poured herself a cup of coffee, her fingers trembling as she tried to pour the milk.

She took a sip of the coffee. "I handled both our personal and business finances, and he was too involved with his affair to notice that anything was wrong. That is until he took his girlfriend out to dinner at Kokomo's, and they rejected his credit card. He was mortified when she had to pay, and he came home irate, sifting through our books while I was at the casino. When he found out what I'd done, he said he was leaving me. I showed him the door.

"There's a Chinese proverb that says, 'Building up a family's fortune is like moving earth with a needle, but losing a family's fortune can be as swift as a boat rushing downstream with the current.'

"By the time the divorce went through, we were both in financial ruin. He sold the business and married his girlfriend. I got a new job with another restaurant company, but when I started gambling entire paychecks, I knew I needed to get help before I destroyed my life."

She took another sip. "So I attended a Gamblers Anonymous meeting, met Sam and Jenny, and they took me to church. God redeemed me in spite of what I'd done and gave me the accountability I needed to stop gambling. I haven't been back in a casino for two years."

Caroline set back in her chair as if exhausted. But for the first time in months, Leia felt she wasn't alone.

Sam pointed toward Andy, and the associate pastor cleared his throat.

"I didn't have a fortune to waste, but there's another proverb that says: 'There are two great pleasures in gambling: that of winning and that of losing.' Unfortunately I was on the losing side."

He stuck his hands into the pockets of his sweater.

"Poker was my vice too, but I didn't learn to play at a casino ... I learned in seminary."

Leia sat up. "What?"

"Every Friday night a group of guys from my New Testament Greek class would get together and play an innocent game of poker. Buy-in was ten bucks, which doesn't sound like much except we were all poor grad students and should have spent it on peanut butter and bread.

"We could rebuy as many times during the game as we wanted, so sometimes I'd spend fifty or sixty dollars to stay in the game."

He met her eye and then looked back down at the floor. Leia could understand his embarrassment.

"I married Heather while I was in seminary. She thought the whole poker night thing was ludicrous, but she didn't stop me from playing. I caught the bug, and when a church offered me a position in Las Vegas, I jumped at the chance.

"I wouldn't think of being caught in a casino, but one of the senior pastors invited me to a weekly poker game, and I couldn't turn him down. Everyone seemed to think that since we were all Christians, none of us would stumble.

"I didn't just stumble." He cleaned his glasses on his sweater. "I fell flat on my face.

"I played with businessmen who were actually making money, so even though some of us were on church salaries, buy-in was set at twenty-five dollars with unlimited rebuys. No one stopped me when I spent hundreds of dollars a night. I don't know where they thought I was getting the money.

"Heather and I had several fights about poker night, but I argued that I was developing relationships with church leadership. This was part of my ministry. I made her feel guilty for trying to stop me. Of course, she had no idea how much I was spending since I guarded our financial records. I told her we were barely scraping by, so she worked two jobs to help support us—while she was pregnant with our first child. She thought she was contributing to the ministry, but the money was funding my poker night."

His eyes drifted out the window, watching a red-tailed hawk circle the trees around the golf course.

"Then a wife of one of the men I played with asked Heather if it bothered her that I gambled so much. She said it was only ten dollars a week, and the woman told her I was spending hundreds. Heather confronted me about the gambling that night. I admitted that it was a problem and promised to quit gambling. She quit both of her jobs.

"When I didn't stop playing, Heather took our newborn son and went to live with her parents. I lost my position at the church."

"What did you do?" Leia asked.

"Found another poker game with some guys in my neighborhood and lost everything we had, including our house and car. It took me almost a month of living in a homeless shelter before I realized I needed help. Then it took a year of counseling and support for me to be able to operate again.

"Heather and my son moved back to Vegas ten years ago, and I got a job at Calvary. With God's help I'll never play again."

"You didn't leave Vegas?" Leia asked.

"No. My support group is here, and I need to be around people who understand the importance of abstaining from gambling instead of feeding the addiction."

Sam poured a cup of coffee and handed it to Leia. She added sugar and milk.

"So here's the deal, Leia," Sam said. "The three of us have been where you are, and we want to help you. But first you must promise to do several things."

She hesitated. "What?"

"You have to agree to start every day with a half hour of prayer and Bible reading. God is the only one strong enough to overcome your addiction, and you must connect with him."

She nodded. She'd spend all day in his Word if she had to. She'd have plenty of time in her prison cell.

Sam continued. "You must understand that your addiction is an illness, and you will be susceptible to compulsive gambling for the rest of your life. Because of this, you must promise that you will avoid visiting casinos, playing slot machines, buying lottery tickets, or betting on ball games. One slip can set you spiraling back to where you are today."

He didn't wait for her to answer. "You need to put your mortgage and credit cards and banking accounts in Ethan's name and ask him to give you a predetermined amount of cash for your expenses. Once the cash is gone for the week, you have no more."

Her head felt like it was spinning. "Okay."

"It's critical to work to pay off the debt *by yourself*. Ethan can't pay your debt for you."

She nodded. She would do it herself if she had to work three jobs.

"Finally, you need to join and attend a local Gamblers Anonymous group," Sam continued. "There are plenty around here for you to choose from."

He leaned toward her. "If you are willing to do these things, Andy, Caroline, and I have agreed to meet with you once a week for support."

"Thank you," Leia whispered. With God as her strength, maybe she could stop this cycle.

"And one other thing," Sam said. "If you establish a plan to pay the church back over the next twelve months, the leadership has agreed not to prosecute."

Leia looked over at Andy, and he smiled.

God's mercy showered over her sin.

48

THE SKY WAS BLACK BY THE TIME ETHAN'S PLANE LANDED AT McCarran. He rushed up the Jetway and through the terminal, carrying his flight jacket in one arm while he pulled his carry-on bag with the other. Instead of taking the crew shuttle, he jogged toward the parking lot.

There was no way he could do small talk with another flight crew on the van. The conversation looped in his head.

How are you?

Fantastic ... my wife just tried to commit suicide.

It's hot tonight, isn't it?

Blistering.

Even if he wanted to brave light conversation, he couldn't sit still. He'd paced the aisle of the 757 for most of the flight home.

When he reached his car, he tossed his bag into the backseat and started the engine. He stretched his neck and dug in the glove compartment until he found the small bottle of Advil he had stashed there. He downed two pills for his throbbing head and then backed out of the parking space.

When the flights out of Denver were canceled last night, he'd tried to rent a car, but I-70 had been shut down because of the snow. So he waited, spending a restless night in a reclining chair at Denver's pilot lounge and hiking through the airport all morning and afternoon until the gate agent finally called his name. Last row. Middle seat. At least it got him home.

He'd called Jenny several times from the airport, but she still wouldn't tell him what was going on. Leia never called. His wife had tried to kill herself, and no one would tell him why.

He exited the highway, turned onto Prospect Street, and pulled up in his driveway. Jenny had told him to go directly home, but the house was dark.

He opened the garage door and started to pull inside when he stomped on the brake. Someone had trashed the garage.

He hopped out of the car and carefully stepped around the nails and screws scattered on the cement floor. His neat work area had been decimated. The tools he'd worked so hard to organize were lying haphazardly on the bench and around the floor. His drill bits looked as though they'd been hurled across the room by a tornado. He retrieved a hammer from the floor and hung it back up on the wall. He reached down to pick up his drill, but he didn't touch it. The mess was the least of his worries.

He picked up a crowbar from the cement floor, opened the door, and carried the bar into the house, gripping it as he turned on the lights.

The kitchen looked worse than the garage. Knives, silverware, pens, and papers were strewn across the floor. Drawers were hanging out under the countertops, some of them lying on the tile. He leaned over to pick up two pieces from one that had broken and set them on the counter. Another expense to add to the list.

Something crunched under his shoe. He lifted his foot, picked up a straw, and threw it toward the trash can. It would take a week to clean up this mess.

"Leia!" he yelled.

The room was silent.

He bypassed the living room without even stopping to look at the piles on the carpet. The entire house was probably a disaster. When

whoever had broken in didn't find much to steal, they must have van-
dalized the place instead.

He'd find his wife first, and then he'd call the police.

He ran upstairs and called Leia's name again. This time he heard
her—barely.

"In the bedroom."

He pushed open the door. With the lights from the hallway, he saw
her on the bed. Sitting alone in the darkness. No sound. No movement.
The computer beside the bed was black.

He sank onto the mattress, but he didn't touch her.

"What's going on, Leia?" She was going to be honest with him, or he
was walking right back out that door.

She didn't move her head. "How was your checkride?"

"I was managing until I got a call from Jenny. She said you tried to
commit suicide."

Her voice trembled. "Yes."

"Leia?"

"Can you reschedule your ride?"

He'd take this one problem at a time. "What happened downstairs?"

"I was looking for money."

He set the crowbar on the bed. "What happened to our money?"

"I spent it."

Did he have to shake it out of her? "Where did it go?"

She gulped. "I gambled it."

"What?" Fire ignited in his belly and flamed through his mind.

He yanked the crowbar off the bed, and clutching it in his fist, he
marched toward the window.

"How much did you lose?"

She didn't answer.

"How much?" His voice sounded weak now, strained.

"Seventy thousand," she whispered.

He raised the bar over his head and thrust it down on the window
seat, splitting the wood into slivers. Leia gasped as he threw the bar into
the seat.

He spun around to face her. His arms and legs were shaking, his fists clenched to his side. He wanted to punch something and punch it hard.

"Where did you get seventy thousand dollars?"

"Credit cards. Our savings account. A home equity loan."

"A home equity loan?"

"The mortgage company let me have one without your signature."

"Wasn't that nice of them? They let you destroy our future all by yourself."

"Ethan ..." she started, but he didn't want to hear what she had to say. She'd taken all that he'd worked for and had flushed it down the toilet.

"Is that all?" he asked.

"No." She rocked back and forth on the bed. "I spent the church's carnival money on blackjack."

"You're a class act, aren't you?"

"I didn't want to do it, Ethan. I tried to win it back, but it was too late. I couldn't help myself."

"Of course you could have. You could have started by telling me."

"Sam and his friends are going to help me through this. I'll pay you back—and the church."

"Where are you going to get the money?"

"I'll work in Sam and Jenny's store."

"For the rest of your life."

Her lips quivered. "I'll figure it out."

"Am I the last person to know about this?"

"Jenny just found out yesterday."

"You didn't even tell a friend?"

She pulled her legs close to her chest. "Derek knew."

Then it clicked. Of course Derek knew. He'd seen Leia in Black Hawk. He'd hinted to Ethan, but he'd kept her secret.

How humiliating. Leia had run to Derek instead of to him. He couldn't think about what Derek had done with the information.

"Which casinos?" he demanded.

"The Regal Palace and Casa Bonita."

"You've been a good customer." He reached under the bed and

pulled out the baseball bat. Leia grabbed a pillow, shielding it over her face.

"If I were going to hit you, Leia, I would have done it a long time ago."

She peeked out over the top of the pillow as he twisted the end off the bat and pulled out a small tube. He snapped open the top and pulled out two hundred dollars. All that was left of their savings.

He threw the cash on the bed.

"If you're going to throw away our money, you might as well trash it all."

"I'm so sorry, Ethan."

He backed away from the bed. "I hope so."

He heard his wife crying as he ran out the door.

♠ ♥ ♣ ♦

LEIA KICKED AT THE MONEY UNTIL IT FELL OFF THE BED. DIDN'T Ethan know he was supplying crack to an addict? She didn't want cash right now. She couldn't handle it.

She rolled over onto Ethan's pillow and sobbed. She had known he'd be mad, disappointed in her. But for just an instant she'd been afraid he might actually hurt her.

The thread of hope that she might be able to save her marriage disappeared. Ethan should be irate. She deserved it. But after Sam and Jenny's grace, she'd thought that Ethan might surprise her too. She had hoped that he would wrap his arms around her and say that the money wasn't important as long as she was okay.

He hadn't even hugged her. The money was important to him. More important than her.

Maybe she should have jumped.

The salty tears stung her burnt cheeks as she cupped her hand over her abdomen.

Even if Ethan didn't want her, she had to take care of herself. For the sake of their baby.

She reached over the bed and picked up a five-dollar bill. Then she slowly pushed herself up.

She shuffled through the desk until she found an envelope. Then she scribbled a note on it before stuffing the money inside.

She didn't bother putting on shoes. She jumped over the scattered money, raced down the stairs, and dashed out the front door.

The sharp rocks pricked her feet as she crossed the front yard. She placed the envelope against the front door, rang the bell, and ran back into her garage.

It wasn't much, but she'd paid back her first loan.

49

ETHAN RACED HIS CAR DOWN THEIR STREET, PARKING BY THE CURB instead of flying out of the neighborhood. He couldn't drive another block. Anger blasted through his body like a cannon ball, his arms shaking so hard he couldn't keep his grasp on the steering wheel.

How could Leia do this to him ... to them?

He'd worked since college to build up a cushion. Stability for the present and a little protection for the future. Enough savings to start a family.

Everything was gone.

Leia knew how hard he'd worked to budget and build up their nest egg. Yet without even hesitating, she'd thrown it all away. Apparently she didn't care about their future like he did.

It would take years for them to recoup seventy thousand dollars. Even more years before they could start a family.

If she didn't care, she should just leave. He wouldn't keep trying to persuade her to be happy with him. If she wanted to be on her own, she shouldn't have gotten married. God help him, he had to let her go.

He started the engine, drove toward Vegas, and parked in a garage beside the Strip. An elevator sped him down to the sidewalk, and when he emerged, columns of water clothed in green light shot up from

Bellagio's lake and exploded into raindrops in the night sky. The fountains danced in unison under purple and white lights as "Singin' in the Rain" blared over the loudspeaker.

A blast of water sprayed him as he pressed through the crowd.

He turned off the Strip and fled a block down East Flamingo, past a row of casinos waiting to separate guests from their cash.

The Regal Palace towered over the street, blazing elegance with its crafted stonework and bronze statues. He had no interest in stopping to appreciate the design. Instead he hustled up the long flight of stairs to the entrance.

He passed under stone arches and through a gold-plated lobby. Mary-Maggie had been right. The place was spectacular. Fish swam around him as he walked through the glass tunnel, and then he was on the casino floor—the hub that financed all the extravagance, the cash cow that management milked every day. He'd bet the casino owners kept their money.

There were attempts at making this room look regal, but it reminded him of a county fair with flashing lights, loud buzzers, and adults hollering like kids. All it needed was popcorn and a Tilt-a-Whirl.

People lined up at slot machines, so intent on the screens that they looked like frontline soldiers waging war. Some of the players were professionals with dark suits and ties. Others were clearly there for fun—women with miniskirts surrounded by men in silk shirts.

His eyes honed in on an elderly woman perched on a stool, one hand clutching an oxygen tank, the other tapping a button over and over. Her mouth gaped open like she was in a trance; her eyes didn't blink.

Was this all she had to do in her twilight years? Surely she had grandchildren or even great-grandchildren who needed snuggling. If not, there were so many ways she could help the less fortunate. She could read to kids or serve at a food kitchen or teach Sunday school. Instead she was throwing away the last years of her life as well as the last of her money.

He wandered through the machines to a line of roulette tables. People crowded around as the dealer spun the wheel. He didn't stay to see where the ball landed, but he heard the cheers.

An attendant stopped him. "Can I help you find something, sir?"

Answers.

"No. Thank you."

A couple strolled by him, holding hands. They were dressed in jeans and casual shirts, the woman's straight hair pulled back in a pony-tail. She pointed up at a tower with white lights that overlooked the casino floor, and the man's eyes followed. Ethan saw a wedding ring on the man's finger.

They looked completely normal. The kind of couple he'd see at church.

How could so many people allow themselves to be trapped by this industry? How could the casino owners sleep at night when they were destroying families every day? He shuddered. How did these people trap his wife?

Leia was strong. She was a fighter. She'd always been the top at everything she'd done.

Maybe that was the problem. She had to be at the top of everything, including gambling. He could have told her that no one ever really beats the house.

He stumbled back when two women crashed into him, rushing toward an open slot machine. Neither of them stopped to apologize. The elusive carrot dangling at the end of the stick overrode even the smallest gesture of kindness.

If only he'd known what Leia was doing. He could have protected her from destroying herself. He could have taken her name off the mort-gage, ripped up their credit cards, frozen their savings account. And he could have helped her find something worthwhile to occupy her time.

How was he supposed to take care of her when she kept hiding things from him?

He passed through the craps tables and saw a sign for blackjack. He perused the tables but didn't stop. He was going home.

Walking past the last blackjack table, he stopped and turned his head. Derek Barton was sitting at a card table, a blonde draped across his back. But Derek wasn't looking at the girl. His gaze focused on the deck as the dealer shuffled and then dealt the cards. Ethan stood back and watched his friend tap the table. The dealer gave him another card.

Ethan sat down on the stool beside him, and Derek looked startled. He didn't say a word to Ethan as he turned over his cards to win the round.

"How'd you get that black eye?" Ethan asked.

"It was a misunderstanding."

"So is this where you always come for fun?"

"I got kicked out of my old stomping ground." Derek glanced over his shoulder like he was looking for someone.

"She's not here," Ethan said.

Derek whispered to the blonde, and she wandered away from the table. "Did you come here to gamble?"

"I came to get answers."

Derek took his chips from the table, and Ethan followed him to the bar.

Derek ordered a beer and lifted his bottle in a mock toast. "To answers."

Ethan leaned toward him. He hated asking the question.

"Did you sleep with my wife?"

Derek propped his leg up on an empty stool. "Everyone's been asking me that question lately."

"This isn't a joke."

"She propositioned me."

Ethan's fingers crunched the edge of the counter, rage raced up his chest. He leaned toward him. "Did you sleep with her?"

"No." Derek twisted the bottle on the shiny counter.

"But you knew about her gambling."

"I bailed her out in Black Hawk."

"And yet you didn't tell me."

"It was between Leia and me."

Ethan set his feet on the floor, standing over Derek. "Were you trying to blackmail her?"

A sneaky smile crept up Derek's lips. "In a manner of speaking."

Ethan shoved Derek's shoulders, the glass bottle shattering on the floor. The bartender raced over and glared at him.

"Take it outside," he growled.

Ethan took a step back. "I'm leaving."

"If you don't, I'm calling security."

Ethan looked back at his old friend. "You need Jesus, Derek."

"Jesus doesn't seem to be doing you much good."

He shoved his hands into the pockets of his jeans so he wouldn't slug the man.

Derek ordered another beer. "And yet you keep telling me about your God."

"It's the last time I'm going to tell you."

"Leia's messing with you, Ethan."

He clenched his fists. "Stay away from my wife."

He wheeled and strode toward the entrance. He rushed up the Strip, past the Mirage and Venetian. Streams of people flowed by him, the seductive allure of the lights pulling them like a magnet.

He'd seen enough.

Collapsing on a cast-iron bench, he grieved.

God—what was he supposed to do? Even if he could forgive Leia for what she had done, he could never trust her again. Trust was a fragile enough condition without adding a stick of dynamite. She'd blown it away, and Derek had helped her.

He reached into his pocket and pulled out his cell phone. Then he dialed his sister's number.

Paige's answering machine picked up.

"Hey, it's me," he said. "When you—"

"Ethan?"

"Is this a bad time?"

One of the kids screamed in the background.

"It's never a good time." She laughed. "But I still want to talk. How are you?"

"Not so good." He watched a woman in an evening gown walk toward him, mascara streaking down her face. She sobbed as she passed by.

"I need to know how you did it."

"Did what?"

"Forgave Brett."

Paige paused. "What happened?"

"Leia's been gambling."

"Oh no—"

"She spent our savings plus tens of thousands she squeezed from creditors." He couldn't tell her about the church.

"It's hard, Ethan. Really hard."

"I don't know if I can do it."

"You've got to let her work this out on her own. You can't rescue her."

"Has Brett quit gambling?"

Paige hesitated. "I don't know."

"How can you let him keep doing this to you?"

"I've taken over our money. If he's betting on sports, it's coming from some place else."

"Yet you haven't confronted him."

"I'm trying to build our trust level back."

"He can't keep hurting your family."

A blast of cannon smoke made him jump, and he looked across the Boulevard. The pirate's ship in front of Treasure Island was sinking, scantily clad women dangling from the masts. He stood up and started the long walk back to his car.

"If Leia wants help, she can get it," Paige said.

"Is Brett getting any help?"

"He doesn't think he needs it."

At least Leia was willing to admit she has a problem.

"Has she had an affair?" Paige asked.

If Derek had slept with her, he would have flaunted it. There was no victory in his eyes. "I don't think so."

His sister didn't respond.

"Please tell me that Brett hasn't," Ethan begged.

"We're working through a lot of things."

"Paige!"

Ethan stopped at a crosswalk and waited with the crowd.

"I'd do a few things different if I could go back in time." She sighed. "I'd have given him an ultimatum at the beginning instead of letting it drag on. I'd have forced him to choose between his sports betting or me and the kids. If he had picked gambling, I'd have left."

"You can still leave."

"It's not that simple anymore."

Ethan wished he could go back to Denver and wring Brett's neck, but he had enough to deal with in his own marriage.

His sister was crying now. "Support her, Ethan. Love her. But you've got to let her take responsibility for this situation. You can't wave a magic wand and make it all better."

"Bring the kids here, Paige. You can live with us, with me, until Brett gets it together."

"I can't."

He heard Brett's voice in the background. Paige's voice was muffled, but he could hear her words. "Ethan's on the phone ... no, I'm fine."

He didn't hear Brett's response, though he probably wasn't thrilled to hear that his brother-in-law had called. The two men had never been friends.

"Brett says hello," Paige said.

"I bet he does." Ethan felt a wave of relief when he turned off the Strip. He pushed the button for the parking lot elevator. "I'm serious about you and the kids coming here."

"Give my love to Leia."

"I'm praying for you, Paige."

"And I for you."

Ethan closed his phone and got into the elevator. It would take an act of God for him to forgive Leia. Where was the justice? The penalty for the pain she'd caused?

He got into his car and drove out of the garage and merged onto I-15. Did God really expect him to live with the consequences of his wife's actions? She's gone behind his back. Stolen his money. Slashed the financial security he'd worked so hard to build for both of them. It was all gone.

The taillights on the car in front of him flashed red, and he slammed on his brakes. The traffic slowed to a snail's pace, and he crept forward with it.

The Bible was clear that Jesus had paid the penalty for humanity's sin. Anger. Adultery. Murder. Self-righteousness. Pride.

But gambling?

He swerved into the left lane and tried to pass the car jam, but the lanes were blocked. He sat and drummed his fingers on the wheel, nervous energy pumping out through his hands until he saw the problem. Flashing yellow lights announced the grand opening of a new casino. Both lanes of traffic were trying to exit off the ramp, and there was a stoplight at the end. He banked left toward the median and sped around the stopped cars.

Leia had been caught in a trap, and he should have seen its ugly jaws. He'd willingly moved them to Las Vegas, but he hadn't been there to help her when she injured her knee. She'd entered the lion's den, and he'd left her alone as prey.

He couldn't solve the world's problems, but maybe he could help Leia. That is if she were willing to quit gambling and fight for their marriage. No more unreturned calls. Or late-night escapes to the casino. Or secrets with people like Derek Barton.

If she were willing to do that, he would try to forgive her. And forget about the money.

He turned back into their neighborhood.

Thank God, she hadn't killed herself. Thank God, she hadn't had an affair.

And, thank God, he still loved his wife.

50

LEIA WRAPPED A CARDIGAN AROUND HER SHOULDERS AND OPENED the
front door, fresh air cooling her face. The walls inside the house
were closing in on her, the computer beckoning her to escape. In spite
of all she'd been through this week, she still wanted to play.

A soft orange light flickered from the street lamp as she sat down on
the front step, tucking her knees into her chest. Ethan had sped out of the
house three hours ago, and she doubted he'd come back tonight. Maybe
not even tomorrow. But at some point he'd have to retrieve his things.

She couldn't blame him if he never forgave her. She didn't know if
she could forgive herself.

She leaned back against the concrete and looked up at the stars.
She hadn't enjoyed the night air in a long time. For a brief moment she
didn't even miss the slots. In the morning she was driving to her first GA
meeting—at least the people there would understand.

She watched the headlights of a car crawl down their road before
Ethan's Accord turned into the driveway. She squeezed her hands
around her legs, waiting for him to get out of the car. As he walked
toward her, she didn't meet his eye. He could get his stuff and go. She
wouldn't try to make him talk.

But he didn't walk around her. He sat down on the concrete and pushed her sweater back up around her shoulders.

"I'm sorry," he whispered.

She shook her head. "It's my fault."

"I knew something was wrong—"

"There was nothing you could do, Ethan. It's my problem."

He put his arm around her, and she leaned into him. "I don't want us to turn out like Brett and Paige."

She met his eyes. "With God's help I'm going to beat this."

His gaze dropped to the ground. "I went to the Regal Palace tonight."

She shivered. She didn't want to talk about it.

"All the people gambling looked normal, Leia. They look like us."

"It's just entertainment until they find out they're not as strong as they think."

"Derek Barton was there." Ethan stared across their dark yard. "I asked him if you slept with him."

She didn't want to talk about Derek either, but harboring these secrets almost killed her. "What did he say?"

"No."

"He was telling the truth."

He turned her face toward him, and as he looked into her eyes the water rushed back into them. She gulped. "I was willing to do almost anything to get the money back, but I couldn't ..."

"That would have killed me."

"Me too."

He squeezed her arm. "I'm sorry I scared you tonight."

She twisted a button on the sweater. "I understand if you want to leave and never come back."

"But I don't want to do that, Leia. If you'll work to beat this thing, I'll help you through it."

"Why did you marry me, Ethan?"

"Because I fell in love with you."

"But why?" She was stubborn, sarcastic, irresponsible ... and weak.

He kissed her forehead. "I love your spirit. Your drive. Your fearless passion for life."

"All that stuff drives you insane."

"Some days." He wrapped his arms around her. "But most days I'm jealous of your determination. Nothing stops you."

"Since when have you been jealous?"

He grinned. "Since you landed that Cessna during a typhoon."

"It was barely sprinkling."

"I was a goner the second you stepped off that plane."

"But you didn't even know me then."

"I'm still just as crazy about you."

She snuggled into his chest. "I don't deserve you, Ethan."

He started to say something else, but she put her finger on his lips. "There is one thing I forgot to tell you."

He let go of her. "I can't handle any more bad news, Leia."

"This isn't bad." She took a deep breath. She never imagined herself saying these words and being happy about it. "In about seven months we're going to have a baby."

He opened his mouth and shut it. She smiled as his expression evolved from disbelief to hope.

He opened his mouth again. "How in the world?"

She cleared her throat. "I'm afraid I gambled with my birth control."

"What?"

"I got distracted and missed taking a few of my pills."

"A few?"

"A lot of my pills."

"Leia, I ..."

She squeezed his hand. "I want this baby."

"Really?"

"Really."

He reached out and wrapped her in his arms. His face was in her hair.

"Are you feeling okay?"

"A little nauseous, but according to the nurse, that's a good sign."

He heard the front door open on the next house, and the porch light flipped on. Misty came outside and waved over to them. "Hey, lovebirds! Thanks for the money, Leia."

Leia waved back. "No problem."

"I'm buying you a special eye shadow at my party."

"Brown, please." Leia said. "Light brown."

"I'm thinking a frosty blue."

"Brown ..." Leia repeated, but Misty had already shut the door.

Ethan gave her a strange look. "What in the world?"

"I borrowed five dollars from her."

"Okay."

"I'm paying back everyone I owe. The church money is next."

"You can do it."

She smiled at him. "I can, can't I?"

He nodded.

"We still have the money in our retirement accounts."

He sat straight up. "We can borrow from that to pay back some of what we owe."

"You don't owe a penny," she insisted. "I'm paying these debts off by myself."

"If you get that Ambassador job, we can pay it off in a few years."

"I didn't get the job."

He froze. "When did you find that out?"

"In January. I was too mortified to tell you."

He slowly brushed a strand of hair off her face. "You don't have to hide things from me, Leia."

"Yes, I do."

"If we want our marriage to work, we've got to stop keeping secrets."

"If you really knew me, you wouldn't like me much."

He wove his fingers through hers. "And if you really knew me, you probably wouldn't like me either."

She kissed his cheek. "Doubtful."

The streetlight flickered beside them, and she shivered. For an instant she could hear the chimes. Feel the rhythm of the machine.

Taste the pleasure of a win. The slots called to her, taunting her, begging her to return one last time.

She closed her eyes and shook as she clutched Ethan's hand.

For their family's sake she'd do everything she could to dim the lights in her mind and conquer her addiction for good.

EPILOGUE

One year later

A GUARD GLANCED AT LEIA AS SHE FIDGETED IN THE METAL FOLDING chair, fanning her shirt to cool her skin. Leia avoided the woman's gaze, looking out the row of windows to a double fence laced with coils of razor wire. There was no tower along the fence, but another armed guard watched the front gate. The blue sky above the prison didn't alleviate the rush of claustrophobia that pounded her. The institution was low security, but she was still trapped inside.

The visiting room was packed with prisoners and their guests. She closed her eyes as she tried to battle back the image of a crowded casino floor. The pictures flashed in her mind without an invitation. Her cravings to gamble returned daily with a frightening allure. And they haunted her in the strangest places. Without warning she was transported back to the casino floor.

Even though her knee had healed, the game still tempted her while she was awake and asleep. She never fathomed how the wide net of gambling would trap her mind. She hadn't just lost her ability to escape during the past year. It felt like she'd lost the warmth of her security blanket. The relationship with her best friend.

She and Ethan had spent the year in counseling. Her choices had severed the trust in their relationship, but they were slowly starting to heal. Ethan sold their house and moved them into a small townhome. These days they lived like college students except they'd eliminated pizza from their budget. Ethan even stopped complaining about boxed macaroni and cheese.

The two of them had worked hard to design a plan so that she could earn some money on the days he was home. She'd signed on with a tour company in Las Vegas, flying sunset cruises over the Grand Canyon and Lake Mead to help pay off her debt. It was hardly the majors, but in the past twelve months, she'd managed to pay back the church and start chipping away at their credit card debt. It might take her a decade, but someday she would be free from her carnage even if she could never break away from the addiction.

Through God's grace and the support of her friends, she had abstained from gambling since she'd hit bottom at the Casa Bonita, but it hadn't been easy. One afternoon after physical therapy, she fooled herself into thinking she was strong enough to take a walk along the Strip and look at the lights. She wasn't ready. Instead of just looking, she ended up inside a casino with her weekly grocery money clutched in one hand. It wasn't until she sat down in front of a slot machine that she seemed to wake up from a dream. It was like she'd been watching someone else about to destroy herself. She'd stuffed the money into her pocket and run all the way to her car before she changed her mind.

The baby in Leia's arms squirmed, and she pushed the dark locks back from her daughter's sweaty forehead, kissing her soft skin.

Grace Sondra Carlisle.

Even on the days she was exhausted from yet another sleepless night, she thanked God for her baby girl, the one good thing that resulted from the agony of her spiral. That and the renewed relationship with both her husband and her heavenly Father. Ethan had spent the year loving her in spite of her flaws. The blinders had been stripped off both of them, and with the help of God, they were struggling together to rebuild what they'd lost.

The glass door at the end of the room slid back, and Leia stood up. Sondra Vaughn spread her arms open as she rushed into the room. She grabbed Leia and squeezed her tight. Then she reached down for Grace.

She stared at the baby for a moment and then snuggled Grace against her chest. "She has your dad's mouth."

Leia smiled. "And his ears."

Sondra held her granddaughter out in front of her. "And she has Ethan's blue eyes."

Leia looked down at her daughter and marveled again at the life

God had given her. "You and I didn't make the cut, did we?"

"No, but she's still beautiful."

Sondra sat down in a metal chair beside the square table. She couldn't keep her eyes off her five-month-old granddaughter as the baby drifted to sleep. Leia couldn't stop staring at her mom. The gray in her uniform matched the gray streaking through her frizzy brown hair. She wasn't wearing any makeup, not even lipstick. Her mother used to wear lipstick to breakfast.

The last time Leia had seen her had been at a cousin's wedding five years ago. Her mother had been wearing a lavender suit, and she'd been flaunting a new haircut and manicured nails. When Leia left the reception hall that night, her mother had waved good-bye as she waltzed across the dance floor.

Since Leia started attending GA, she'd talked to her mom almost every week. They were slowly mending their relationship as they journeyed together through recovery.

Sondra glanced up at her. "How are you doing?"

"I'm tired."

"Are you still working?"

"A couple of times a week at Jenny's store and with Las Vegas Sunset Tours."

"You need to get your rest, sweetheart."

Leia's back bristled like it always did when her mother spewed out unsolicited advice. She took a deep breath. It was time to emulate the traits she'd been learning in GA. Kindness. Honesty. Humility.

"I'm trying, Mom."

"If you get too tired, you'll be tempted to gamble again."

"I'm always tempted to gamble."

"It's hard, Leia." Sondra took her hand and squeezed. "It may not help to hear it, but I understand."

"It does help." She paused. A year had gone by, and she still hadn't apologized to her mom. "I'm so sorry for judging you."

"You don't have to apologize, honey. I was supposed to be the strong one after your dad died."

"But I was proud ... and cruel. I thought I was too strong to give in to an addiction."

"Only God is strong."

Leia glanced back out the window at the clear sky. "It's almost your turn to start over again."

"Two more weeks."

"Are you nervous?"

Sondra nodded. "Scared to death."

"There's strength in accountability."

Sondra stared back at her, and Leia saw the anticipation in her eyes.

"And I'm planning to keep you accountable."

Sondra smiled.

"Plus …" Leia looked down at the baby in her arms. "We both have someone else to think about now."

Sondra waved over an elderly woman who was visiting with her family.

"Olivia, I want you to meet my beautiful daughter and granddaughter."

Olivia squeezed her in a bear hug. "Your mother talks about you all the time."

Leia felt the child within her swell with pride. "Really?"

"Apparently she thinks she has the smartest kid and grandkid in the world." Olivia pointed at the family in the corner. "I'm a bit biased toward my four kids and eight grandchildren."

Sondra held up Grace. "But look at this baby."

Olivia winked at her. "The competition's tough."

The woman took Grace's fingers in hers. "Now you stay out of trouble, Grace Carlisle. I don't ever want to see you in here."

"You won't," Sondra said. "She's got a good mom."

Leia put her arm around her mom's shoulders. "Just like me."

AUTHOR'S NOTE

Pathological gambling is no respecter of age, gender, income level, or religion. The seductive trap is wide enough to capture business leaders, professionals, teens, grandparents, single parents, low-income families, college graduates, and church leadership.

As I researched the personal stories behind this addiction, my heart ached for all the men and women who'd lost everything as a result of gambling, one of the fastest-growing industries in the United States.

Women succumb to gambling nearly three times faster than men (Reuters Health). According to the National Council on Problem Gambling, approximately two to three percent of adults (six to nine million) have a gambling problem, and between one and two percent of the adult population are compulsive gamblers. Another study in 1997 (Harvard Medical School Division on Addictions) estimated that not only did 7.5 million American adults have gambling problems, but there were even more American adolescents considered to be problem or pathological gamblers (7.9 million).

Compulsive gamblers often bottom out faster than other addicts, as they burn all their resources in search of another high. Approximately one in five compulsive gamblers attempts suicide.

If you or someone you love is addicted to gambling, please seek help. Focus on the Family and Tyndale House Publishers have published an excellent resource by Tom Raabe titled *House of Cards* to give hope to gamblers and their families. There is also information available at:

www.gamblersanonymous.org
www.citizenlink.org/FOSI/gambling
www.gam-anon.org
www.ncalg.org

For a list of other helpful resources, please visit my Web site at www.melaniedobson.com.

DISCUSSION QUESTIONS

In *Going for Broke*, Leia initially gambled as a diversion from her loneliness and the pain of her knee injury. How was she slowly drawn into this addiction, and why was it so intoxicating?

Ethan loved Leia in spite of her failures. Is there anything else he could have done to help prevent her fall?

Do you have someone in your life who is willing to speak the truth even when it hurts?

Leia's problems began long before she visited a casino. What could she have done to protect herself from the threat of gambling addiction?

Second Corinthians 12:9 says that we are weak, but God is strong. How does God's power give us the strength we need to overcome our weaknesses?

Leia and Ethan were both quick to judge and criticize other people for their failures. How did Leia's addiction change both of their hearts?

Do you think Jenny and Sam and Calvary Church handled Leia's crisis with a balance of accountability and grace? What would you have done in this situation?

Have you or someone you loved ever overcome an addiction? What steps did you take to break free?

AUTHOR INTERVIEW

How did you start writing? What was your first piece of writing like?

When I was seven, I started my first journal, and then I pounded out a very short "autobiography" when I was nine. As I grew older, I wrote for every yearbook, newsletter, small-town newspaper, and magazine that would let me publish. Payment, of course, was optional.

Why do you write fiction?

Because I have to! I love the process of creating stories, and even if no one ever bought a single book, I would still write fiction. As I seek after God, I pray the stories he's etched in my heart give readers a glimpse of his love and grace even when they don't understand his plan.

Why do people remember a story more easily than a sermon?

Inspirational novels have changed my life as I identify with a character's pain, joy, struggles, and triumph.

What do you hope readers will take away from your book?

I hope Leia's story will be a reminder that without God's power in our lives, none of us are strong enough to fight sin and addiction. And as children of God, our Father desires to love and protect us even when we fail.

Which character in the book is most like you?

While I was writing *Going for Broke*, I was marooned in a small flat in what was formerly East Berlin. It was during the gray German winter, and I was with two toddlers who were dying to be outside. On the days that I felt like I was going crazy, I could identify with Leia's fear of entrapment and the subsequent depression brought on by her confinement. .

What actor would you picture playing your main character in a movie?

Hmm ... I was so focused on Leia's internal journey as I wrote this manuscript that I really can't envision any specific actor for this role.

Which writers have influenced you most?

Tough question! The writers who've inspired me most include Angela Hunt, Rene Gutteridge, Jan Karon, Linda Hall, Kristen Heitzmann, Susan Meissner, and Nancy Jo Jenkins.

Describe your writing process.

Before I begin a book, I write detailed character descriptions, an outline, and background pieces on my major settings; but as the mom of two preschoolers, I write the actual book in spurts— while the girls are finishing their breakfast, during their naptime, after the final bedtime story. Somehow, thank God, a story forms through all these stolen moments I designate as my writing time.

Can you share a particularly memorable encounter with a reader?

Together for Good (my first novel) was a story about a woman whose heart had been torn apart by a failed adoption. After this was published, I was blessed and honored by the many people who shared their family's adoption journey with me.

What is one fact about yourself that readers might find most surprising?

My husband contracts for computer animation projects around the world, so when I'm not writing, I'm moving. In the past three years our family has lived in Colorado, Tennessee, Germany, California, North Carolina, and Oregon. We were on our way to a job in New Zealand when it fell through a week before we got on the airplane. Our stuff made it to Auckland via ship, but we've never been there.